ALSO BY LISA ZEIDNER

LOVE BOMB

LOVE BOMB

LISA ZEIDNER

SARAH CRICHTON BOOKS

FARRAR, STRAUS AND GIROUX

NEW YORK

Sarah Crichton Books
Farrar, Straus and Giroux
18 West 18th Street, New York 10011

Copyright © 2012 by Lisa Zeidner
All rights reserved
Distributed in Canada by D&M Publishers, Inc.
Printed in the United States of America
First edition, 2012

Library of Congress Cataloging-in-Publication Data
Zeidner, Lisa.
    Love bomb / Lisa Zeidner. — 1st ed.
        p.   cm.
    ISBN 978-0-374-19271-6 (alk. paper)
    1. Hostages—Fiction.   2. Weddings—Fiction.   I. Title.

PS3576.E37L68 2012
813'.54—dc23

                                    2011052367

Designed by Jonathan D. Lippincott

www.fsgbooks.com

1   3   5   7   9   10   8   6   4   2

FOR DOROTHY ZEIDNER

1926–2009

Helen Burns

and

Dr. and Mrs. Jacob Nathanson

and

Salome and Delbert Billips Jr.

invite you to celebrate the marriage of

Tess Nathanson

to

Gabriel Billips

•

Saturday, June 25, 2011, Four o'clock

106 Rosewood Lane, Haddonfield, New Jersey

Reception to follow

•

In lieu of gifts, the bride and groom encourage

donations to Doctors Without Borders

INSIDE

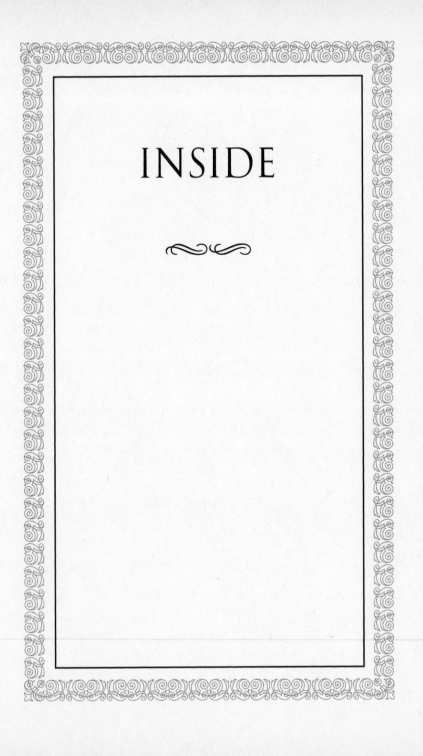

The bride did not wear white. But the terrorist did.

The bride wore a fitted dark blue cocktail dress, shimmering and shiny, the color of a duck caught in an oil spill. The terrorist, however, wore the most conventional gown of white satin and lace, complete with veil.

The guests had already crowded into the great room to await the bride. Until this moment, the biggest anticipated setback had been the threat of bad weather that had forced the ceremony indoors. The bride and groom, who had been discouraged from an outdoor summer wedding for this very reason, seemed not only stoical about the approaching storm but jauntily pleased; and when, just as suddenly, the thunder skittered away and the sun broke through, guests who believed in a higher power could note that said Being had just offered a wink and a nod, or blessed the proceedings.

Those who needed to sit had sat. Instead of the familiar strains of Pachelbel's Canon, the assembled guests heard a series of whirs outside the door from what sounded like a power drill. While they turned to face the noise, the terrorist, not Tess, made an entrance from the opposite side of the room, from the French doors that led to the backyard. She did one runway strut down what passed for an aisle. Then she just spun around to face the crowd and allowed everyone, including the wedding photographer, to get a long look.

With her wedding dress, the terrorist wore what looked like an old World War II gas mask, bulky as a scuba diver's. You couldn't see her eyes through the plastic portholes, because over the gas mask she wore wraparound mirrored sunglasses. Her veil was far too heavy for bridal purposes—more like a burqa. Threaded from the gas mask to her arm was some kind of small black box, attached with what many of the guests immediately recognized as an iPod armband. On the box, a small button flashed.

Since her gown was strapless and her arms bare, you could see the box quite well. The arm wearing it was clearly a woman's arm. A very fit woman's arm. This woman had put in some serious time on the Nautilus machines, or with free weights, the younger men would later agree, when her arms became a central question: How could anyone who knew her fail to recognize those arms, those hands? Granted, it was possible she had been fat before, in training for this, her big day of mayhem, grunting through chin-ups deep into the night. Still. Shouldn't the person in question—the person she wanted to hurt, the person responsible for endangering the lives of sixty-odd innocent bystanders—recognize the tone of her skin, her elbows?

The black box was practically the only dark item on her body and thus meant to be seen, as were the boots. The wedding dress had been intentionally hemmed too short, so it wasn't just the toes of her shoes that protruded but the entire clunky things. The terrorist wore steel-reinforced-toe work boots identical to those of any road construction crew or cable installation dude, except that the boots had been spray-painted white over stencils, so they actually looked like white-and-cream lace. The shoelaces had been spray-painted white, too.

It would have been easy enough—easier, in fact—to buy white shoelaces. The caked paint on the laces was disconcerting, and gave the shoes the look of something that would be in a museum, in a big Plexiglas case, posturing as art.

The veil was so long that it hid part of her waist, so only as she walked, at certain angles, could you see that she wore a belt that appeared to be made entirely from rounds of ammo, on the side of which was somehow balanced or clipped—as if it were a cell phone—a sawed-off shotgun? Not a *Soldier of Fortune* crowd, but it appeared to be a sawed-off shotgun.

Despite the artillery, no one took the terrorist seriously at first. Almost everyone assumed that she was part of an artsy ceremony. Both Tess and Gabriel had been very secretive about the details of the wedding, revealing only that it would be "intimate." The older guests—who believed in the importance of ritual at a time like this, who resolutely understood that your own wedding was the worst possible time to try to get creative—attempted to smile indulgently. But many of the bride and groom's friends looked genuinely delighted.

Not that most of the guests required an armed bride in a gas mask to be alert, amused, and grateful to be there. The groom's sister, Miranda Mobley, was an actress, and as her date she'd brought her current boyfriend, a better-known actor: Trevor Hunter, star of action-adventure movies with comic overtones and a long-running TV cop show. After the bride and groom shoved cake into their mouths, Miranda's car—the actors had arrived in a town car, with a driver—would whisk her back to Manhattan, in preparation for late-night talk shows. The celebrities sat quietly on their plastic chairs. But as people twisted backwards to look for the bride and groom, their eyes kept snagging on the movie stars. In fact, most people's first thought was that Art Bride *was* Miranda, harnessed into a supporting role as ironic maid of honor.

Once Miranda was located in the crowd, they figured the terrorist was Tess herself. Though Tess had greeted people as they arrived at the house, she could have changed clothes in her childhood home. One or two of the guests, grinning, began to look around for the groom, whom they assumed would also be in costume. Gabriel, in his wedding suit, looked as mystified as they did. But they assumed his shock was just part of the performance, even when he craned his neck to find his bride-to-be.

Tess was crammed into the back of the room in her blue dress, just another spectator. Therefore not Art Bride. And the wide-eyed bride looked even more puzzled than Gabriel.

She stood in a clump by the door with the entire catering staff— not only the head chefs, a husband-and-wife duo in the regulation tall white hats and white Nehru jackets, their names stitched in cursive on the pockets, but all five of their young penguin-dressed food service underlings.

When the terrorist, voice muffled by the gas mask, boomed, in a kind of parodic broadcaster's voice, "Everyone standing, find a chair," everyone began to smile, laugh, and clap, or almost everyone.

Helen Burns, the mother of the bride whose house this was, quickly located Tess in the clump of guests, then Gabriel. Then her son, Simon, and her three grandchildren. Then her tremulous mother in her wheelchair, who wore her usual expression, half happy-go-lucky, half defeated.

The Africans also did not appear to be at all amused. The four friends of the bride and groom's from Chad and Mali, three men and one's wife—Helen had been introduced to them but could not remember their long, foreign names—who had traveled here for the festivities, may not have been totally versed in American wedding customs, but they knew a real shotgun from a prop. So, presumably, did the groom's grandfather, who might be old now but had fought in actual wars. Helen noticed that Delbert Billips Sr. seemed to be trying to calculate all of the egresses in the room without moving his head too much. She also noticed that the woman did not pay any attention to him, which meant that whoever she was, she was not connected to the groom's side of the family, because if you were planning a hostage event, you would make special arrangements for the man with combat experience.

Also highly unamused: the mental health service providers. Helen Burns, the bride's mother, was a therapist with a mere Ph.D. But the father of the bride, the maternal grandfather of the groom, and a handful of the wedding guests were psychiatrists who could call in a script for Thorazine or process a committal right on the spot. They did not think this woman was fetchingly creative. They would think she was schizophrenic. They would think she was schizophrenic just on the basis of the outfit. The outfit alone screamed *inpatient*.

There were not enough chairs for everyone. The room that Helen thought of as the not-so-great room could not comfortably hold this many people. Panic-stricken as the rain threatened, they'd called in an S.O.S. to the bride's brother Simon, and with the help of the caterers' staff, they'd rearranged everything into some kind of ad hoc performance space with the conviction that the rain was going to pass so that the food could still be served outside, under the tent. Helen was very upset. It was ridiculous. Who wants a backyard wedding! Even if it *doesn't* rain, who needs mosquitoes, ants, the heat and humidity! But then the threat of rain had passed, and Helen realized that her daughter liked just the improvised quality of the wedding, as if it inoculated her against the fear that she was demanding too much attention.

Now, instead of bad weather, they had an armed interloper in a gas mask.

"Okay," the terrorist said, "the rest of you can line up behind and around the chairs. First—" But she was interrupted by a ringing phone. People no longer turn off their cell phones, even for a wedding. "Ooooh, that's a *really stupid* ring tone," she noted. Many laughed while the offender set her phone to vibrate. "Let's turn off our phones. Not vibrate, just flat off. Try to be without your phones for a while. Let's do it together. On the count of three," and the guests complied, laughing more as the clashes of the various phones' powering-down songs cycled through.

"Now," she said, "I'm passing a hat," the word *hat* muffled, so it sounded as if she were announcing she planned to pass gas. Where the hat came from was unclear—somewhere under the magician's veil, or, considering what would happen soon, it had been planted in the room beforehand. "If you could all just send your phones forward to the aisle and place them in the top hat. Just pass them down the rows. That's it. Thank you. If you want to help carry it, honey"—to the flower girl, who could not look more pleased at the prospect of what was clearly a party game—"you need to put down the flowers. Yeah, it is heavy. It's a special magician's hat, gets deeper."

Some guests resisted being separated from their phones. One guest, a psychiatrist friend of the bride's father, pointed out that all the phones looked alike. He said he'd be screwed if he lost his address book.

"Don't worry about that, sir; I'm sure we can sort them all out later."

"I'm not really comfortable with this," the psychiatrist said, very loudly and slowly, as only a very poor psychiatrist would speak to an insane person. Helen knew that he was not necessarily this poor a psychiatrist, but he was under stress. "Could you please tell me—"

The woman approached, stood over him, and swooped her hand to the shotgun on her belt. If the psychiatrist noticed the incongruity between the dull metal of the gun and her French manicure, it would have been further diagnostic evidence.

He surrendered the phone, as did the others who had hoped to quietly decline participation in this part of the event.

The terrorist looked around sternly. "Who's holding out?"

No one responded. Later, they would marvel that no one had the presence of mind to keep a phone; it's not as if their captor counted them.

She insinuated herself among the guests, paying particular attention to the middle-aged men. She looked deep into their eyes as she passed. They could see themselves reflected in her sunglasses. She stopped in front of Richard Silver, an old friend of the bride's father, a gastroenterologist whom Jake Nathanson had known since medical school, and glared. Or what was probably a glare; it's always hard to tell when you can't see someone's eyes, which is why many banks now post signs that say sunglasses and hats are not allowed. Despite 9/11 and "Let's roll," all the legendary bravery of the men on the doomed, hijacked plane headed for the Capitol, most bank robberies happen without anyone even brandishing a gun. These days, a mere note will do.

"But I'm on call," Dr. Silver said.

She made the universal hand gesture that means *Fork it over.*

"No," the gastroenterologist said.

The woman's shoulders tensed in irritation. She marched to the mammoth console that held Helen's television and DVD player, practically the only piece of furniture, other than the couch, that hadn't been crammed into the garage to accommodate the chairs. From the space between the back of the console and the wall—the piece never managed to be flush enough against the wall because of the irritating tangle of cords and big, boxy plugs—she removed a rifle and a plastic garbage bag. She tucked the plastic bag into the belt that held the shotgun. She marched back to the gastroenterologist and pointed the rifle at his forehead.

He surrendered his iPhone.

The event so far had taken maybe four minutes. The rifle marked a decisive turning point. The tone changed as decisively as the weather. Those who thought this was theater immediately relinquished that idea. Even those who held out for guerrilla theater—the rifle unloaded, the woman an actor friend of the groom's from film school, the whole event some kind of commentary on the comforts of the West versus the hardships the bride and groom had witnessed with Doctors Without Borders in Mali, where they met—allowed themselves to be genuinely scared.

As disconcerting as the rifle itself was the fact that it had been planted in the house. Which meant that this person had access to the house. To Helen, who lived here, that fact alone was not surprising. Like almost everyone in their quaint, prosperous New Jersey hamlet, she rarely bothered to lock her doors. Anyone—her lawn care professional, a bunch of high school kids in need of a party venue—could gain access to her house. Her geriatric golden retriever would not be much of a deterrent. Whoever entered her house would have access to her computer files, her credit card numbers on her bills, her prescription drugs, her sad lingerie. Helen didn't dwell much in those seconds on the predictable feelings of violation. In truth, there wasn't that much to violate. Her life was an open book that, frankly, no one was much interested in reading. The more puzzling, and urgent, question was why.

That the woman had a beef with someone was obvious. Helen was pretty sure that it wasn't her. She would also bet that it had nothing to do with the bride and groom, though a person of limited imagination would go there first.

With the hand not holding the rifle, the terrorist removed the plastic bag from her bullet belt and shook it out.

"Next," she said, "I'd like the ladies to pass forward their purses. Over here, into the bag."

The women reluctantly surrendered the tiny handbags with their lipsticks, their Stim-U-Dents. Their metal nail files and, perhaps, their tiny cans of Mace spray. Their cute sewing kits from past hotel stays containing needles and safety pins for emergency wardrobe malfunctions and also, if necessary, for poking out eyes. The terrorist held the bag open as the guests dutifully passed their purses.

"Excuse me, miss," an older man said. "One thing I want to tell you."

Helen didn't even have to look at the speaker to tell he was one of the psychiatrists. He was using his therapist's voice: soft, slow, soothing, syrupy. Helen had met him for the first time at the rehearsal dinner the night before: Dr. Ira Needleman from Los Angeles, the groom's grandfather.

"My wife is diabetic," Dr. Needleman said. "Her insulin is in her purse."

"So?"

"I'm sure you don't want to hurt anyone."

The terrorist laughed, showily.

"Well, she's obviously not going to let you keep your insulin needle," someone else said. Facing the terrorist: "Right?"

This was Dr. Jacob "Jake" Nathanson, father of the bride and Helen's ex-husband, who thought that Dr. Needleman, semiretired therapist to the stars, was a pretentious quack.

The terrorist said, roughly, "Bingo."

"Look," Jake said. He was using his own straightforward, I-won't-condescend-to-you, I'm-not-a-typical-therapist therapist's voice. His children and ex-wife knew it well. "Perhaps if you just told us what you want . . ."

"We're getting to that," the terrorist said.

"Excuse me?" Jake said. "I couldn't quite understand you. Maybe if you took off the mask . . ."

She ignored him. All of the purses were now in the trash bag. She dragged the bag to the French doors at the back of the room, opened the door, and thrust it out onto the lawn, along with the cell phones. Closed the door.

"And now if you would all kindly put your hands behind your backs. Ladies and gentlemen, I am here today—"

"Again," Jake interrupted, louder now, "I really want to hear what you have to say, but I could understand you so much better if you just took off the mask."

"Jake," Helen said, urgently. "Just let her talk."

"Thank you," the terrorist said.

"I agree with Jake," another of the psychiatrists said.

"Shut up!" the terrorist said.

The purse collection part of the event had taken another couple of minutes. This part also happened very quickly, so quickly that it was impressive that the three African men organized a coup without any rehearsal at all.

Ngarta Adoulaye from Chad failed to put his hands behind his back. He stood, ready to act. The faux bride immediately swooped over to him and pointed the rifle at his shoulder. Once he sat back down she removed, from her belt, some kind of plastic restraint, in the style of a hospital wrist ID band but much wider and stronger, which she used to grab his arms and secure them behind the chair. In order to do this, even quickly, she had to very briefly prop the rifle in her armpit, where it rather dramatically changed the look of her cleavage.

Good old-fashioned sexism: it is difficult to be terrified of someone in a strapless push-up bra. She had a rifle, but it was hard to believe that she knew how to use it. It was probably not even loaded. It was impossible to believe that some man in the gathering could not approach her from behind and wrest it from her hands, while she instinctively yelped and protected the strapless dress from being dislocated.

And that is what happened. While she was tying up Ngarta, another African, Souleymane Samake from Mali, tried to wrest the rifle from her. Failed. The woman executed a fast, practiced move to regain control of the weapon: a kick to Souleymane's groin and a two-handed, twisting motion on the rifle. As Souleymane doubled over howling, the rifle fired. In the back of the room, the bride squealed because one of the waitpersons had stomped on her foot in an attempt to get out the doors. The female half of the husband-and-wife chef team wailed and fell to the floor, her wedding cake of a hat tumbling from her head.

Nothing had hit her. The bullet had actually ricocheted and knocked a vase off a shelf of the fireplace, like in an old Western. Either the terrorist was an excellent marksman, or Cyndi, the girl chef, was lucky to be alive to plate canapés another day. She had probably never heard rifle fire that close before. Probably few of the guests had. It was exceptionally loud, so loud that it was impossible to believe someone on the block had not already called the police.

"You can see that was a VERY BAD IDEA," the terrorist said, cupping the black box on her arm as if to protect it. "Listen—"

Several, in this interlude, had tried or were trying to run. How hard could it be to escape the great room of a suburban house on a crisp Saturday in summer? It's true that many people would be at the beach. But it was hardly a ghost town. All over Haddonfield, people were washing cars, unloading groceries, lobbing gentle practice pitches to their Little Leaguers. Even without gunfire, neighbors would be alert to the presence of so many interlopers' cars on the street and the weird photographic ritual guests had needed to undergo before entering the house, not to mention a caterer's van and a town car with a driver on a day that was not a prom night. They would know there was a wedding. The Haddonfield police would have been informed that there was a wedding. They would not expect screaming at a wedding.

The two Africans who were not tied up headed toward the doors. They made for an odd couple: Souleymane in a traditional, wildly colorful, tentlike *grand boubou*; Idris Deby in a trim Western suit. The African woman with the weird headdress, the other guests could tell, must have belonged to the restrained man, because she stayed behind, yipping in a strange register. Several of the groom's friends headed toward the doors, as did the Doctors Without Borders cohort. So did a mother and a baby.

This was a suburban family room, not a ballroom. People standing in the available floor space—basically none—behind the inadequate number of folding chairs for a short ceremony was already more than the room was good for. Within a second the room was full of writhing and screaming: full-throated from the men, shrieks from the women and the babes-in-arms, and, in its own special robotic munchkin register, the wails of Theodore, the bride's eighteen-year-old half brother, who had Asperger's syndrome.

But those who tried the door leading from the room to the house's hallway found it forcibly barricaded from outside. So that was what the drill had accomplished. Those who headed for the French doors found the terrorist was already blocking those doors triumphantly with her rifle, which was now pointed at the approaching guests. Curled around one of her fingers, another item fetched from beneath the mother of all bridal veils: a big, nasty, serious-looking padlock. A padlock not for a gym locker but for a car impoundment lot. She nudged the rifle into the chest of the most aggressive young man. He froze and raised his hands. So did his compatriot in jailbreak.

Helen Burns, who had stayed as still as possible amid the chaos and was trying very hard to figure out what this woman wanted, did something strange then. From her seat in the front row, she gave the terrorist a friendly, unobtrusive little wave. She did not look directly at her while she waved. She turned her head to look a little bit to the side and down. If this woman was seriously mentally ill, Helen knew it was a bad idea to engage in direct eye contact with her. Direct eye contact would be too stimulating. She would need to connect periodically, but not too intensely.

Given her oblique view, and the gas mask, it was impossible to tell if the terrorist was smiling. But her shoulders lilted a bit as she waved back—just the smallest flutter of acknowledgment of the fingers on the rifle.

$\mathscr{L}$ater, it would be pointed out that Dr. Helen Burns had opposed the wedding from the start. Not the marriage, but the party.

If they were a tribe in unforgiving terrain, if life were hard and short, there would be an excuse for people to festoon their hair with feathers and machete the suckling pig. People in love? Let's eat! But here? It was silly. Why sanctify their love with a ceremony? Especially a ceremony performed not in a church but in a suburban backyard, by a friend who made a point of alerting everyone that he bought his ministry license on the Internet.

If weddings were pointless, ironic weddings were even more excruciatingly so. Like being a little bit pregnant: How can you believe slightly in the power vested in church or state? Although, in fairness, that's exactly how most people believe. They hedge their bets. Far be it from Helen to challenge them. Let the psychiatrists browbeat them about the inconsistencies in their belief systems.

But Tess! It broke her heart because there they all were, the pathetic parental units with their failed marriages, and though Tess seemed to be happy and well adjusted—miraculously so, actually— here she still was wanting the fancy dress, the invitation engraved in italics. Hadn't Helen hand-made enough Halloween costumes to save her daughter from needing to be Princess for a Day? Worse yet, Tess wanted to be *original*. And that she would never be. And that broke Helen's heart even worse, because what more could Tess do? The girl had lived in Africa, in places without running water, in places where she could have been tortured and killed. She was marrying a biracial performance artist. And yet she was still, finally, like her brother, an accountant. Okay: an M.B.A. with a specialty in microfinance. But the wedding meant that Tess still longed to be something she wasn't, something she would never be. She would never be a golden girl. She would always be a mousy blond, her personality, like her bangs, neither here nor there, always growing out, never lying right.

Was this true? Probably not. Tess was probably fine, and Helen was projecting. Dr. Burns could consider the possibility. After all, Gabriel, the groom, was great. You could not have custom-ordered a better husband for Tess than Gabe. He loved her with a clear-eyed conviction that maybe sixty-odd people could profit from witnessing. It was Helen, not Tess, who seemed to be most unnerved by the prospect of the guest list. She simply could not imagine how they could negotiate that many needs, at that many complicated cross-purposes.

Helen's ex-husband, Jake, was not a concern. Helen and Jake's marriage and its dissolution were far behind them. All of that agony, in memory, was like a bad overnight stay in a plastic chair at an airport during holiday weather delays. But Jake had followed Helen with two other marriages and two new kids, generating whole new shitstorms of tension and animosity. His second wife, Sarah, had remarried, too. Jake hated Sarah's second husband, and Sarah hated Jake's third wife. Everyone in the overextended family united on only one thing, and that was dislike of Jake's child bride and her baby. The baby's name was Louis—evidently old-fashioned baby names had cycled back into fashion again—but Helen's kids called their new stepbrother the Infant Jesus, their father's new McMansion the McManger. The wife's name was actually Mary.

Their family tree was not, finally, all *that* complicated, but it was tedious to explain, and of course somewhat embarrassing, especially when the issue from the marriages got trotted out like some warped Von Trapp family lineup. As if their situation didn't already attract enough attention, Jake's son by the second marriage had Asperger's. The odds of him getting through the ceremony without acting out in some spectacular way were about as slim as the odds of Mary's infant not crying. Helen could take all of this in stride, and Tess, who was close to both her stepmother and stepbrother, wasn't concerned in the least. But Helen did flinch to envision how it would all seem to her daughter's future in-laws.

The groom's parents were as delightful as Gabriel himself. Del and Sal Billips were intelligent, open, easygoing people, journalists from Atlanta. Helen was looking forward to getting to know them better. The touchy issue was the grandparents. Gabriel's father was black, his grandfather a retired military colonel. Billips Sr. was reputed to be strict, harsh, unforgiving, a man who wore full regalia and polished shoes to summer barbeques. He rarely spoke and, when he did, it was generally about race. The grandmother didn't speak at all, yet managed to somehow steadily beam her disapproval and disappointment—she'd have a lot of fun with the sour, geriatric Jews at the wedding, most of whom could be counted on to make a radically uncouth generalization about "Afro-Americans."

At least one could hope that the groom's grandparents had grown accustomed to Jewish psychiatrists. The groom's mother, Salome ("Sal"), née Needleman, had a father in the trade. Perhaps all you needed to know about Ira Needleman, M.D., the L.A. psychiatrist, was that he was the kind of guy who would name his daughter after Freud's groupie and alleged mistress, Lou Andreas-Salome. The East Coast psychiatrists would view their touchy-feely L.A. colleague with barely disguised contempt. They would not join in warm amazement that the bride and groom, the two people in the world least requiring psychoanalysis, both had shrinks for grandfathers. They would bicker.

And that wasn't all:

- Tess's brother Simon had recently separated from his wife. He could pretend to be happy for Tess, but still, his current mood could not be called marriage-friendly. Or Haddonfield-friendly. He was now installed in a grim apartment in Philadelphia, battling for visitation rights. When he entered the town where he grew up and where his children and ex-wife still lived, he wore the expression of a soldier returning to the battlefield where he lost both legs. Even to let the kids attend their aunt's wedding, Simon's vindictive soon-to-be-ex had kicked up a tornado of impediments and conditions. Helen felt bad for her son, for the kids, and also for herself. Her time with her grandchildren had been dramatically reduced.

- Gabriel's sister, Miranda, was an actress who had been steadily gaining visibility, and would have a new movie out that very week. Miranda wasn't even sure that she'd be able to attend because of her duties promoting the film. Helen fervently hoped she wouldn't come. She was obscenely beautiful. No bride needs to be thus upstaged. Let Miranda stay in New York and do *Letterman*.

- To compound the Miranda problem, Miranda was bringing a date. Helen personally had never heard of Trevor Hunter, the actor in question. Tess has IMDB'd him for her mother and pulled up ten or fifteen pictures of him grinning emptily with his unwashed hair sticking up in a piglet curlicue in the front. To Helen, he looked sexless—a cartoon unicorn. But his name made all of Tess's friends gasp with pleasure and anticipation. More distraction. More upstaging.

- Tess and Gabriel planned to invite some people they'd befriended during their stint in Africa. Helen had nothing but respect for Doctors Without Borders. But the year and a half of Tess's tour, when she was first in Mali, then in Chad, were the most miserable months that Helen had ever experienced as a parent. The most truly satisfying day of her life was the day that Tess returned safe from Africa. Even though most of the people they were inviting from those days were fellow Americans—tough women who spent a couple of months a year as logisticians for Médecins Sans Frontières, the organization whose name Helen could never learn to say properly (or, as some of the insiders called MSF, "Many

Single Females"); politically committed men involved, like Gabriel and Tess, with microfinance for third world nations—Helen suspected that political asylum for the Africans might be the real goal. She kept imagining counterforces converging with Uzis upon her house. Absurd, and maybe just a touch of post-traumatic stress disorder, from the time she spent with her chest thumping over every ringing telephone, every picture of a kidnapped humanitarian aid worker that she saw in *The New York Times*.

- Even assuming that was paranoid—that Tess was right when she said, as a mantra, "Mom! Repeat after me! Chad ain't that bad (at least anymore)!"—was Tess's wedding really the proper forum for the inevitable discussions about the fate of the dark continent? About brutal rape and flesh-eating bacteria? All of the MSF people ardently believed that American foreign policy was the root of all evil. Gabriel's grandfather, presumably, did not. Helen feared there would be a showdown.

- Strangers in Helen's house, which no matter how hard she cleaned (not that she cleaned that hard) always smelled like dog. She'd have to kennel Maynard. Poor Maynard, in a cage all alone with his stiff hips! On this score, Helen was quite aware she was projecting, that the person she was worried about displacing was herself. At this point in her life, she feared, her habits were so solitary and strange that she'd be an object of pity, of mockery. Or worse yet of brave self-sufficiency. Hard to relish the prospect of the newer wives parading past the diorama of her stalled life, their pupils widening and narrowing like camera lenses as they clicked off the seriously outdated wallpaper, the non-stainless-steel appliances in the house that she'd clung to after the divorce, for the children, so they didn't lose the comfort and familiarity of Haddonfield. She had never quite been able to afford the house, and each month's bills, for decades, were a matter of triage, or life support. No one—not the wives, not the Africans, not the actors—needed to see her house.

"Are you sure," Helen asked Tess over the phone, when they first discussed the wedding plans, "that you don't want to hold the wedding somewhere more convenient for your friends in New York?"

"Too expensive."

"There are a lot of us to help you."

"Not my style. Plus it's nice for people to be able to get away."

"How come you don't want to do it at your father's house? It's much nicer and bigger."

In answer to that suggestion, Tess only snorted. It went without saying that Mary would not be eager to host a shindig at the McManger.

Helen persisted. "How about some nice place in downtown Philly, so the guests can walk from their hotels?"

"No. I like the house. I grew up there. The garden is great."

"Isn't there some hip venue in Brooklyn you'd prefer?" Helen asked. A ship dock? An abandoned shirt factory? A crack house festooned with balloons and maybe the wedding coordinated with some Take Back Our Block party?

"Hey, Ma, what's *wrong* with you, anyhow?"

"I just hope it will be nice enough," Helen murmured, paying quiet attention to her queasy sense of indecent exposure. How could a caterer function in her kitchen? She didn't even have a gas range. But at least there was her garden, a half acre of lusciousness that she'd inherited from the previous owners and to which she'd been a truly fine stepmother. None of the subsequent McWives had a garden like that, or ever would. So ironic that her daughter, who had been the poster child of suburban safety, prospering in school and on swim team, her yearbook full of chirped adoration from classmates with whom she vowed to keep in touch until the grave, wound up severing all ties to move to Africa, then Manhattan, or rather, the grimmer frontiers of Brooklyn, which to Helen looked like the set of a film about the end of the world; whereas her son, who had always hated the town and had been declaring since eighth grade that he would get out at the first opportunity, went to the local college for both undergrad and business school, married a local girl, and put down roots right where he began, just like Jimmy Stewart in *It's a Wonderful Life* except without the good humor, or the devoted wife. No justice in the world.

Maybe he would fall in love with a charming Doctors Without Borders woman at the wedding and finally get his wish. What did Helen have to do with how her children turned out? Not much. Pruning, weeding, watering.

Mother of the bride, Helen scolded herself, and quickly tamped herself back into the supporting role. She'd practiced therapy for more than a quarter of a century. Even if Tess had been there in person, Helen could have managed to reveal not a whiff of her own uneasiness. Except that wasn't true, because over the phone, Tess *had* caught the serve, and lobbed it right back. "It'll be okay, Ma," Tess said. "If anyone can deal with this crowd, you can." Helen knew it was true, and let herself bask in the compliment, as well as in joy at how well her daughter knew her.

Still, the sense of foreboding persisted. Each decision made brought a fresh stab of unease. It was an intense feeling, truly a gut feeling, specific as morning sickness.

Much to the derision of her Freudian ex, Dr. Helen Burns had trained as a Reichian. The way she practiced today had very little to do with theory, Reich's or others', although it was probably closest to an offshoot of Karen Horney and attachment theory. Helen was still inclined to think in terms of "energy." The energy surrounding this event definitely had some indefinable cloud, some neoplasm not yet showing up on the MRI.

She was upset enough to ask Jake how he was feeling about the upcoming nuptials.

"Fine," her ex-husband said. "I like the guy. Thought you did, too."

"Yes," Helen said.

Helen knew how relieved Jake was that his future son-in-law was not merely a "performance artist," but had some practical application for his hobbies; currently Gabriel managed a nonprofit that helped Africans sell their arts and crafts abroad. In MSF, he had actually done art therapy with kids, which Helen knew Jake thought was noble if misguided. Helen further knew that Jake was very interested in predicting the potential problems with an interracial marriage, with how it was like or unlike Jake marrying a non-Jew as he himself had now managed to do two out of three times, but that was only because the research on white women marrying black men (no concept of biracial yet in the psychiatric literature) still focused on the woman's relationship with her father, which meant that Tess's choice of a mate would be, first and foremost, about Jake himself.

It was amazing how often conversations with Jake turned out to be about Jake himself. How could the man practice therapy? Really, he couldn't listen. But then most therapists didn't. Therapists were people after all, and most people didn't listen, which is why people needed therapists to begin with. It takes some work to learn to tamp down the self until someone else can speak without being dismissed, mocked, or one-upped. "It's not about the marriage," Helen persisted. "I love Gabe. And he loves Tess to pieces. I just have this weird feeling about the wedding."

"Weird how?" Jake asked and, before she could answer, "All the exes? I think we'll manage to behave ourselves. And who cares if a couple of spurned spouses glare at each other across the centerpieces. I actually think Tess is kind of proud of us all. Us, and the Africans in the tribal getups—it makes her interesting. Less of a Girl Scout."

Blunt, but true.

"That, and . . ." Helen said.

"What?"

Where to start? "Miranda."

"Miranda Mobley," Jake exhaled, punching out each sexy syllable. "I wonder where she got Mobley as a stage name. I mean, I understand that Billips is not a great name for an actress. Too hillbilly. Hey, did you ever ask Gabe whether he's related to Chauncey Billips? Wouldn't it be cool if Chauncey Billips came to the wedding?"

Helen had absolutely no idea who Chauncey Billips was but had the sense not to inquire.

This is how conversations with Jake tended to go. One could hope he managed not to engage in his own elaborate free associations in session. Most of Helen's own therapy was nonverbal, not about what she said (because what, after all, was there to say about most problems?) but about how it was said, and how the body received it. Her therapy was about tone and gesture. About projecting a certain kind of stillness that was free of judgment, and in which the life of whatever hurt dominated the person could simply be acknowledged.

"I guess I'm concerned about Miranda and this Trevor person," Helen allowed.

"They probably won't come."

"Coming. Both of them. RSVP'd."

"Really!" Jake said. "That's great. Will Rosewood Lane be staked out by paparazzi?"

And all of this uneasiness was before Tess informed her mother about a last-minute addition to the guest list: Mara Lowell, an old friend from college who, Tess said, would hopefully not bring down the tone with bad karma.

"Her ex," Tess explained, "is an old friend of Gabe's, also from Wesleyan. Ben. Ben Kramer. The novelist? Have you read him? She's got kind of a . . . thing about him."

Hel Burns knew the Thing very well, since Mara Lowell was her patient.

That Tess was unaware of the connection was not astonishing. Helen had kept her own name. Helen's feelings about her name could best be described in terms of Stockholm syndrome: once you've been trapped through childhood with a name like Hel Burns, it's hard to let go. But six degrees of separation was maybe more like three, in the therapeutic community. Tess knew that a chunk of her mother's business consisted of phone therapy with clients in New York, work she had gotten by referral after one patient moved there. But there was no reason for her to place Mara in that group. Perhaps Mara was also not aware that she was attending a wedding at her therapist's house.

Helen hadn't spoken to Mara in a while. Which also wasn't unusual: her therapy was not of the pay-me-even-if-you're-hit-by-a-car-and-are-lying-on-the-road-with-your-legs-crushed variety. As with her own children, patients generally called her when they needed something. "Why did you invite her, then?" Helen asked.

"She's coming as someone's date."

Shouldn't Helen know whose date?

Helen thought about calling Jake again. Dr. Jacob Nathanson would have a lot to say about how to handle this situation. No doubt there was an elaborate protocol. But she didn't call him or say anything to Tess.

She did put in a call to Mara, blessedly getting her answering machine. Mara left a message in return, bubbling with amazement about the coincidence, and adding that she was doing great—new boyfriend, *totally* over Ben, and what exactly did Tess know, what had Helen told her? Helen left another message to assure her, nothing at all. Not even that Mara was a patient.

Helen dealt with her own mounting anxiety as best she could. Deadheading flowers in the garden. Pats to the silky head of her dog and kisses for Maynard's big black nose, kisses that the dog reciprocated by sniffing them while Helen prattled on in the cartoon whisper she used to speak to her dog, because she was embarrassed to be the kind of woman who speaks to her dog.

When she first saw the woman with the rifle, Helen's first thought was that it was Mara Lowell. She and her patient had shared a surprised but warm and officially uncomplicated greeting at the house—"Who knew?" Mara said, sporting a dramatic new haircut, and introduced Helen to the boyfriend, who seemed nice, who knew the groom how? No time to find out. But the first thing Helen did, when the first shot was fired, was to look around for Mara.

Mara clung to the new boyfriend.

So it wasn't her. But someone had an issue with someone. Clearly.

Both Jake's sister and Salome's brother had to be somewhere else and could not attend on the date worked out to accommodate the bride and groom's African friends. Then Helen's sister canceled last-minute—kid emergency. Delbert Jr.'s brother was dead (car accident—Delbert went to war, repeatedly, but his brother Frank died within miles of his house). A wedding without one aunt or uncle? This seemed very wrong. Helen had been so paranoid about this event that she wondered if all of the decamping people knew something she didn't.

"What's happening?" Helen's mother asked belatedly. Helen, beside her, rotated to face her head-on; her mother was so deaf she probably didn't notice the bullet. The face Helen made, exaggeratedly, meant *Just a little delay. No big deal.* Helen's mother looked relieved.

Fact is, Helen was relieved, too. Jealousy, resentment: those were things she could deal with. Fury over a bloody civil war was out of her skill set.

Poor Tess!

Even at her own wedding, not the center of attention.

*S*IT DOWN," the terrorist commanded.

At least "terrorist" is how the guests referred to her. Although any law enforcement crisis negotiator would call her a "barricaded subject with hostages."

For an exclamation point, she fired a shot from the rifle into the ceiling.

The roar of the bullet shut everyone up and froze everyone but Simon's children. His sons, Dan and Cole, all Fauntleroyish in their miniature suits, and his daughter, Rosalind, done up as flower girl, adorable and highly flammable, scrambled to find the cartridge as if it were a ball hit into the stands at a baseball game. Then screamed, because the shell was hot.

"Careful," the terrorist said. "Hot."

The room filled with the acrid smell of gunfire. The terrified guests looked at the hole the bullet had made in the ceiling as they went into the kind of adrenaline trough that is the opposite of how adrenaline can also pump you up, make you brave.

Those who could sit, sat. The spasm of fearlessness that had led to the escape attempt seemed to now be as spent as the bullet. Except for one screaming baby, the room was silent. In the quiet, everyone felt how close the room was, how tight. Without any self-consciousness at all, the mother popped down the spaghetti straps of her fancy dress and began to nurse the baby.

"Now," the terrorist said. "Sit—except for you."

She pointed to the photographer at the back of the room, who had continued snapping pictures. A friend of the bride and groom's from Chad, he had shot through worse.

There really was not floor space for everyone without a chair to sit. The women in their nice dresses, the men in their suits, could not comfortably cross their legs. Only moments ago, their biggest issues had been how attractive they looked. No one is used to dressing up anymore.

"Calmly," the terrorist said. "And listen. "The only person coming in or out of this room is going to be me. First off, I want to commend the bride and groom for hosting a party with modest production values. Close family and friends right here in the backyard of her childhood home—young man, you must sit down."

A five-year-old had begun to whine. He was the kind of jack-in-the-box kid that anyone, immediately, could identify as ADHD except his mother, whose defensive expression suggested she was still trying to think of him as "spirited." The terrorist located him in the crowd and turned her whole body in his direction.

"He's a child," the mother noted, tremulously.

"Yes, ma'am, I'm fully aware that he's a child. So is the flower girl, and you notice she's behaving quite nicely."

Rosalind did a curtsey to acknowledge the compliment.

"Sit! Stay! Young man, I will not tell you again."

The little boy reacted to her alpha tone as a dog would. He sat down between his parents and was quiet.

Helen, seeing them, was moved. Everyone in the room had huddled with the person or people they cared about. Everyone else, to everyone else, was cannon fodder. Her son, who did not have a chair, was crouched and now trying to encircle his three standing children. Tess and Gabe, also standing, in the back, had managed to find each other, and watched, their shoulders touching. Gabe's parents watched with what Helen thought might be journalist's faces: alert but neutral.

"You see? Mom and Dad, you *can* try that at home. You do *not* have to be trained professionals."

As she spoke, the psychiatrists in the house watched body language and began to run diagnostics.

Obviously this wasn't therapy and they had not a shred of information, but just as they will explain in police academy how aim in night shooting tends, paradoxically, to be more accurate than day shooting, because you aren't distracted by light or movement—same as how basketball players know that free-throw shots are better if you just throw them up casually, without too much forethought or genuflecting, because your instincts have taken over—they all assumed there was a lot they could tell quickly, purely, and with deadly accuracy.

Their expressions indicated that they all planned to be the one to figure her out and save the day.

At that prospect, Helen found herself truly alarmed. How many psychiatrists does it take to change a lightbulb? Hopefully the first one who opened his mouth would not insult her by asking if she saw little green men.

"Parenting has changed a lot, don't you think?" one of the psychiatrists agreed, casually, as if he and the terrorist were chatting over drinks.

Helen wondered why he didn't just inquire, point-blank, if she loved her mother.

Her response: "What are you talking about?"

Jake jumped in. "If you'd just take off the mask," he persisted.

She shook her head.

It was hard for Helen not to roll her eyes. Actually, she feared she had rolled her eyes. Obviously the psychiatrists would want to listen to the terrorist's production. Not the words themselves but how they came out, their rhythm and inflection. Was her tone elevated, grandiose? Were her answers precise? Overly precise? Were they one-word answers or did she, on the other hand, blather? Did she stick to one subject or wander?

They had already missed their first clue, which is that she didn't seem to realize she was in a room full of psychiatrists. That meant

that not only was she not here because of anyone on the Billips side
of the wedding party, if she didn't know Billips Sr. was a decorated
army guy, but she wasn't here because of Jake Nathanson, either.
And Jake Nathanson, with his three wives and who knew how many
other seductions that didn't end in marriage and procreation behind
him, would have been a very obvious target. But it didn't appear to
be Jake and it didn't appear to be any of the other psychiatrists, either,
which eliminated a nice chunk of the assembled guests. Statistically,
mental health care providers are among the most common targets of
stalkers.

"Just let her talk," Billips Sr. said.

He didn't stand to say it, but his voice was commanding, room-
filling.

"Why, *thank* you, sir," the terrorist said.

Helen caught the grandfather's eye and tried to communicate to
him, by a tightening of the mouth and a steady stare, that she approved of his approach and that he should wrest control away from
the shrinks as soon as possible.

"So," the terrorist said. "I should also note to you that the back
door has been wired with explosives. If you don't believe me, feel free
to take a peek. You are not going to want to try to leave. I recommend
very strongly against it.

"Tess and Gabriel, I am sorry to rain on your parade. My presence here is due specifically to one particular piece of shit, but for now
I'm addressing all of the weasels and betrayers in the crowd. Because
I'm sure there are some here. There are some everywhere. All I want
is a simple, heartfelt apology."

Silence.

"And then we can move on, no?"

Silence.

The terrorist paced, arms crossed. Making eye contact, insofar as
eye contact is possible through gas mask and sunglasses, with the
crowd.

One of the guests stood up then and screamed, "I'm sorry!"

LISA ZEIDNER

Then he pumped his fist, Rocky-triumph style, as people turned to stare. The terrorist in particular looked surprised. "I'm *sorry*," he added, as if she might not have understood the first time.

Even the nonprofessionals in the group, or those who didn't know the family, immediately recognized the Asperger's voice; if they couldn't pinpoint the specific disorder, they at least knew there was something really wrong with him. A quite good-looking young man with shoulder-length hair of a honey blond so beautiful that no colorist could duplicate it. The bride's half brother, Theo.

"Sorr-*E*! Sorr-*E*! Sorr-*E*!"—now a chant, as if calling the rock star back for an encore.

The boy's mother, beside him, hushed him, tugging on his suit jacket. The question was not why he had blurted out, but why he had remained quiet for so long.

"But she said—"

"Not you, hon," the terrorist added; then, to the mother, "Will he be okay?"

The mother shrugged in the Esperanto of defeated motherhood.

The terrorist did not react, however. She stood at attention, legs slightly spread, immobile as a Beefeater, posing for the camera.

"You think you're so tough," she added, in a voice both furious and tremulous. "Happiness is a warm gun, right? Just your rifle, your pony, and you. Well, look who's swinging the big dick now," and she illustrated with some figure eights of the rifle, jutting out her pelvis as she did so in a kind of jerky stripper move, all of which made her suddenly seem, even more than she had before, quite seriously deranged.

She had begun to walk backward. Her last line she managed to deliver right at the spot where the bride and groom would have stood to take their vows. They'd set up a lectern, borrowed from a middle school where a friend of Tess's worked. Helen had not been clear why, exactly, they needed a lectern, or why the bride and groom seemed charmed by its homeliness. The terrorist crouched and, from the cabinet underneath, pulled a daunting length of thick, heavy metal chain. She rattled it for effect. She outstretched her arms and held it taut, looking directly at the photographer and posing until he nodded to indicate that he'd got a good shot.

Then she went out the back door, attached the chain to something—what?—and, pointedly, clicked shut the padlock.

$\mathscr{B}$ecause of Alan Smith, the wedding photographer—in real life, a photojournalist whom the bride and groom had met in Chad—they would have much more complete documentation than hostage situations usually afford.

Alan did not know most of the guests. They meant nothing to him. Most people at weddings mean nothing to most people at weddings. Nobody even bothered to try to remember anyone's name. That was one of the reasons he loved photographs so much. You didn't need to know the people. He would not claim that a picture told you everything. Instead, it told you enough to feel the poignancy of what you didn't know. The stillness and quietude of photos. Their hushed temporality. Nothing made you understand mortality better than a photograph of a dead woman with a little lipstick on.

Al had set up a kind of gauntlet on the front lawn, through which all of the arriving guests passed to have their pictures taken before entering the house. He'd thoughtfully even laid down a roll of pink construction paper—a pink carpet—to protect the ladies' heels as they moved to the spot he'd pre-lit, where his "assistant" Alyssa, a journalist whom he'd recently started seeing, helped him set up. He had worked quickly on the portraits, but there did get to be a bit of a bottleneck as it grew closer to the appointed hour. He took a couple of great photos of the snaking line itself. In one of them, his favorite, the across-the-street neighbor watched resentfully from just within the dark of his garage.

Al was very pleased. What a record of the hostages' last moments if they were to die. And that was before he knew that two of the potentially dead people were among the last to pull up in their gleaming black town car: the actress Miranda Mobley and her new boyfriend, the actor Trevor Hunt.

Photos of Trevor and Miranda hugging each other, all dressed up. Not to mention the only pictures of Miranda and her brother, the groom, who looked like her transsexual body double. And now, last-minute group hug: the groom and his sister, the bride and her brother.

If Miranda and Trevor died, Al was going to be a fucking millionaire.

The bride's brother Simon had not met Miranda yet, but he had already seen her naked. So had his father. In fact, they'd seen her naked together.

Other than stage and TV work, Miranda had had four movie roles of increasing visibility, and in three of them she had been undressed. Both Simon and his father had seen her breasts, her ass. They had studied her body on the top-of-the-line TV cunningly built into Jake's new kitchen.

"What is that called?" Jake asked his son—Mary was at yoga, and all the kids were in the pool, being supervised by baby Louis's nanny. He pointed out the profile of Miranda's leg in the skimpy panties, the hollow or dimple where ass met hip.

"I have no idea," Simon said. "It's more an absence of a thing."

"It must have a name. What are the two muscle groups that meet?"

"Hey, you're the one who went to med school."

"Gluteus maximus?" Jake said. "And . . . hip flexor?"

"I don't know, Dad. Don't you have an anatomy book?"

"It's good to try to remember things. Hedge against Alzheimer's."

While his father Googled muscle groups on his laptop, Simon

just drank his beer and stared at Miranda Mobley's breasts on the TV. The nipples were dark, the breasts just the right size to be cupped by a hand yet slightly overflow the hand. He had never slept with a woman with nipples that dark. Joan's were the ordinary white-girl pink. So, no doubt, were his father's new blond wife's. The familiar Caucasian color combination suddenly seemed slightly nauseating, like a white rat's pink-rimmed eyes or one of those ghostly, translucent fish that lives deep down in the ocean. Everything about Miranda Mobley suggested concupiscent readiness. Her very skin tone—its dusky indeterminacy—was sexy, insinuating lights out, draw the curtains. That was probably racist. Was it racist, by default, to find a person's skin tone attractive? He had been looking forward to asking her, at the rehearsal dinner, about what kind of parts she could get or wanted to get and whether being of mixed race had proven an advantage, or a hindrance, or both. On TV, he had noted, black girls could be cops or nurses or even forensic people who didn't blanch while plunging a blade into the worst kind of bloated, stinky corpse. If they were the leads, though, they were generally in serious danger. Miranda Mobley seemed like she had a chance to push the envelope in that regard. She did not have to be tortured in tiny underwear. She was getting girl-next-door parts. Nude girl-next-door.

God, he was horny.

But Miranda hadn't come to the rehearsal dinner. So the first time Simon met her was when her town car pulled up—a little late, truth be told.

As if her chauffeur-driven black town car were not distraction enough, the actress arrived with a police escort. A Haddonfield squad car followed, lights blinking. The grim-faced officer, in sunglasses, blocked the road to watch Miranda emerge. Then saluted, did a dramatic U-turn, and sped off.

Simon, too, watched. Since he'd been outside, providing parking support to arriving guests, he saw Miranda emerge from the car, and the first things that came out, as will often happen when people step out of a vehicle, were her feet. Then her calves. It's hard to focus on someone's legs when her breasts are bared but here her calves alone, high and tight, were heart-stopping.

Miranda wore a little black sundress that suddenly made him understand at once, completely and deeply, the little black dress. The little black dress was about this body. You could present this body simply, the way you presented fresh fruit in a bowl. Behold the knees. Behold the clean plane of the collarbone, necklace-free. To Simon, who had just emerged from a twelve-year sentence in the suburbs, his flash of insight into the metaphysics of the little black dress seemed revelatory, and brought with it a surge of longing not only for Miranda herself but for the urban world from which she sprang, a world free of car seats and Christmas ornaments. Fuck nature! He wanted to go to London, Paris, and Rome, he wanted to have sex on white sheets with black women!

"I'm Simon Nathanson," he said. "You're my new sister-in-law. Or sister-in-law-in-law. Is that right? Sister-in-law once removed?"

She smiled. "Very nice to meet you. And this is Trevor Hunter. Trev, Simon, Tess's brother."

Ah, crap. The boyfriend. Big and bland. As a human being, he was a box store. One on every corner. Jocular, uncreative, yet faintly malevolent, like every boy who ever got the girl in high school.

"And these are my kids, Daniel, Cole, and Rosalind. Kids, come meet your new—aunt-in-law? Aunt-in-law-in-law?"

"What a pretty name," Miranda said. "Rosalind is a name from Shakespeare. So is my name, Miranda. Sorry we're so late. We got pulled over by that cop! In this Podunk town! For no reason!"

"He was harassing us is what," Trevor offered. "'Your papers, please,' then running 'em real slow. Then figured out who we were and got all polite."

"Creepy," Miranda said, making a little creepy face that Al managed to get on camera.

"Smile," the wedding photographer said. "Miranda, Trevor—oh, hi, Tess—all of you, line up here."

In Shakespeare, Simon could marry Miranda, and his sister could marry Miranda's brother. Trevor could marry the ass.

Speaking of asses, here, somehow, was Jake Nathanson. Simon's father presented himself to Miranda in his best low-toned, casual, urbane flirting voice, oblivious to the fact that he was old enough to be her grandfather.

Simon did not want to die before having sex again.

Nor did Al.

At some point in the lawn shoot, Alyssa, his girlfriend, caught his eye and flashed him a big, pleased smile.

Al and Alyssa: karma or just an excellent coincidence?

Later, struggling to get decent shots of the hostage taker over the heads and body parts of the people in the room, Al realized that he hadn't gotten a picture of Alyssa outside. If something were to happen to Alyssa, she and he would be the only ones of whom there was no record. Only them. If the whole room went up in flames, no one would even know they had been there.

Of course if the whole room went up in flames, there wouldn't be photos of anyone. The camera, though expensive and rugged, was no black box.

Nevertheless, while their captor made her exit out the French doors to the backyard, rather than snapping pictures of her attaching the length of metal chain and the lock, he turned to Alyssa and said, not "I love you," which is what he was thinking, but: "Smile."

A sound we know from the movies, canned as laugh track, is "everyone talks at once." The standard stage direction for mass confusion. In the confines of the great room, the cacophony of almost sixty frightened people talking at once was lush and off-key, like an orchestra tuning up.

"Quiet," Delbert Billips Sr. commanded.

He stood. He had exceptional posture. He was almost as dark as the Africans, in a black suit. His hair was close-cut and white at the temples. He must have been in his mid- or late seventies. He had kept himself beautifully. He was crisp and trim. Helen made note of the way, when he stood, he put his hand lightly on his wife's shoulder to reassure her.

"All right," he said. "Let's get organized. And let's try to talk quietly. Someone see if you can release him."

Idris Deby worked the plastic restraint off his fellow Chadian. Ngarta stood, rubbed his wrists, rotated his shoulders, and then looked to Billips for his assignment.

The colonel approached the three African men. He made a series of army or police gestures. You two, split up. You, go over there. Idris, Ngarta, and Souleymane proceeded immediately to the piece of furniture from behind which the woman had extracted the rifle. One felt behind the books on the shelves. The other tried to peer further behind the cabinet while Billips continued to scan the room.

A couple of the older Jews exchanged looks of irritation that Billips had deputized only other black men. But his bond with the

Africans was not due to race. He recognized the three African men as not only the bravest of the wedding guests but the only ones who would know how to work in a team and behave like soldiers. They'd acted at the right time, backed off at the right time. He sensed immediately that he would get no cooperation from the bride and groom's clueless friends, white or black, who had charged the door earlier. Their contribution to all of this would be to get them all killed with their undisciplined bravado.

The great-room addition had been built in the early '80s, right before Helen and Jake divorced. Chicken-or-egg-wise, it's always hard to tell what comes first, the renovation and the stress it causes, or the marital problems that make more space seem essential. The ceilings were high, the skylight was perennially dirty and out of reach, and so were the transom windows. The only egress was the French doors. Billips went immediately to the doors and looked up, down. He crouched like a Vietnamese rice farmer. He felt the trim. Then he spent a while pondering whatever he saw outside the doors while the crowd remained quiet and watchful.

Idris Deby rapped lightly on the piece of furniture, to get Billips Sr.'s attention. He nodded no, as in no weapons, but pointed to the cabinet that housed the DVD player. From it, he held up a yellow plastic kidney-shaped bed pan. Billips looked at Helen, to confirm that she personally didn't keep a bed pan in her family room, and when Helen indicated not, he nodded grimly. Then he called the taller of the two African men to the doors, to feel the top of the trim, which he couldn't reach. The African pronounced it clear of wires.

None of this could have taken more than several minutes.

"We should run," one of the younger guests said. "The chain goes across the middle. Just break the glass and go under it, over it."

"Is there really a bomb?" another guest asked.

Billips said, "Yes."

"Is it real?"

Billips: "Can't say for sure, but it looks like a bomb."

At that, the woman who had recently finished breast-feeding her baby began to sob. Then the baby cried, too.

"And that door?"

One of the groom's friends near the door to the family room gave it a shove. It didn't move.

"If all of us pushed?"

"Listen," Billips said again. "This is really important. No one acts independently. No making a break for it, and nobody talks to her, nobody says a word to her, other than the person we decide is designated to talk to her. Is that understood?"

If anyone wondered who died and made Billips God, they didn't publicly object to him taking over now.

"Did anyone manage to keep a phone?" Billips asked.

No. The gastroenterologist said, "I wish I'd thought to call 911 when she told us to turn the phones off."

Billips to Helen: "There isn't a phone in the room? A phone you shoved out of the way somewhere?"

Helen told him no. The phone had been removed from the room, to make sure a telemarketer didn't call during the ceremony.

"No Xbox? No Internet access through your TV?"

No, Helen said.

"Does the intercom work?"

No. The intercom had been installed back when suburban life was assumed to be one big pool party, and you needed it to locate your kids for dinner when they were in their rooms blasting music, or in the basement playing beer pong. It had not worked for years, and had not been fixed because who would Helen call now, her dog?

"Okay. First," Billips said, "we need to figure out what she wants. Then we need to decide who will talk to her. Anyone know her?"

A sea of denying nods and murmurs from the assemblage.

"Tess? Gabe?"

No from the bride and groom.

"I cannot believe," said one of the male guests, "that a woman can hold fifty people—what are we here, fifty? Sixty?"

"Fifty-five," Tess said. "Plus the caterers and their staff."

"Fifty-five hostages in a house. Gimme a break! It's not like we're on a plane where the only weapon is the tines of our forks. There's a kitchen full of knives and power tools in the garage—"

"Let's go for it," another of the able-bodied male guests concurred.

Actually, Helen thought, Jake had taken all the power tools. She had hedge clippers, though.

"We're locked in," someone reminded him.

"Well, over there. In the corner. Nice big decorative vase. Try having one broken over your head."

Trevor Hunter, the actor, seemed to take this as an instruction. He stood to do a quick mime of a cartoon character bopped on the noggin and reeling. Eyes crossed, seeing stars. A few people, including several of the children and Theodore of course, laughed.

"Do it again," Simon's son Dan commanded. Simon shushed him.

"She isn't here to be knocked out," someone said.

"Well, let's get her here," the Guardian Angel–type said.

They'd overlooked the vase. As Billips watched, Idris and Ngarta teamed up to remove the dried flowers from the vase and overturn it. No knife emerged, just dirt and several mummified, dead crickets.

"Just break the vase."

"You could poke someone's eye out with a hair clip," a guest noted.

"Or a high heel."

"You could strangle someone with the sleeves of a shirt," someone else offered.

"You can go for someone's air passage with a pen," the bartender said.

During this exchange, Billips surveyed the crowd with faint distaste, and seemed to decide that he was going to need to let them talk for a while. While they did, he continued to case the room. Helen watched him. So did his son, Delbert Jr., the groom's father, who watched with what Helen had to assume was a journalist's intensity and focus. And then both Del Jr. and the groom himself edged through the crowd toward Billips, so that three generations of Billipses were staring out the back window.

Helen watched the Billipses check out the door locks, the back-yard with the tables, white tablecloths fluttering in the breeze, and the neighboring houses. Behind Helen's house, at the end of the yard, past the garden, you could see a bit of the country club's golf course.

"All right," Billips said. "I repeat. There will be no heroics. She has a rifle and a shotgun, and who knows what else. With the number of people in this room, any action on our parts could result in someone being injured or killed. We don't know what kind of bomb that is or how it's triggered. Maybe if the chain is disturbed. Maybe she has a dead man's switch. That flashing thing on her arm may well be the trigger. We also don't have any way of knowing for sure if she's alone. We should keep our voices down. If we're quiet we'll know when she's outside, listening. We also might be able to hear when she's upstairs."

Everyone looked up, following his eye.

Billips said, "Let's try to figure out what she wants and then figure out if we can give it to her, and how. Now, who's going to talk to her? We need a negotiator."

The five psychiatrists all held up their hands to volunteer.

"We have to know what's wrong with her," Ira Needleman explained, "to know how best to deal with her."

The other psychiatrists—Jake Nathanson; Sam Gold, the man with whom he shared an office suite; Marty Feldstein of Chicago, an old friend from his residency; and Myra Feldstein, Marty's wife—all nodded their concurrence. The men were all gray-haired and doleful. Though they were of varying heights and weights, they all looked like Bernie Madoff, Jewish and prosperously rumpled, except for Marty's plump wife, who looked exactly like what movies cast as a female psychiatrist, right down to the big jewelry.

"Okay," Billips said. "What's wrong with her?"

*A*n old psychiatry joke: if a new patient walks in for treatment with a peg leg, an eye patch, and a parrot on his shoulder, you should ask him, "What seems to be the problem?" In school they preach humility, open-mindedness. They try to teach you not to rush to judgment. Helen knew it was not a lesson that any of the psychiatrists seemed to have learned, but then, they had been to medical school, a recipe for allowing those who survived it to be smug.

"First and obvious choice, schizophrenic," Marty said. He addressed both the other psychiatrists and the crowd. "From the getup."

Helen thought, Here it comes.

"Schizophrenics are bright enough to plan this," Marty continued. "Onset twenty to thirty—doesn't she seem like she would be in that age range? They hide their symptoms well. If she was in the arts field, she might be thought to be eccentric or creative rather than crazy. She could wander around a university campus in the gas mask and still keep her job, until something snaps."

Jake was shaking his head in deferential disagreement. "I'd go with borderline personality disorder," he said. "Lots of anger, obviously. Jealousy. You'd have the classic *Fatal Attraction* situation: at the beginning, she seduces the guy intellectually and sexually. She's very eager to please. There would be nothing to indicate she was unreasonable. 'Look,' he'd say, 'I'm not leaving my wife,' and she'd assure him she understood. But when things begin to fall apart, the symptoms would start to emerge. Once you're in with her, it's hard to get out. There's no shades of gray with this woman. You're either good or bad. She immediately overbonds. Anyone here have a lover like that?"

A couple of the young men looked at each other and suppressed smirks. Who *hadn't* had a lover like that?

"Or a patient?" Jake continued, addressing the other psychiatrists. "Any really nasty transference situations with borderline patients?"

A knowing nod from several shrinks.

"Oh, many," Ira Needleman said. "One of the worst involving a very famous actress who shall remain nameless here. But I feel confident I would recognize her."

"Bipolar?" Myra suggested, as an alternate diagnosis.

"Bipolar is not dangerous," her husband, Marty, said.

"She might be in the middle of a major depressive episode," Myra insisted. "All those murder-suicides in the news lately . . ."

"But those are men," her husband said. "It's the men who want to go out in a river of blood. It's the men who get steamed over a speeding ticket and want to do suicide by cop or, in the Middle East, plan the—what are they called?"

"Love bombs?" Jake said.

"Love bombing is what cults do to convert people," the best man offered. "To make 'em drink the Kool-Aid."

"Love IEDs," Tess said.

"Love IEDs," Marty said. "That's right. What does it stand for?"

"Incendiary explosive devices?"

"Not incendiary. Improvised, I think."

"Love IEDs. Right. I can't have you, no one can. That's what we got here. Women in the middle of MDEs tend to be . . ."

"Noisier," Sam said. "Much wailing and beating of the breast."

"Histrionic," Jake agreed.

"Flamboyant," Ira agreed.

Go ahead, gentlemen, Helen thought. Quote from memory from *DSM-IV.*

"Well, the outfit is certainly all that," Marty said.

"The gas mask rules out NPD," Jake said.

"If it was narcissistic personality disorder," Ira Needleman agreed, "she'd be done up to the hilt."

"But she is all done up," Myra said. "She's certainly courting the photographer."

Sam said, "People in the midst of MDEs aren't planners. Lots of planning here. Which also rules out drugs. Anyway, no woman would do this."

" 'No woman,' " Myra scoffed.

"Not sexism," Sam said. "Just statistical fact."

"How do you know that it's a woman?" Myra demanded. "Okay, if women don't do this, and you know that for a *fact*—which I happen to disagree with, but let's follow the argument through—how do you *know* that it's a woman?"

There were some groans from the wedding guests.

"Uh, because she has breasts?" a guest offered.

"So what?" Myra said. "They could be fake."

"She has cleavage," someone objected.

"She could be a transvestite. She could be a transsexual. The lover she's angry at could be a woman."

More groans. Someone in the crowd said, "Gimme a break."

"It is a big dress," a woman noted. "If you were trying to hide a . . . package in a wedding dress, you wouldn't go all slinky and Narciso Rodriguez."

"If she were really a man," the novelist Ben Kramer said, "it would explain the mask. If she's gay, she could have been having an affair with someone's wife. We can't assume that she's straight. There's that great part in Jonathan Franzen's novel *The Corrections* where this chef has affairs with both the man who owns the restaurant and the owner's wife."

The psychiatrists ignored him.

"Wasn't there a big case very close to here with a transvestite?" someone asked. "Couple of years ago?"

"Yeah," another guest confirmed. "Haddon Heights. I think a lot of cops died. It was a big deal around here. A transsexual, I think."

"My point exactly," Myra said.

"Come on," Marty said.

"Excuse me," Billips Sr. said. "How exactly is all this going to help us?"

Amen, Helen thought.

"Yeah," someone said from the crowd. "I mean, there isn't exactly time to get a course of Lexapro going here."

"For erotomania," Dr. Needleman advised, "you can get good results with pimozide, used also for Tourette's."

"But," Tess said. Everyone let her talk, since she was the bride. "Why are you so sure this is a love thing? She didn't tell us what we're apologizing *for*."

"She did mention betrayal," Marty said.

"Do you know her?" Billips asked the bride and groom, who repeated that they did not.

"Anyone else?" Billips said. "Anyone with a crazy ex?"

Simon Nathanson, the bride's brother, grinned at his mother. Helen returned a sad smile in acknowledgment. By every possible definition, her son had a crazy soon-to-be-ex. But Simon—and his children—would recognize her. Besides, Joan, while deeply neurotic, was ferociously conventional. She wanted to fit in. She wanted to be a room mother. This wasn't Joan. Joan's idea of a terrorist event was to procure an expensive divorce attorney and refuse all settlement offers.

Trevor Hunter, the actor, raised his hand. "I don't recognize her," he said, "but there are people who . . . well, there are some people who are kind of obsessed with me."

He shrugged bashfully, as if to say, *Go figure.*

"Crazy fans," Ira Needleman declared.

"It's true," Miranda said. "I mean, we all have 'em. But Trev has tons. There's that one real bad one—Loony Tina."

"Crazy fans," Ira Needleman said, "are a certain percentage of my clientele in Los Angeles. Delusional disorder, erotomanic subtype."

"Would she know you're here?" Billips asked Trevor. "At a wedding in New Jersey?"

"Again," Trevor said, "I have no clue. I don't know her."

"Ah," Dr. Needleman said, "but she knows you. Or thinks she does. She has a secret 'signal' that she shares with you—say, the penguin. She has penguin earrings and penguin stationary. So if she sees you photographed in a tuxedo, she takes it as a sign to her."

"The male fans can be really dangerous, I'm sure," Jake said. "But don't the female ones just tend to spam their objects of desire with a lot of mail?"

"Generally, yes," Dr. Needleman agreed.

"I still insist," Dr. Gold insisted, "that women don't do this."

"Not *generally*," Jake said.

"Unless she's a man," Myra Feldstein repeated.

Billips Sr. put up a warning hand, as if to keep that tape loop from starting again.

"Okay," he said. "Let's go with this fan angle for a second." He turned to Trevor. "Do you think this crazy fan would have enough access to your schedule to follow you from Los Angeles to a wedding in New Jersey?"

Trevor said he had no idea.

"Didn't she use the phrase 'modest production values'?" someone asked.

"Maybe she's some kind of production person," Miranda offered.

"Maybe she dated some kind of production person."

"Any 'production people' here?" Billips asked. "Anyone know any 'production people'?"

No, and no.

"Could it be your ex-girlfriend?" Billips persisted, to Trevor.

Those who read celebrity gossip magazines knew about Trevor's last girlfriend, Ruth, whom he'd dumped for Miranda. If this were Ruth, many people could recognize her. Maybe that explained the necessity for the gas mask.

Trevor said, "I don't think she'd do anything like this. No. Definitely not. But I've had, well, I've had some other girlfriends."

Helen Burns noted herself getting impatient. This is what she'd most feared about the actor attending the wedding: that he would take attention away from the bride who deserved it. Even in this situation, he was an airtime hog. She even felt vague hostility toward Gabriel's sister, Miranda, for bringing him. But Helen looked at her daughter, and Tess, bless her heart, was just listening to the entire exchange with calm attention.

"By Occam's razor," Marty said, "shouldn't we start with the simplest explanation?"

Tess didn't look directly at her father, but Dr. Sarah Barrett did. So did Jake's second wife's current husband. So did Jake's third and current wife, Mary. Not even Helen, who tried hard, could find much to warm to in Mary. Although Jake did have a thorny history of romantic entanglements, he was now sixty-three. And he wasn't Picasso. This wife was most likely the end of the line, this baby the last seed he would sow.

"Well," Jake said, "the exact nature of the problem is only important insofar as we'd want to determine if we're dealing with someone psychotic. If she's not psychotic, we've always got mixed personality disorder. Or NOS."

NOS? *Not otherwise specified?* All this time wasted grandstanding on diagnosis and they were going to settle for not otherwise specified?

"All right," Billips said. "We're not getting anywhere. Let's just decide who's going to talk to her. It can only be one person."

"I think it should be me," Myra said. "Since I'm a woman."

"We don't know enough about her," Marty said, "to know if a woman is the most appropriate negotiator."

"Oh, for Pete's sake, Mart, of *course* a woman is the most appropriate negotiator."

"Why is it sexist for us to assume she's not a woman based on how she presents, but not sexist for you to assume that a woman would be the best therapist based on her sex?"

"Guys, get a room," one of the guests said.

Myra said, "A theory. She responded very poorly to the interruption of the talking child. We can surmise that she has a narcissistic wound. Let's say she had attended some sort of wilderness camp be-cause of severe problems with her parents as an adolescent, which would, of course, have been brewing for some time. It would explain a lot of the equipment and planning, which is, true, not ordinary for a female. She would have learned all that there—the chain, the knots, the locks."

"Interesting," Sam Gold said.

"The firearms?" Marty scoffed.

"A real growth industry in places like Idaho," Jake said. "Of course, what the Outward Bound–type camps do, mainly, is keep the kids away from both their parents and drugs for eight to ten weeks, which is something, often enough to begin to effect a change."

"What's a narcissistic wound?" one of the wedding guests asked.

Marty said, "A narcissistic wound is just basically a fancy way of saying 'hurt feelings.' I think we can safely assume, at this point, that she has hurt feelings."

"Lick my narcissistic wound, baby," Ben said.

"All right," Billips said, interrupting some nervous laughter. "You two"—Marty and Myra—"can't negotiate. You're fighting."

From both, in unison: "No we're not."

"You two . . ." He studied both Sam Gold and Ira Needleman. He seemed to be searching for the most politic way to say "Too Jewish." It was interesting how obvious it was that the terrorist wasn't. Although her face was covered by the gas mask, her hair was still visible. It was thick, shoulder-length, auburn, her skin pale. Not Polish Russian pale. Irish?

That left Jake Nathanson. Jake puffed with a kind of excited pride, even if his nomination was by process of elimination.

"But what if it has something to do with Jake?" Sam asked.

Helen said, "I don't think so. I don't think that woman had any idea that there were psychiatrists at this wedding."

Jake looked at her gratefully. "Which argues, again, for a diag-nosis of schizophrenia, since with onset this late she may not have been referred to anyone prior to this."

"I don't know," Helen said. "I wouldn't start by assuming that. I wouldn't start by assuming anything. She could just be having a very bad day."

The five psychiatrists eyed her scornfully.

Helen was not at all unnerved by their dismissal. She knew that all psychiatrists considered her a lightweight. She was a woman who could not prescribe drugs. She was not just a woman with a mere Ph.D. but a small, plain, quiet, soft-spoken, non-Jewish woman—so many strikes against her it's a miracle she was permitted to practice. She was used to people talking over her, through her. She was quiet for a living. Let the shrinks bloviate. She would just slip into her invisibility suit. Without saying a word, she pulsed some energy Billips Sr.'s way, like the faint but steady cell phone signal from a person buried in the rubble of an earthquake.

"Okay," Billips Sr. said, and pointed to Helen. "You. You'll be the negotiator."

The shrinks exchanged dumbfounded looks, as if they'd just learned a gum-chewing waitress with a beehive, her arms stacked with plates, had been plucked from a diner to be secretary of state. Before they could object, Billips Sr. pointed to Jake. "And you—apologize first."

"Why me?" Jake said. "If anyone should apologize, it should be him."

Jake tipped his head in the direction of Sarah's strong, silent, sandy-haired new husband, Matt Barrett. "After all," Jake said, "Matt's ex-wife could be less than pleased."

Billips Sr. asked Matt if the terrorist could be his ex-wife. Matt said that his ex-wife was currently on vacation, with his (Matt's) kids by his previous marriage and the boyfriend to whom she was engaged. In the game of musical marriage, everyone had found a chair to sit in except for Helen.

"You *think* she is," Jake said. "Still, there could be some bitterness."

"No one else?" Billips Sr. asked Jake. "No nurses at the hospital? No one before Mary?"

"No, absolutely not," Jake said, with exaggerated calm, as Sarah made "yeah, right" noises. "Besides, unless one of my ex-wives has shattered the space-time continuum and mastered the art of occupying two bodies at once, it is ludicrous to think this has anything to do with me. Why don't you ask Matt if *he* had anyone else before or after Sarah?"

Matt shook his head no. Sarah took his hand in solidarity.

"As for us," Jake said—here he made a sweeping gesture to include his whole family clan: Helen, Sarah, Matt, Mary, Tess, Simon, the mystified Theo, even baby Louis—"there's no jealousy or ill will here. Right? In fact, we may have had the best divorces in modern history."

Jake's first two wives, separated from each other in the front row by Theo, leaned forward and inclined toward each other to exchange a half smile. One of Jake's most cherished delusions was about the supernatural civility of his divorces, the easygoing acceptance and warmth of his children and ex-wives.

Actually, Helen and Sarah—"sister ex-wives," as Sarah liked to dub them—did get along splendidly now. But the goodwill didn't quite trickle down to Jake, or Mary. In the front row, Helen, Sarah, and Sal, the three Fates, sported identical corsages on their wrists. Helen didn't understand why a wedding this unconventional, with no bridesmaids at all, never mind bridesmaids in matching purple polyester, still forced the women of a certain age to wear corsages. Tess was not a gardener, so Helen knew her daughter didn't know that gardeners are not that enamored of cut flowers, no less flowers with their stems amputated, parched and pinned through their ovaries. As she tried to concentrate, Helen kept getting distracted by the bulky, fragrant corsage. On her wrist, it seemed in its death throes, like a live butterfly with its thorax impaled.

"On with it," Billips Sr. said.

Jake didn't want to play. "Can I at least bow my head and apologize silently in my mind? Like at a Quaker service?"

"Dad," Tess pleaded.

The wedding photographer managed to get a truly excellent shot of that moment. Not only Dr. Barrett craning her neck to look with disgust at the father of the bride, and therefore her current husband following her gaze, to see what she knew or thought she knew, but Helen tilted toward Jake, too, expectantly. His current wife turned toward him, warningly. His daughter looking at him, and her husband-to-be with his hand on her shoulder, comforting her, at the same time, for both the hostage situation and the old, sad story of her family. The groom's side looking with undiscriminating disgust at *all* of these blathering whack jobs. Jake, meanwhile, turning to his old friend the gastroenterologist, who knew everything about his long history of romantic exploits, with cheeks puffed slightly out for the Yiddish equivalent of "Who, me?"

*M*any of the wedding guests knew the outlines of the doctor's story. Jake Nathanson's wives kept getting younger. Each new spouse resulted in a new child and a new house. Despite the vicissitudes of the real estate market and the fiscal consequences of divorce, Jake had nurtured a profitable sideline in insurance company testifying and surfed the waves of the country's recessionary woes just right, acquiring a series of residences that all impressively appreciated.

The problem with ever-younger wives is the possibility—indeed the probability—of being cuckolded. Not that Jake thought of it in those terms. His views about adultery, he would claim, were much more subtle and evolved. But outsiders did. That Sarah had left him for the general contractor hired to build their addition was well known, and cause for giggles.

Physicians are extremely busy, laden with responsibilities, but their days are like heavy overcoats with many secret pockets sewn into the linings. Their schedules allow ample possibilities for escape: Accreditation seminars. Conferences in the Caribbean. "The gym." (Your spouse did indeed work out, just not on the lat pull-down machine.) Physicians are not always on call and even when they are, although their phones often ring, they're allowed to be curt. They're not expected to chitchat. A physician on call in missionary position with enough arm strength and ability to compartmentalize can answer a phone one-handed to change a dosage in between teasing thrusts.

It's more difficult for female physicians, at least the ones with children, because, no matter how lofty their status in the profession, and no matter how much subcontracting of progeny and property they can afford, they remain the detail-oriented troubleshooters for their domestic lives. Doesn't matter if the mother is performing brain surgery on a newborn. If her own child becomes sick at school, the mother gets the call. Type A overachievers in any case, the female physicians feel obligated to find time to make special cookies in fun shapes for their kids. They want to do this, but can't help feeling resentful, especially having endured so much sexism in med school. That resentment makes the female doctors businesslike and gruff; makes them seem even more like the coldhearted bitches they're taken for anyhow, merely by virtue of being so accomplished; and being treated as soulless and sexless by just about everyone makes them even more susceptible to advances from those rare men unthreatened enough to whisper to them while tracing the lines of their cheeks with their thumbs.

As an anesthesiologist, Dr. Sarah Barrett did most of her work in the early hours, prepping patients for surgeries. That is, in fact, how she and Jake Nathanson met: before his colonoscopy due to irritable bowel issues that cured themselves once he was out of his first marriage, and resurfaced before he was out of his second. His bowels, he liked to say, were the canary in his mine. "You'll see I have great veins," he'd jokingly bragged to Sarah, thrusting forth the arm that still delivered a formidable tennis serve. It takes a particularly refined sense of self to be able to flirt in a hospital gown open at the rear.

Barring the stray emergency and rounds with the residents, Sarah's afternoons were often her own until school let out, when she liked to be around to greet her son. As for Jake Nathanson, his stashes of time were in the mornings, when Sarah was almost always gone. And since he often saw clients in the evenings, after people got off from work, he was rarely in the position of returning home fresh from a liaison with fingernail welts on his ass, smelling of lilac. A maid did their wash. And the families of psychiatrists don't dare to disobey one cardinal rule: you never, ever interrupt a patient in session unless your house is burning down or your kid is on his deathbed.

The couples counselor they saw at the end suggested that you merely needed to look at Sarah's and Jake's schedules to understand the root of their problems. During what wedges of time could they indulge in a little marriage-fortifying intimacy, or even have a relaxed dinner together? Okay, 9:00 p.m. But that was pretty much Sarah's bedtime. Besides, Theo was always around, had always been around, might always be around. Because of the Asperger's, he had not really had play dates, would not give them a timely empty nest. Sarah contended that their marriage could not survive the stress of caring for a special-needs child, because Jake was an uninvolved father, as she might have known by his relationships with his children from his first marriage. Jake couldn't disagree that Theo had been a serious issue, but he claimed the main problem, his downfall, was real estate.

Jake knew that his oldest children and first ex-wife dismissed his house obsession as mere materialism and status display. But Jake would argue that if he hadn't been a psychiatrist, he would have liked to be an architect, and that thinking about the spaces of houses—lofty attics and creepy basements, big windows with window seats for lounging with a book open on your lap as you survey the sky—was like thinking about the mind itself. If they hadn't undertaken the master bedroom and bath renovation, which after all they did partly to give them some toehold of marital privacy against Theo, Sarah would have never met or fallen in love with Barrett, the strapping yet soulful carpenter and contractor overseeing the project.

As for Jake and Mary, whom he'd met at the "homey" hospice where both of their mothers were dying: from his years of practice, Jake could confirm how frequently the death of a parent was a precipitating factor in midlife meltdowns. Because Mary was so much younger, and because they met again at the tile store where Mary worked at the time while studying to be an interior designer and where Jake was surveying granites for their master bath's sink counter, it was easy for people to mock his third marriage. But his relationship with Mary was no more trivial than any other affair that ends in marriage. It emerged, as all affairs do, from deep pain and a thirst for reinvention.

The first time Jake and Mary embraced, in the "family room" of the hospice, her mother was in a particularly ghoulish pre-death step: from hematidrosis, she was sweating blood through her skin, the soaked sheets tinged pink. No matter how many times you've witnessed last gasps on TV, death is, like sex, a rite of passage to experience firsthand. Mary's parents were divorced. She was an only child. As a psychiatrist, Jake was certainly used to the registers of neediness. But Mary's vulnerability had a plaintive, brave pitch to it, more cello solo than screeching violin. In comforting her, he discharged some of his own grief over losing his own mother, who had adored him as only a Jewish mother can adore her son the doctor.

Yes, the abandoning father/adored little beauty queen issues were real, with Jake inevitably the substitute father, as if he didn't already fulfill that role for enough people. And yes, Jake would be the last person to deny that, having come only that week from borderline PSA readings at the urologist's, he could certainly use to sip, vampirelike, some of Mary's youthful vitality. But the first time their hands touched, both of them tracing the veins in a slab of granite at the supplier, they shared something rich and primal, not the typical feints of May-September romance.

Jake's work made him adept at asking penetrating questions with his face composed into sincere interest—at least, Sarah would say, for periods of up to an hour. Sarah assumed that Jake would soon tire of listening to Mary, but it turns out that Jake was one of the first men to take her aspirations seriously without thrusting out both hands, palms up, Frankenstein's monster–like, to grab her breasts, so they had a productive loop going: Mary's gratitude guaranteed Jake's continued support. Then Sarah assumed that Mary would grow annoyed with Jake once she had the baby and saw his cosmic lack of involvement. But Jake had, in fact, always been very good with babies—"when," he liked to note, "it matters most." He was good with children until they could talk.

When Sarah told all this to Helen—they'd grown close after Sarah and Jake split up, closer in joint concern while Tess was in Africa—Helen said, "He could have gotten better with children. Maybe the third time's the charm. Maybe practice makes perfect." On principle, Helen tried not to engage too jubilantly in Jake-bashing with Sarah. She didn't think that kind of negative energy was productive for either of them, or for their children. But it was a fine line: she didn't want to seem to be defending him, either. So when Sarah insisted that both Mary and Jake would become disillusioned, in time, Helen murmured agreement.

Jake contended that Mary was not dumber than most people just because she was better-looking. Mary was not, despite the tits-and-ass-backwards assumptions almost everyone made, an inflatable sex-toy doll. In fact, he believed that, ironically—"You really should stop overusing the word *ironically*," Sarah informed him, "and in point of fact, you misuse it"—Mary *saved him from* the kind of free fall into sexuality that destroyed many of his colleagues, including his second wife.

"You can't actually believe that," Sarah had said, in one of their dreary couples counseling sessions. "You are like the world's champion rationalizer."

"Are you sure you aren't projecting?" Jake asked. "Who was having hot-and-heavy sex in the marital bed with Lady Chatterley's lover?"

"The class implications of that are beneath you, especially given you're boffing a Jersey girl with a GED."

"She earned her degrees the hard way, Sarah. Try to be a feminist."

"Besides, Matt and I *never* had 'sex in the marital bed,' " Sarah said, and that was the truth. How could they? There were always workmen around the house, not to mention Jake himself, voicing some opinion about the renovation.

Instead, like teenagers, Sarah and Matt began messing around on the big front seat of his truck, which, inconveniently for adultery, had his name painted in big letters on the sides.

At first they'd meet for a late lunch and park side-by-side near the diner, shielded from view by the Dumpster. Then they discovered a storage facility nearby where the parking lot was always empty, except for the occasional cleaning crew who met there to smoke weed en route to an adjacent office building. The cleaning men, dreadlocks in hairnets, would sometimes smirk as they passed with boom boxes and massive bags of shredded documents.

Matt's truck was vigilantly styleless, in a color that he called light brown. ("Can you say 'beige'?" she'd scolded. "Why don't men ever know the names of colors?" At first the most casual exchanges feel laced with substance, touches that trail DNA strands of who they've been, who they'll be together.) Most of the time they managed to wait until after lunch, so their kisses smelled of his tools, sawdust, and of the leather seats, pungent in the sun. Sarah loved the smells, so different from the hospital's. Occasionally something sharp would distract them: a lost item of his daughter's, a hair clip or lidless tube of fruity lip gloss. But once, to her amazement, a single shoe.

How does a person lose one shoe? Matt told her calmly, with no animosity, that his wife was always losing things, usually in the guise of keeping them safe. The shoe was tiny, a bland black pump; like his car, it seemed to aspire to some universe of the style-free. She held up this shoe and thought: What are we doing? But then his touch brought her back.

In movies, the lunchtime disrobing happens in fast motion, desire reduced to Keystone Kops. In fact, what they did was difficult. After their first time at a hotel, looking down at their interlaced fingers as they sat quietly on the bed, she began to cry—"I've been so lonely," she said, and he said, "Me too." He began to call their path to being together the Maze. His wife, her husband. Her kid, his kids. Houses, lawyers. Timetables, therapists, taxes, tuition—and then the guilt, anger, bewilderment, sadness. Mostly sadness. Always, hanging over the adulterer like nasty mistletoe, the fact of failure.

At the beginning with Matt, though, she didn't care. Suitcaseless and naked in daylight, she felt like a brave refugee. She slid down the open vowels of his "Hello," breathed in the texture of his crisp blue shirt, and knelt on the couch in undergarments that matched. They did like the hotel rooms with couches—as if the furniture of daily life had been whirled up by a tornado and settled down, unharmed, somewhere new.

Matt specialized in renovation, not new construction. Renovation was, in a way, like getting someone else's kids. You had to work with what was there.

Because Matt spent so much time in the house, he got to know Theo, and seeing his patience with Theo, his tolerance, his kindness, just his innate, calm interest, slayed Sarah far more than the sex. Then adultery, Jake claimed, contrary to received opinion, is rarely about the sex.

People always asked, luridly: "How did you find out?" Stray hotel bill receipt? (No, they paid cash.) Fine-tooth-combed cell phone logs? (No, all phone bills went directly to their respective offices.) PTA mom friend of Matt's wife espying Matt's truck parked at a hotel she passed on her way to Toys "R" Us? What was the Jamesian moment when consciousness dawned, their illusions were seared like ice cream on summer asphalt, when the lives they'd constructed unraveled as fast as a line of knitting?

The moment came when Jake, Sarah, and Matt were doing the final walk-through of the addition, composing the punch list of the inevitable annoying unfinished details. They'd constructed a new bedroom and master bath over the garage, connecting it to the house with a skylit hallway, and transformed the old bedroom into what would become a study to do any psychiatrist proud, with floor-to-ceiling bookshelves.

The space was exactly the master bedroom home buyers fantasize about: both spacious and cozy, contemporary while still gesturing toward the house's quirky Victorian charm. The room was like a fantasia about marriage itself, a tone poem to the twinned yet mutually exclusive goals of privacy and intimacy. Each pair of shoes nestled in its own minihome in the master closet. The snazzy see-through fireplace.

They were all just walking around, inhaling the promising scents of paint and polyurethane, admiring.

Jake looked at Sarah. But she didn't look back. She was smiling at Matt. And Jake knew: this was their bedroom. It had always been their bedroom.

At that moment, his phone rang, and he was so befuddled by the realization he'd just had that he didn't pretend it was a patient. "Hi, sweetie," he said, to Mary. "Yes. I'll be there soon."

Then, lamely, to Sarah, who was staring: "My secretary."

Jake thrust out his hand to Matt. "You did a great job, Matt," he said. "Great. Thanks. We'll talk, obviously. We'll settle up," and he meant "settle up" in its full emotional spectrum, not just the last 10 percent payment.

The symmetry was slightly creepy: Jake's first marriage had also ended at almost exactly the moment of the completion of the family-room addition.

"Maybe one doctor in the house is enough," Jake would say with a shrug, as shorthand for the demise of his marriage. Although Marty and Myra Feldstein were still together, not only two physicians but two psychiatrists in private practice, sharing an office suite. They'd met in medical school, where they were two adjoining M. Feldsteins on the roster, so Myra hadn't had to change her name when she got married, and wouldn't have to change it back if she ever divorced. But maybe that was an anomaly, more like the intense, twisted closeness of twins. Maybe for normal people, one physician in the family is enough. Just as, in his opinion, one Jew was enough. One Jewish doctor: more than enough.

So Sarah left Jake for a general contractor, and Jake left Sarah for an interior designer. Interesting that they'd both gravitated toward people in the building trade. Matt and Mary, the goy boy toy and the shiksa bimbo, were, of course, more age-appropriate for each other, despite Sarah's disclaimer: "He's four years younger, Jake, not thirty years younger."

"Sarah, you're happy. I'm happy. What's with the tone? What's left to fight about? You got the house."

"That's because, Jake, *I paid for the house*, because, if you recall, your cash was tied up in the house from your last divorce."

Sometimes Jake was distressed to find he missed the house he shared with Sarah more than he missed Sarah herself. "Home Sweet Mental Home" was his nickname for the big old Victorian, because so many of its past renovations had been so nutty. Renovation was a little like therapy. Including the fact that there are some houses—like this one that Helen, incomprehensibly, was still in, although it was too big for her, was falling down around her, and had obscenely high real estate taxes—that simply couldn't be fixed. Some marriages that couldn't be fixed, either: tear-down marriages.

Maybe that was unfair to Helen. What would his life be like if they'd toughed it out? A lot simpler, that's for sure. But simplicity, he would contend, is as false a construct as the luxurious hotel room: the little cabin in the woods, where you curl up with your beloved, wanting nothing more than the sun and the sky, the birds chirping outside. *"Our life is frittered away by detail . . . Simplicity, simplicity, simplicity! Simplicity of life and elevation of purpose."* The shrink would have said to Thoreau, if Thoreau asked his opinion: Rotsa ruck.

$\mathcal{L}$ook," Jake said. "You're really barking up the wrong tree here. Look at the weaponry. I've never owned or fired a gun. I don't think I've ever known a woman who owned or fired a gun."

"She could have learned," someone offered, "if she was pissed off enough."

"I don't know any women who could get that pissed off. In fact, I don't think I've even had a patient who could get that pissed off since my residency."

Jake's posture was relaxed, one arm over the back of Mary's chair. His cadences were cheery, unflappable. Helen knew Jake's cool-and-collected-when-cornered routine. He'd trotted it out during the divorce mediation, to explain why he couldn't give her a penny more although he was renovating a manse in Moorestown, and Helen, trying to finish her Ph.D. while raising two toddlers alone, couldn't send the kids to camp, or have a diseased tree cut down until it fell on the house, made a hole in the roof, and her homeowner's insurance kicked in. "Why don't you sell the house and move to the city?" Jake had suggested, reasonably. "It would be better for your social life. Don't be afraid for the kids. It will be better for them, too. Expand their horizons." Thus somehow her simple request for more child support would turn into a referendum on her shortcomings as a human being: Her clinginess. Her timidity. Her risk aversion. Even at mothering—the one thing that nurturing women, i.e. stupid people, were supposed to do well—she'd failed, by being overly protective.

But Jake had been right. She should have left. Haddonfield had not been a fun place for a single mother. Even today, the suburb was shockingly conservative, and divorcing couples tended to skulk off in shame, not to mention that only the physicians and lawyers could afford two residences there. But by the time she'd felt strong enough to leave, she could no longer afford the city. Helen had done the best she could. Still, she always found it uncomfortable to have Jake physically present in her house, looking around as if he were returning to his elementary school, the desks so teensy, the water fountains so low. She did better with him on the phone.

"How about Nellie?" Dr. Sarah Barrett demanded, seethingly. Her own anger at him was fresher, more raw.

"Who's Nellie?" Mary asked.

"No one," Jake said. "A fixed delusion of Sarah's."

"A fixed delusion who calls your cell phone at three a.m."

"It's an *answering service*, Sarah. That's what they do. They call."

"Taisez-vous," Souleymane said.

"Pardon?" Jake said.

Souleymane held up his hand. The terrorist's footsteps could be heard down the hallway, near the kitchen. The footsteps got louder. Then they heard the front door close.

"She left," a Rambo boy hissed. "Let's go for it. Back door."

"Bomb," Billips Sr. reminded.

"Maybe she just left us here," another guest said.

But no: now the front door opened again. And the footsteps got quieter as she went back down the hall.

"What's she doing?" someone asked.

"Maybe she left something in her car."

A woman near the door to the room began to wail—high-pitched and keening, followed by gasping sobs. One of the serving persons, a young woman, stood and began to bang on the closed family room door. It was hard to understand what she was screaming, but it seemed to be standard claustrophobic panic stuff: *I've got to get out of here.*

Then, more curiously: "Someone call my father."

The husband-and-wife catering duo flanked her and attempted to calm her down. Their expressions indicated more exasperation with the difficulty of finding good help than any real concern. The girl was hysterical. She threw her body against the door. The yanked knob came off in her hand, throwing her backwards. The man whose body she hit gave out a kind of "Whoah" and pushed her back. Within seconds the area near the door was a mosh pit, although the girl's wail was still the most insistent. She kept saying, "This can't be happening!"

Theodore Nathanson, whose Asperberger's made him prone to repetition, stood and also made frantic motions, grabbing hanks of his own hair in his hands as he took up his own cry of "This can't be happening." His cries woke the babies. Theo, the babies, and the five-year-old ADHD kid were already as annoying to the rest of the hostages as they'd be if they were sitting in the row behind them on an airplane on a transatlantic flight.

The door was a standard, cheap hollow-core door, not built to withstand major rage. The catering staffer's fist went right through it, splintered the door, and hit the sheet of plywood behind it. Now the woman screamed louder, holding up her bleeding hand.

Tess and Gabe went to inspect the wound. The "Let's roll" men also muscled their way toward the door. As they did this Billips Sr., above the screaming, seemed to be trying to command them to stop.

They did not stop. Everyone who was not screaming took the liberty to cry or talk, most of the tones anguished or bellicose, except for what was by now recognizable as the novelist Ben Kramer's voice, which was inappropriately conversational and jolly. Ben wondered if this wasn't already a reality TV show, where you thrust the strangers together and saw who was heroic, who behaved like a total asshole. Someone pointed out that the total asshole was him.

Tess and Gabe flanked the waitgirl and moved her toward the couch. The three African men made their way through the crowd as well. They helped to relocate the older guests who had staked out the couch to nearby chairs and laid the girl down while they tried to look at the hand. Helen was surprised to hear one of the Africans—Idris Deby, she believed, one of her daughter's best friends—speak for the first time as he said, "May I help you, madam?" He had an absolutely perfect Oxford accent. For all Helen knew, he was a lord.

Aware that this was an odd time to pause for these particular emotions, Helen watched her daughter and Gabe with pride and pleasure. She had hated Tess's stint in Doctors Without Borders, but she loved that Tess and Gabe had met in the field. Tess had said that relationships solidified really fast, because you saw how people acted in an emergency. You had profound respect for your beloved's resourcefulness and grace under pressure. Tess and Gabe first made love to the sound of gunfire ("You get used to it," Tess said. "At a certain point it's almost soothing, like crickets"), on a lumpy cot in a room without air-conditioning. They must have stunk—and not in the insouciant French way, either. They made love the first time as if it could be their last. They came back to the States together, where no one they knew could even locate Chad on a map, had no idea what was happening in Chad, and, though they could compose their murmuring faces into sympathy, didn't care. Yet Tess and Gabe weren't sanctimonious. Helen admired that, too. They could be nonconfrontational at Jake and Mary's beach house with its expansive view of the ocean. They were as pleased as any newlyweds about their gleaming new pots, the high-thread-count sheets. They could be warm to Colonel Billips Sr., whom they joked pinned his war medals to his pajamas when he went to bed, and had some distasteful, old-school notions about race, but was, Gabe had always insisted to his friends, underneath it all, a stand-up guy.

The waves of noise from the crowd subsided some with the first aid work, although there were still voices to be heard: the Rambo boys, at the door, who seemed to be concurring that they were, in fact, locked in; and some kind of outbreak between bickering women. One woman said, "This isn't fair. I have nothing to do with this. I have a four-year-old daughter at home." Another woman noted she was a mother, too. A lot of them were parents. At that, Mara Lowell—Helen thought it was Mara Lowell—said sourly, "Well, why don't those of us who are childless just stand up and volunteer to be shot? Since we don't *matter* to anyone."

Many of Dr. Burns's patients were, like Mara, single professional women. They eventually learned that Helen, too, was a divorcée, and saw in her radiant calm some kind of hope.

With such patients, Helen didn't mention how large her children loomed in the landscape of her joys and worries. She didn't mention grandchildren, what a thrill it had been to be around babies again. Helen thought a lot about babies. She'd loved nursing her babies. The sweetness of it, the lightness and rightness. But a lot of women didn't love it, for a lot of reasons. That in most of her patients a baby still wailed was so patently obvious, the need so raw and bewildered, and what could you say, finally, about that? The psychiatrists could blather about the anal stage, about shit and selfhood, but they didn't seem to really get what that meant. They couldn't grasp the difference between a parent tenderly wiping your ass, holding your feet together in the air, in love even with the feeling of trussing your feet like a chicken and the clean, smooth plane of your butt, and the parent who lets you stew in your own juices, who makes a face of disgust and is rough when they finally get around to changing you. When a woman agonized about why some man didn't love her, Helen tried to see that baby inside, calling out. She tried to understand the persistence—the "obsession," if you will—as the dog barking and barking in the backyard, hungry in the cold, water bowl empty, until someone finally relents and opens the door.

There was another thing, too. When you had a child, because you identify so achingly with your child's disappointment or pain, you suddenly understood things about yourself, about your parents and your own childhood, that were very hard to understand otherwise—not impossible, but much more difficult. Take Simon. He was not all that self-reflective. You wouldn't call him a colorful guy, though he got endearingly cheerful after a couple of beers. He was an accountant.

He'd recoiled, pretty understandably, from his father's distant, dismissive psychoanalytic approach. But when he had children of his own, he'd had to confront more fully his father's total indifference to them. If Jake didn't like children, had no interest in them, why did he keep on having more of them?

Helen wished she could say to Mara, The childless matter big-time to someone. They matter big-time, or should, to their own parents.

Who had the hysterical waitperson asked for but a parent?

Tess asked the girl her name.

"Amy," she said.

"Okay, Amy," Gabe said. "Doctor? Doctor in the house?"

Of course there were doctors in the house. There was an anesthesiologist, a gastroenterologist, and a bunch of shrinks. The shrinks lived in terror of hearing the line "Is there a doctor in the house" uttered on an airplane. When it came to jump-starting a stalled heart, the flight attendants had more recent training than most of the shrinks. No one took the bait.

"What with medical malpractice," one of the guests noted.

"Actually," a Nathanson cousin said, "I'm in tax law, so I'm not sure, but I think New Jersey's Good Samaritan law *requires* a doctor to help."

Tense murmuring from the psychiatric cohort.

One of the door vigilantes said he had had a lot of sports injuries, and had a general sense of how to run a check for range of motion. After inspecting Amy, he said that Amy's wrist was probably sprained, not broken.

At which point Amy fainted.

The room got blessedly quieter as Tess and Gabe roused her.

"All right," Billips Sr. said. "Let's pull it together here."

Because everyone had been attending to the minidrama of the fallen waitperson, no one had been facing the doors to the garden. So there was a collective gasp of sorts when they looked up to find the woman standing outside, her legs spread, aiming the rifle toward the door and doing a kind of sweep with it, as if deciding whom to get in her sights. She stopped at Amy, on the couch.

As people began to scream, Helen instinctively moved in front of Amy or, rather, in front of her daughter.

Helen made, for the terrorist's benefit, an expression of impatience. She nodded her head toward Amy on the couch and then did a kind of joint eye-roll flutter and head roll that meant *What a nutcase*. Whether the woman could see her from that distance, over the heads of the others, wasn't clear.

The terrorist pointed the gun upward. She held out her arm. She crooked her elbow, as if to check the time. With the rifle, she pointed to the place on her wrist where her wristwatch would be, if she were wearing a watch. She tapped on her wrist with the rifle to say, *Time's a-tickin'*, then pointed to the flashing black box on her arm. And the bomb.

Helen nodded to let her know she completely understood. Then, without breaking eye contact or looking down at her own arm, she unzipped the Velcro of the corsage's wristband and quickly, quietly put the corsage underneath her chair. Irrational, she knew. But immediately, she felt much better.

$\mathcal{A}$s their captor disappeared around the corner of the house, everyone began to scream and cry again, confronting what an idiotic way this would be to die. But not, finally, so unusual. People were always opening fire at fast-food restaurants, gyms, and shopping malls. Wrong place at the wrong time: every day, someone somewhere died stupidly. Deer through the windshield. Freak hostile stingray leaping into your boat. A tree falls on you as you jog in the park. Well, at least those deaths are natural. Mother Nature is a bad, bad mother. Better the big tree branch on the bike path than a kid in a high-rise hurling a coin off the balcony that, by some law of physics you'd understand if you lived to take physics, gathers enough force to land on your head with the force of a piano. Your meeting goes great, the traffic is light, you catch an earlier flight on standby, how lucky you feel sauntering right from security to the gate, but that plane goes down. The whole sky for flying and that one birdbrain from the flock needs to suck itself into the engine of that one plane. Of course the bird is natural, too. At least you can make a case for randomness as part of God's grand plan. *One grain of sand . . .* But the people stuck in the towers on 9/11, the people choosing death by falling instead of death by burning: How to make sense of that except as a medieval vision of hell? The deaths more horrible in crowds, although there is something counterintuitive about that, since every death must be suffered as a solitary death.

Billips Sr. shouted, "Atten-*shun*," in his command voice. Everyone complied.

"Enough," he said. "We're going to be calm now, and we're going to be organized. Anyone who knows anyone crazy, or has ever made anyone mad enough to maybe seek revenge, raise your hands."

All of the psychiatrists raised their hands. The two actors did. The novelist Ben Kramer and his wife did. Simon did. Amy on the couch did.

"In love or even in work," Billips Sr. added.

More hands, including the caterers.

"Come on," Billips said. "Even if it's not someone current. Someone you offended in the past."

By now, almost a third of the guests had identified themselves.

"We're going to be systematic," Billips said. "We'll start with the most likely candidates and then move on from there."

"My wife is going to need her insulin soon," Ira Needleman said. "Or at least some water. If she gets dehydrated . . ."

"We'll move as fast as we can," Billips assured him. "Jake, we'll start with you."

"Why me?" Jake Nathanson objected.

"Because it's your daughter getting married. Because you've had three wives."

"They're all here," Jake said. "No bad blood. Right, ladies? A fan of Trevor's seems the most likely."

The actor nodded his doleful concurrence.

"Anyway," Jake said, "what are we supposed to do once we 'identify' the person? Is there supposed to be a public confession and apology? What does she plan to do to the person? Are we surrendering him up to her, like, as a sacrifice? Do we feel comfortable with that? I personally don't feel comfortable with that. Could we all kind of meditate privately on the person or people we may have hurt, and offer up silent apologies? Could we all apologize together, at once?"

Helen couldn't help but smile at that one. Apology as HMO.

Jake continued, "If we have the wrong person 'apologize,' it could make her even angrier. Contrarily, it could give us more of a clue about what she's after. It might make more sense, in fact, to start with the *least* likely person, just to see how she reacts."

"All right," Simon Nathanson said. "I'll go."

He stood and went down the line of three chairs in which his children sat, putting his hands on their thighs in order to pin their butts to the chairs. "Do. Not. Move," he said, a word for each child. He started muscling his way to the podium.

"What are you doing?" the bride asked her brother, alarmed.

"Simon, that's not Joan," his mother said.

Was he volunteering himself as the most likely suspect, or the least likely? Did he honestly believe that the terrorist was Joan in costume? Preternaturally implausible, and retiring Simon was so improbable a candidate to take on the duty of first in the line of fire that Helen found herself too stunned to talk. Was he protecting his father? Was he just unhinged? But many of the guests didn't know him, and simply waited to hear what he'd confess.

"As some of you know," Simon said, "I am separated from my wife, and currently in the process of a divorce. Kids," he said, facing his children, "as your mom and I told you, it is not your fault, and I ask you to remember that as you listen, hopefully not understanding a lot of what I say, although—well, kids are the game changer in a marriage, aren't they? I'm not sure how to do this."

"Just say what went wrong with the marriage, and say you're sorry, and ask her if she's your ex," a wedding guest volunteered.

"I'm not sorry," Simon said.

Someone else: "So why are you up there, then?"

"To get the ball rolling," Simon said.

"Are you just going to stand up there and complain about your marriage? That doesn't seem productive."

Simon suggested that he try to just tell one thing. It was hard, he said, to sum up how a relationship falls apart, so maybe he could stick with describing just one scene from the marriage that happened—let's see, about eight months ago now; the thing that spelled the beginning of the end.

*F*irst comes love. Then comes marriage. Simon knew what came next, and unlike his wife, he was able to foresee the consequences. He personally had had a childhood. It had been *long*. Certain grade school teachers still bobbed up from the lagoon of his dream life, and his wife's formative years had been miserable, too, so why would she imagine her children's lives as catching fireflies on a summer night, all glimmer and possibility? Not that he didn't understand denial. Denial explains the first child. But the second? Your life is already ruined. Thus the dog: you can't go anywhere anyway. Might as well have someone treat you like a war hero when you return from buying milk.

The third child was presumably what dog breeders call an *oops*. He didn't believe it. The first two were boys. Joan kept at it until she got the girl. Their elegant whippet bitch, evidently, didn't count. So now they got some public school bang out of their real estate tax buck. They formed their own towheaded village of idiots, all with names on those years' not top ten but top twenty of baby names, neither too boring nor too trendy.

Of foremost concern was the children's "safety." The children were escorted to and from the school and delivered to play dates where a chaperone was within earshot, ready to mediate any conflicts. At school there were "units" on strangers, and on bullies. All sports were supervised, all practices observed and applauded as if they were the unveiling of the *Pietà* for the Pope, and all children got their turns.

At least "fairness" and "fun" were the party line, although in Simon's experience the father-coaches, some of whom seemed not a little off plumb but diagnosable, were the worst bullies of all.

There appeared to be a shockingly short time between childhood as an idyll, full of possibilities for imagination and enjoyment, and the time when the spoiled little fuckers were benched, were exhorted to buckle down. The job of school was to punish the parents for being able to afford to live in Eden. Especially important was to punish the mothers who did not work, and therefore had nothing better to do than go through school all over again, overseeing the selling of gift wrap for the PTA, the covering of textbooks with "book socks," the construction of obscenely complicated crafts projects ("Make a three-dimensional animal entirely from recycled materials"), and, later, staring helplessly at math homework they couldn't even do the first go-round. At which point they turn to the husbands and bark, "Can't you do *anything*?"

Simon served as the air traffic controller of the children's arrivals and departures to school, social events, sports, play dates, and emergency doctors' appointments. He did not ask how they'd managed to brainwash the woman who, having moved here from the city when Dan was in kindergarten, sat on the sidelines of her first soccer game and marveled that she felt as if she'd just entered the Witness Protection Program. He tried to adopt the genial, "What the hell" compliance of the other Stepford dads, although at Back to School Nights, hunched inward and glaring, he looked a little like a serial killer. At the next mention of the word *rubric*, he might open fire.

When he and Joan weren't arguing about the children, they argued about household management. They disagreed on subjects like Laundry: Optimal Frequency Of. Mostly they argued about money. Joan, too, had to work to feed their life's meter. It is true that Simon's income fluctuated in inconvenient ways, but if he were not self-employed, he would be far less available to serve as a coolie. Except it was hard to make that argument with her because even the cardiologist daddies managed to coach Little League and show up to man booths at the school's Fun Fair. If he *really* hated the public schools so much, he could send his children to a Friends school, except—oh, right, he didn't earn enough. If he earned more, she wouldn't have to work, and thus would have more time to help the kids make scarecrows at the church's Fall Fest. Their childhoods flew by so fast!

If he made the point that, precisely because their childhoods flew by so fast, they ought to be able to, say, walk down to the pond with the dog without it turning into a Navy SEALs drill where her entire experience of the event was pointing out, repeatedly, how very difficult it was going to be to clean the mud off the dog's paws and the kids' shoes, she'd say, "Yes. I'm the killjoy. You're the fun one, aren't you? You get to play. I scrub the bathrooms." Actually, he cleaned the bathrooms. But to note that would merely earn the retort that if he earned more money, they could afford a maid. There was therefore no point in responding, so more and more often, he said nothing. "Keeping it bottled up" in exactly the way guaranteed to cause him an early infarct, which would be one way out. However, since she knew what his silence implied, they could now have entire arguments, predictable and circular as Christmas wreaths, without saying a word.

For the hell of it, he'd sometimes try to fill the silence with sympathy. Beam her some telepathic goodwill. But, unlike the dog, she didn't seem to be able to pick up on those clues. If he stroked her arm, she glared with eyes lowered, to warn him off asking for sex. The options in that department ("Make time for each other") seemed so hopeless, they made him wish that Joan of Dark would start an affair with the coach of Dan's midget football team, which was highly unlikely. Midget football was a sex-free zone.

How many more Back to School Nights? How many more elementary ice cream socials? How many more potlucks at the swim club? How many special breakfasts in bed for Mom on Mother's Day? How many, God help us, Halloweens?

That Halloween, Joan had a business trip. She had campaigned ferociously to get out of her deployment and was profoundly bereft when she failed. She had gotten another mother to chaperone her children, so that Simon only had to open the door bearing the basket of candy and chirp, "Happy Halloween!" She said she believed he could handle that.

Contempt, the marriage counselor had warned, was the loudest death knell for a partnership.

"I don't know," Simon said. "'Happy Halloween' seems very contrary to the spirit of the event to me. Would it be okay if I opened the door and growled, 'What do *you* want, little boy?'"

While he tried to make light of it, he was truly offended by how easy it would be to cross the line into bad taste in their town that time forgot, even with a Halloween display. You could have skulls that had evidently been shorn of all suggestion of death or decay. Ditto bloody plastic arms and legs that did not suggest brutal amputation. But you couldn't have a hanged man. You could have an open coffin, but you couldn't put a doll baby in it and a sign that said "Died too young." No, all was well, Darfur is Disneyland, even the candy is safe because with fluoride kids don't get cavities anymore.

"And you have to control the dog," Joan said.

In fairness, their marriage had been dissolving for quite some time—certainly since Rosalind was born. Later he would wonder if it was the town itself that had turned Joan into this aproned caricature of efficiency who overdoted on the children and was cruel to him, June Cleaver with a cleaver. But watching her climb into the airport shuttle van in the morning as if her National Guard unit were being called back for the third time for active duty in Iraq, aggrieved that Simon wasn't taking her to the airport despite the fact that he couldn't both do that and get the kids to school, was when he knew the marriage was over.

Sensibly, Simon thought, their dog was not fond of children. Joan suggested the dog just be left in the fenced yard.

Which is what Simon did. Except the minute his children left to trick-or-treat, he put the bowl of candy in front of the door and went into the kitchen to marinate himself a nice veal chop. He fully planned to let the dog chew on the bone when he was done, against all edicts of dog safety.

The red fawn whippet had been his triumph. If it weren't for him, they'd have the town's mascot, a slobbering Lab. His dog was so co-operative, such a lady, that she would let him take a veal bone from her mouth. Once he got the chop on the grill outside, she would be consumed enough with the smell of the veal that she wouldn't bother the trick-or-treaters.

Simon could see Ginger (the kids had named her; he called her Gin, or Gingivitis) from the kitchen window. She was stalking some creature as usual, one paw fetchingly suspended. She usually didn't catch her prey. But she did kill the occasional squirrel too stupid to run. And this must have been the case with the rabbit that, as Simon went out to light the grill, he saw Ginger ferociously shaking by the neck.

She did her victory dance, figure-eighting herself around the corpse. Luckily, the rabbit was really dead; Simon hadn't enjoyed the several twitching squirrels he'd had to finish off with blows from a shovel. Also, it was a pretty clean kill, almost bloodless, Ginger her-self not injured for a change. Maybe he should leave this one for Joan to bag—give her a taste of single parenthood with the full comple-ment of tasks she didn't give him credit for, not just the cooking of most meals that weren't mac and cheese, but all the manly things in the toolkit of a modern man. Grass! Snow! Fuse boxes! Toilet plung-ers, tire gauges! Roadkill, Gingerkill! Then the doorbell rang again, but he couldn't answer it, because he had to do something with the rabbit or Ginger would begin to tear it apart.

He used the pitchfork tool from the grill set to spear the rabbit and hefted it onto the cover of the gas grill. The rabbit was quite beautiful, its black eyes open, its soft fur a pointillist field of beiges and browns, hyperreal as something from a still life. Of course the rabbit was still, it was dead. *Still Life with Gas Grill.* All he needed now was a pear, a slice of Brie, and a carving knife.

Rabbit was yet another thing his family would not eat. Certainly there must be some instructional video online about how to skin a rabbit, and some recipes. He ran into the house for the laptop. By the time he got outside, Ginger was standing on her hind legs, sniffing her catch. He got her down and held her by the collar as he sat on the steps to Google "rabbit dressing."

According to a YouTube video from Mark Gilchrist, host of *Game for Everything*, skinning and dressing a rabbit didn't look that hard. Simon watched the chef make a nick in the right place and then hold the rabbit by its front legs over a trash can to pull the guts out in one clean swoop. He watched him get rid of the legs and head—"Easy off"—and then cut off the tail ("He doesn't want his tail anymore"). Done correctly, the skin, it appeared, could all come off in one piece, except for the stray bits of fluff left clinging. Simon held up the rabbit by its hind legs to inform Ginger of his plans. Ginger, who had been flabbergasted that Simon was on the computer even at a moment of such exquisite importance, indicated her approval with a whole-body shimmy.

There were issues. First, they didn't actually own a meat cleaver. He did own an axe. Overkill, but it would have to do.

Next, Chef Gilchrist's rabbit stew recipe required you to submerge the rabbit in a pot of salt water overnight, to remove the bitterness—"It's really worth the effort"—and then, the next day, boil the rabbit whole for fully two and a half hours until the meat fell off the bone. There were no corners to be cut here, evidently. A stew was thus not in the cards, but the truth is Simon loved a piece of grilled rabbit in a nice dark glaze, maybe with some cranberries. Once he got the rabbit skinned, it would surely be possible to slice off some grillable pieces or chunks. If they were inedible, he still had his veal chop.

Granted, it was half-assed. Half-assed was the name of the game in their household. Simon had once suggested they make *Demi Buttus—Demi Asellus?*—their official Latin slogan on the faux-elegant coat-of-arms flags the town favored.

The dog was content to prance alongside her master so long as he had the rabbit in hand. Setting up for the procedure took a long time. First he had to find the axe in the garage and clean it. Next there was the matter of what surface he could use to axe a rabbit. He found some stray pieces of wood in the garage, cleaned them of dirt and dead bugs, and brought them into the kitchen to keep any slippage of the blade away from their countertop.

Three-quarters of every project was setup. And most of the rest was cleanup. In between, there was the spasm of ease of the actual job. Marriage was much the same way: courtship and divorce the setup and cleanup you endure for the split second of pleasure of rolling paint on the walls. The dog's life passed similarly, although between meals and kills the dog at least mostly slept.

At some point, Simon noted, amused, that he was walking around with the rabbit slung casually over his back, like some farmer in knee breeches from a BBC period piece. Wasn't there a dead rabbit in *Women in Love*? Pretty soon he'd be wrestling one of the deranged Little League coaches on a bearskin rug.

He hadn't expected to be as smooth an operator as the professional chef. But it is fair to say that the exercise went quite badly. He failed to find the magic spot under the rib cage, hooded and vaguely clitoral, where you needed to do the first cut in order to keep the guts from spilling out. The guts did spill out. When he attempted to flip the rabbit right side up to scoop out the rest of the entrails, he almost dropped it, and Ginger got so excited that she knocked over the trash can. The intestines splattered the sides of the can and the floor and also, in toppling, upended the trash, so that the guts were now covered with coffee grounds, the dust of what looked like the end of a box of Lucky Charms, and, mysteriously, the jagged triangles of cut-up credit cards.

By the time he finished cleaning up, he'd basically lost his taste for the enterprise, even begun to feel sorry for the rabbit that it hadn't been allowed to occupy its tiny footprint in the town's ecology.

But he was committed. He would not get voted off the island without a fight. He ignored the ringing doorbell. He held the rabbit up by the scruff of its neck and informed the dog that it was time.

The pelt did not come off in one tidy piece. It didn't come off in five pieces, either. Actually, it didn't come off at all. The pelt seemed to have a will, and its fervent wish was to remain attached to its owner.

The sensible thing was to trash the rabbit. But his last idea was to see if the pelt would come off more easily if the rabbit were in pieces. This was explicitly contrary to the chef's instructions but—hey, Beavis and Demi Buttus. He was hoping he could start with the legs, and maybe leave the head attached, since he didn't relish chopping off the head, and see if, once the legs were gone, he could get a strip of breast, thin enough to be edible with searing.

His children entered the kitchen just as he was lifting the axe high and aiming at the rabbit's rear legs.

The boys seemed confused. Perhaps their bloodstained, crazed father heaving an axe at a dead rabbit had something to do with Halloween. They didn't have the frame of reference to think he looked like Jack Nicholson in *The Shining*. But Rosalind, dressed as a little angel in diaphanous pink, immediately began to scream. Once she was screaming, the boys screamed, too, and then the dog began to bark, and in the melee chomped down on a calf that turned out to be Rosalind's. The skin, Simon was relieved to confirm, hadn't really even been punctured. If it were possible to shriek louder, Rosalind did so while he was checking her leg, in the process dumping her bag of candy into the trash, all of the Milky Ways, Sprees, and Nerds mixed in with rabbit entrails, except the candy that reached the floor, which the dog immediately began to eat, wrappings and all.

"Ginger!" Simon said. "Out! Ginger! Now! Go!"

Before accepting her banishment into the yard, the dog first did one deft, precise leap onto the counter and grabbed the veal chop.

Simon couldn't help himself. He laughed. It's true, Your Honor. While his children wept, he laughed.

Unsurprisingly, the rabbit incident would get pride of place in the divorce complaint as evidence of Simon's instability and unfitness for parenthood. *Laughed at children's distress. Did not bring Rosalind to ER despite threat of rabies. Made children dig rabbit's grave. Suggested using daughter's dress as burial shroud. Children now all vegetarians.*

Which really was a problem, since they didn't eat any vegetables. Well, there was always pasta, which was all they really ate anyway.

They weren't upset because their parents were divorcing. They weren't upset because their mother had a new boyfriend before a date for the mediation was even set: the coach of Dan's midget football team, as Simon was shocked to discover despite having predicted it months ago. They weren't proud to have a first-dead-pet story to one-up all the dead goldfish, canaries on their backs, and squashed kitty cats they would hear about on first dates in years to come. No, they were upset because their "obviously bipolar" father had ruined Halloween for them forever.

Simon got the dog.

*S*imon Nathanson was not an experienced public speaker, but he managed to sketch an outline of his alienation from his wife, basically cribbing from the précis he'd been asked to supply to his divorce attorney.

When he finished, someone said, "This is a complete waste of time."

The tax attorney admitted that he and his wife also argued an absurd amount about the minutiae of dumb chores. But he didn't think his wife would put a bullet to his head over it. "Right, hon?" (This to the wife.)

"Yeah, but it's a good reminder," the wife said. "We shouldn't assume she's single. The broken-up marriages are what get really hateful. Especially when kids are involved. The dads go in with rifles, murder the whole family."

"Not the moms, though," Jake Nathanson noted.

"The moms just walk into the ocean with the kids in their arms."

"That's only in Japan."

"How about the astronaut in the diaper?"

Those old enough to remember all nodded, remembering. Truth is, savoring.

What a story that had been. Lisa Nowak, separated with three children, had been having an affair with a fellow NASA astronaut. They did not have sex in space, since they didn't get so far as space and were never on the same training mission, but they certainly traded smutty emails from their respective motherships—at least until Nowak's boyfriend got interested in an Air Force captain and Nowak, intent on revenge, drove almost a thousand miles in a diaper so she didn't have to stop. In an airport parking lot, she donned a wig, trench coat, and sunglasses to pepper spray her terrified rival's car. Since Nowak had also brought rubber gloves, a serious hunting knife, rubber tubing, and garbage bags, the charges were attempted murder in the first degree.

"Whatever happened to her?" Sarah asked.

"Probation," said Sal, who read the wires at work. "And community service."

"Really?" Sarah asked.

"But listen," Tess said, trying to get them back on topic. "That definitely isn't Joan." Besides, Tess said, Joan had left Simon, or rather made Simon leave. Joan was already seeing someone else.

"It's usually the women who end things," Dr. Myra Feldstein noted. "Ironically. The conventional wisdom is that men are always walking out on women, but that is a myth."

"Because women are always the ones who gets things done."

The gastroenterologist nodded his wry assent. "No man ever makes his own appointment for a colonoscopy."

"Oh, for God's fucking sake," someone said, "let's get on with it."

Delbert Billips Sr. asked Simon to apologize. "Let's find out if she's listening, and from where, and how this is going to go."

"I. Am. Sorry," Simon proclaimed, in robot voice, "for any pain and suffering I have caused you. I apologize with profound regret for each and every time I failed to snap to and do exactly what you wanted when you wanted it."

"Dripping with sincerity," a woman in the crowd noted.

"Say it like you mean it": another woman in the crowd.

"How can she even hear us if she isn't here?"

"Are you sure the intercom doesn't work?" Billips Sr. asked.

"Knock once for yes, twice for no," the novelist suggested.

Someone near the doorway did, in fact, tap out a questioning Morse code of knocks on the door.

But no knocks came back. And, as Idris Deby indicated to Billips with a head shake in the negative from the French doors, no one was approaching from the garden.

"Look," Amy said, from the couch.

She had evidently let her hand fall between the sofa's pillows and its frame, which no one had checked, and now extracted four little bags of candy. Helen recognized them: they were what she had made up last Halloween for the trick-or-treaters.

What did it say about their captor, that she had found these bags in the recesses of Helen's pantry and shoved them inside her couch? This event was planned like a jailbreak. The most important question was how she would have known that the ceremony was to be held in this room, and not outside, which would be the more ordinary place for a wedding ceremony, barring rain. Helen wondered why they were in the great room, anyway. That had been their big mistake. If they were outside now, there would be no way to contain them. If the wedding had happened outside as planned, how did the woman expect to corral them all inside? Behind the podium, the garden glittered seductively, the breeze lifting the corners of the tablecloths.

Several of the mothers, and Simon, teamed up to help the children share the candy. Sylvia Needleman, the diabetic, demanded some candy as well. Her husband reminded her that sugar was a bad idea. She countered that her mouth was really dry.

While the couple argued, the men discussed the possibility that if their captor had hidden candy, she may have also hidden a camera and/or microphone, and began a renewed search. Billips Sr. gestured that they should signal or write, not talk out loud. The gastroenterologist produced a pen from his pocket. Simultaneously, Idris Deby found a pen on the bookshelf, and studied it suspiciously. Then surrendered it to Billips Sr., who nodded to let Idris know he understood: it was some kind of video recording device. They both stared into the tiny porthole of its camera eye.

"I'm going to need to go to the bathroom," a woman announced.

Because of the candy, and the search, not everyone was focused on the French doors. So not everyone saw the terrorist standing there. This time she didn't have the rifle. But the sawed-off shotgun was off her belt holster, in her hand. With the other hand she offered an exaggerated finger wag like a clock pendulum that meant *No, no, no, no, no.*

Those who saw her gasped, whimpered, moaned, wailed, or just froze.

Billips Sr. looked at Helen, as if to command her to begin inter-action. But before she could, Simon charged toward the door and started banging on it.

"Hey," he screamed. "I apologized. Now let my children out. *Let my children out!*"

A word for each pound. *Let. My. Children. Go.* His own children sobbing now, from the shock of hearing the intensity of their father's distress.

This was not, was simply not, how you dealt with an insane person. The terrorist took a step closer to the door and pointed the sawed-off shotgun at Simon's heart. She lowered the gun and made a point of squatting to fuss with or adjust the bomb or putative bomb on the grass near the door. When she stood, she leaned forward so the gas mask was almost on the glass. "This is so much fun," she hissed. "On with it!"

Helen pushed Simon away. "Hey," she said, just leaning against the glass and speaking loudly enough to be heard, but quietly enough that it was clear she was talking just to the woman, not the crowd. "Gotta tell you one thing. Very cool gas mask!"

"Thanks," the terrorist said.

"Where on earth did you find such an old one?" Helen asked.

"eBay."

"Must've been hard to make it work with the sunglasses."

The terrorist said nothing.

"Very, very cool," Helen repeated. "How 'bout the dress?"

"Bargain Bride," the woman said, laughing.

"There is such a place?" Helen laughed with her. "Really? That's wild."

"Used stuff, mostly. Hundreds of pairs of stupid white satin shoes."

"The shoes," Helen said dolefully, shaking her head and pleased with what she'd just managed to learn: their captor was single, not married, not stood up at the altar. She had no Havishamish senti-mentality about the wedding dress.

Behind her, Helen could hear the guests getting restless. The shrinks especially, who should know about building rapport, dis-approved of her line of questioning. Jake was marching over to "help." Helen turned and gave him her most ferocious look of warning.

"Also, thanks for the candy," Helen said.

"You found it?"

"Yes. Thanks."

"And my nifty Spy Store pen, too."

Except she didn't seem upset about the fact that Billips Sr. had discreetly placed the pen under a pillow on the couch. Which sug-gested that she had backup means of audio-video.

"So walk me through it," Helen said, casually. "Like: What did you have for breakfast this morning?"

From behind her, groans of objection.

The question wasn't random. It was about sequencing. Often if you get hysterical patients focused on an order of events, they can pull themselves together.

The hostage taker laughed again. "Three-cheese omelet. Wheat toast. Sausage."

"That's good," Helen said, "because you need protein for a day like today. Did you get into the dress before or after?"

"Oh, for God's sake!" the best man blurted, in the background, yanking the hostage taker right out of the rapport Helen had been build-ing. Jake was talking, too, but the hostage taker talked right over him.

"Y'all aren't making much progress," she said. "But maybe that's a good thing. The first fifteen to forty-five minutes of a hostage situ-ation are the most dangerous. You've made it this far without anyone getting hurt. Your next stumbling block, of course, is the surrender. Things can go very badly then. SWAT won't *try* to kill you, of course, but in the melee . . ."

The woman studied Helen for a second through the door. Then she turned her back to the room and fired a single shot from the sawed-off shotgun into the garden, up toward the trees. The reverb of the bullet, amplified by a chorus of startled crows, got everyone screaming again. The terrorist walked out of Helen's frame of vision without turning around.

She didn't have to. Helen got the point. This woman wanted to be caught. Helen prayed that one of her neighbors reported the gunfire. But if the woman didn't plan to extend the guessing game too much longer, why hadn't she just left them a phone? Or let one hostage go to get the police there? Did she want to be caught, or not? It just didn't compute. Of course, no one ever accused crazy people of impeccable logic. But at least it made sense of the biggest mystery of her planning: what she would have done if rain hadn't threatened, if the guests were all sitting in their chairs in the sunlit garden. People would have scattered and run. She would have herded whoever was left into the great room. And the police would have been there immediately. Which meant that she wanted the police. Well, of course she wanted the police—you don't stage a drama like this for no audience.

Helen also realized that, if the woman was itching to fire that gun, things could get more dangerous before they got less so.

Tess and Gabriel had made their way through the crowd toward Simon to steady him.

"Anyone recognize her voice?" Helen asked the crowd.

"She's a white woman," someone offered.

"Like you can tell from someone's voice!"

Right from the beginning, even with so little room to move, the hostages had managed to sort themselves into factions by age, sex, and marital status. Some of that had happened naturally: the older people up close, where they could hear the ceremony; the young mothers with babies toward the rear, so they could escape if the babies began to wail. But they also wanted to divide by race, and in this crowd, race was a complicated calculus.

Souleymane Samake was a Muslim from Mali. He had two wives back home, and six children. Souleymane was Gabe's contact for the crafts that Gabe's charity outfit sold in the United States. True,

Souleymane's wives sometimes argued. The old wife can't help but feel some rivalry with the new wife. As the saying goes, the younger wife, the *kònyò muso*, is the one "whose mosquito net has no holes." But women in Mali had dignity. The women in the United States lived in palaces and did not even have to share their husbands, but nothing satisfied them. While he declined to judge Americans by the most inflamed of Muslim rhetoric about American moral laxity, it was hard not to suspect that the women had brought this event upon themselves, by selfishness and sin, by not being *nyuman*, virtuous.

For their parts, some of the non-NGO-affiliated wedding guests wondered petulantly why the bride and groom had to make such a show about befriending Muslims to begin with. When Tess and Gabe had taken up the collection on Facebook and mycharity.com to get Souleymane here, the couple explained to several people that he was quite enlightened by Malian standards. For starters, his wives had kept their clitorises. Still, the wedding guests believed that the Africans were somehow to blame for this hostage event.

They clumped all of the Africans together, although the other three were from Chad and had never met Souleymane before today. Furthermore, they were Christian. Ngarta Adoulaye and his meek wife, Acta, had worked at the MSF clinic in Chad with Tess and Gabe, along with the third man, Idris Deby. Although Idris was born in Chad, he was a naturalized French citizen. He was educated at the Sorbonne, with a résumé that included a Fulbright. Tess and Gabe admired him fervently and his presence at their wedding was deeply important to them.

You'd think the American blacks would be more open and welcoming to the Africans. But except for Colonel Billips Sr., the couple of black guests from the paternal Billips side of the family joined the American whites in wishing the Africans had just stayed home.

Delbert Billips Jr., the groom's father, computed all of these judgments about race immediately and with deadly accuracy. He had been living in the South with a white woman for thirty-six years. His main territory of disagreement with his wife had to do with what she deemed his inability or unwillingness to tune out certain pitches of racism. White noise, Salome said—make *those* whites just white noise. His son's marriage to Tess seemed in many ways like a carbon copy of his own to Sal, right down to their nutty shrink fathers-in-law. Still, it scared him sometimes how naïve Tess and Gabe seemed. Had they never been stopped by a cop?

As fast as he thought all this, Salome saw him thinking it, saw where he was going. They were already holding hands. Sal took one hand back to stroke the hair on the back of his head. His hair looked like Persian lamb but was in fact peach-fuzzily soft, in a way that seemed to make some kind of music out of the contrast of hair and hard skull. She had always loved the shape of his head. Sometimes Del accused her of communicating with him with calm, assertive energy, as if he were a dog. But it worked. She rested her hand on his head for just a second, long enough to ground him.

The guests were still bickering about the hostage taker's voice.

"I suppose if that black person answered an ad about an apartment, you'd tell them it was already rented."

"And if I answered an ad about an apartment, you think they wouldn't think I'm a Jew from New York?"

"Stop," Del Jr. said.

It was the first thing he'd said so far. People obeyed.

"We don't have to wonder if she's white from her voice. We know she's white from her skin."

"Unless she pulled a Michael Jackson."

Del continued (ignoring the last from Ben Kramer the novelist), "She sounds like she's from California."

"To me, it sounds more like Jersey girl."

"I'll go next," Ben Kramer said. "I'm from New Jersey!"

Mara Lowell craned her head to give her therapist a quick, pointed, desperate look.

"No," Trevor Hunter said. "I'll go."

Billips pointed to the actor. "You."

*D*ear Trevor. I LOVE YOU. I think about you when I wake up/ when I fall asleep/in the shower/when I touch myself. I imagine your hands in my hair. I imagine you kissing my closed eyes, first one, then the other, your lips tickling the lashes. I know how you would touch me, just the way I like. Oh, Trev! On our honeymoon—but I don't want to be pushy. You don't have to marry me. Just give me ten minutes in a hotel/in your trailer/in your limo. I will be discreet. You don't have to use protection. I trust you to pull out. I trust you to be clean.

Our baby is so beautiful. You don't have to pay child support. I will not file a paternity suit. Just visit us, won't you?

You living the high life while I'm stuck here clerking the grave-yard shift at a convenience store, living with my mother, and my stepfather is a drunk and a horrible man, I don't want to let him near our daughter.

The women and girls wrote Trevor daily. They joined Facebook and Myspace fan pages. They tweeted. They e-mailed, too, in florid fonts, clotting their words with emoticons and things that danced and winked across the screen: ballerinas, cats. In the olden days the fan notes were all handwritten and you could tell, just from the cramped or sprawled cursive, that something was amiss. But now even nutcases had computers and e-mail, except in the prisons. In the prisons they had only lined paper, and blunt pencils. *If you write me, I will write you back. I have plenty of time.* In the style popularized by instant messaging and texting, but available always to breathless teenagers and others whose educations stopped in eighth grade, the prisoners used no capital letters or punctuation.

At the studio, it was mostly Trevor's assistant, Charlotte, who read the notes that came to his website, but sometimes they somehow managed to ferret out his personal e-mail account. Sometimes they found his girlfriend's.

His last girlfriend, Ruth, had her own assistants, her own bodyguard. Most places they went—Pilates, the dental hygienist—someone would greet them to express their opinion about their hairstyles, their outfits, their oeuvre.

For the past year or so, Trevor had been having a bad patch with a fan they'd nicknamed Loony Tina. Tina had bad posture and stringy hair. All psychopaths, it appeared, had bad hair, to the extent that he often wondered if mental illness could be cured by a makeover.

Loony Tina would follow Ruth on her errands. After Ruth left the drugstore, Tina would go in and bribe the salesclerk for what was purchased, try to buy the same item. This was her special way of bonding with Trevor. She kept a log of all this, then sent the very precise records to Trevor, as if she were a PI.

You'd think that, having waited outside Ruth's salon while she had her expensive highlights applied, Tina could buy better shampoo. Or at least use shampoo. Or even just clean her glasses, which looked like they were smeared with bird shit.

Trevor tried to take the attention of fans in good grace. Even if people were reaching for his hem as if he were a healer, a splasher of blessed water, he tried not to seem holier-than-thou. Instead he tried to act . . . sportsmanlike. If the fans were a deafening rapids of need and longing, well, then he would just put on his bright orange life vest and kayak through.

Okay, there was something funny about much of it. The guy in Miami who swam naked right past potential crocodiles in the bayou toward the tennis player Anna Kournikova's house, but got off course and presented himself ready for action at the wrong manse. Conan

O'Brien stalked by a lovelorn Boston priest. Still, enough celebrities had been killed that you really couldn't make light of the risks.

Where was the line between unhinged and truly dangerous? An ex–Navy SEAL got a message from God. God Himself commanded him to marry Halle Berry. The human race depended on it. Well, the human race could definitely use more Halle Berrys. Another nutcase believed that Steven Spielberg and his wife had used their obscene wealth to assemble an army of zombie disciples implanting "soul catchers" into people's arms, to control their thoughts. So, what, one minute you're using computer applications to design a wedding invitation for yourself and an actor, dreamy and innocent as an eighth grader writing out her name with someone else's last name in a heart with an arrow through it on her biology notebook, sketching out the ways you and he could meet (His car breaks down in front of your house, and you provide the jump! He buys a sliver of expensive goat cheese at Whole Foods, and you're the cheese slice girl!); and the next minute you're after him with a hatchet?

And, in a way, the movies were to blame. How prescient *Taxi Driver* was in this regard: John Hinckley tried to kill the president to get Jodie Foster's attention, the way Robert De Niro as Travis Bickle killed to get Jodie Foster's attention in *Taxi Driver*, and now Hinckley *was* famous, the mascot of all celebrity stalkers. (And poor John, Jodie Foster was gay!) Movies continued to reinforce the notion that the lunatic could gain honor and respect by spectacular violence. Trevor himself had declined many roles that ended in bloodbaths, and all horror flicks that involved a progression of ever more gruesome tortures. He actually preferred the formulaic violence in his TV cop show. Corpse: plop. Next corpse: plop. Shit 'em on out. Unimaginative, maybe. But safer.

When he and Ruth investigated filing a restraining order against Tina, they were advised that until you found your stalker in your bed, using your vibrator, there wasn't much you could do. Plus, whatever you did was just further contact, and read as confirmation of your interest. Trevor just tried to let the bodyguards—or personal security forces, as they preferred to be called—handle it. The bodyguards and the computer people.

Come to think of it, Trevor hadn't seen Loony Tina in a while. He had been on location, and then he'd been spending time in New York, with Miranda.

They were here for the evening with no security at all. Miranda didn't even have a bodyguard. Their driver was not armed.

They hadn't told anyone they were coming to the wedding. It was a small wedding in New Jersey. Still, Tina could have done some research. Maybe Tina would follow Miranda now instead of Ruth. Could Tina have somehow gotten herself admitted into a screening or focus group for *Crash Fest*, the movie where Trevor and Miranda met?

By the way, they should stop calling the woman with the rifle a terrorist. It was very misleading. She clearly had no political or nationalistic demands. She was just your garden-variety hostage taker—or HT, as they snappily acronymed on his cop show. In point of fact, he'd probably talked down more suicidal and delusional HTs than any of the shrinks. You just needed to be slow, steady, and sympathetic. You spoke *like this*, Trevor said, snapping his voice into his TV cop's voice, making his eyeballs thyroidal with concentration as he crab-walked, his hand on the imaginary holster. If Tina wanted to speak with him privately, he was available.

$\mathscr{H}$elen could not help but wince as Trevor spoke. If the hostage taker was this Tina, insulting her—mocking her unwashed hair—was not what the doctor ordered. How was this an apology? More like a provocation. By the time he was done talking, Helen had to struggle not to dislike the actor, although she tried to find the class clown in him touching.

At some point Helen looked at Sal, and she could tell that Sal was having trouble warming to him, too. She knew how hurt Sal was that Miranda and her boyfriend hadn't shown up for the rehearsal dinner. Was two evenings too long for him to spend with his girlfriend's family?

At the rehearsal dinner, Sal had told Helen about how much Miranda loved to act. A trace of the child's joy still in the relish with which she entered a part, as if slipping through a thorny patch of foliage into some secret garden. Although Del thought his daughter's interest in acting was partly due to an insecure racial identity, Sal believed that acting was, for Miranda, like journalism for her parents, essentially an act of empathy. Maybe all meaningful work was.

Sal also confessed that she had seen a preview of *Crash Fest*, and didn't much care for it. The way the movie pitted Miranda against Ruth for Trevor's love prickled Sal's feminist ire, and Del would find it racist. Ruth is blond, wholesome, pink-cheeked, all-American. Miranda is—other. Fun to fuck but maybe not such a good idea to marry.

Miranda plays a crash test supervisor who, despite being a brain-
iac in spectacles, doesn't mind donning a helmet to drag-race on the
course. Girl wins boy's love by proving she's a good sport. In a big
scene, Miranda, sweaty after some vehicular triumph, flips off the
hot helmet to free her curls. Sal couldn't explain why it bothered her
so much. It was the standard librarian-letting-down-her-hair scene
featured in every romantic comedy for so long that even the slow-
motion parodies of it are old hat (old helmet?). Of course Miranda
wore a jumpsuit that was specially designed to show cleavage, and
risking death to test a car made Miranda sweat, and the sweat
made her nipples erect through the special nipple-revealing jumpsuit fabric. More old news. Like sexism and racism, old news but still
irksome.

As Sarah and Helen shared how traumatized they'd been during
the Doctors Without Borders year, Sal had confessed, almost embarrassed to do so, that war-torn Africa aside, she worried almost as much
about Miranda. Gabriel had always been sensible and self-sufficient.
But Miranda! To her mother she seemed fleet and fragile, like some
kind of darting dragonfly. What kind of life was acting, to commit
yourself to a lifetime of that much rejection, and meanwhile, in order
to share a crappy one-bedroom apartment with three other girls, earning a living as—a waitress, a bartender? In her love life to date, Miranda had ricocheted between two unsatisfactory poles: older men,
one of them married, who treated her frankly as a concubine; and
fellow actors who were even less secure, both fiscally and emotion-
ally, than Miranda herself. When they visited Miranda in New York,
Sal's heart broke for all of the long-legged stunners with their tumbling tresses and the interesting clothes they'd trolled so hard for at
the sample sales. But then, there are no people that age in the suburbs.
You just forget about striving.

Now Miranda had a second-floor condo all her own, with a tree
out her window that bloomed in the spring—a Brooklyn triumph.
Yet Trevor made it clear that he was slumming it in New York. No
bodyguard!

The rehearsal dinner felt like so long ago now, but Helen remembered the tone in which Sal, her wonderful new relative, had said, "No bodyguard." It was as if they'd known each other since their kids were little, supported each other through the travails of parenthood and understood that the worry never stops. Not even when your kid is thirtysomething, and healthy, and successful, and in love.

"So," Trevor concluded. "It's hard to apologize, exactly. Since I've never met you. But I will say: I understand. And I'm . . . sorry if I hurt your feelings."

They all faced the garden doors, awaiting maybe-Tina's response. Nothing.

The barricaded door? Nothing.

"I wouldn't entirely give up on the notion that this is Ruth herself," said Sal's father, Dr. Needleman. Trevor looked puzzled. So did the rest of the guests.

"A lot of the actresses," Dr. Needleman continued, "have a problem with grandiosity. But the acting materializes their narcissism."

"That's not Ruth," Trevor said. "That's not Ruth's walk. Plus Ruth's arms are better. Especially her triceps. She works really hard on them with her trainer."

"Hey," someone said from the crowd, warningly. "You should stop talking about your ex-girlfriend so much in front of Miranda."

Everyone strained to see who was speaking. Helen knew at once that it was her son. Being gallant.

"I mean," Simon said, "isn't it just obvious that it's rude?"

Miranda looked at Simon with fresh interest. "Hear that?" she said to Trevor, with a playful punch to his arm.

"One time," Dr. Needleman said, "early in my career, I had to commit a very famous actress having a nervous breakdown."

"Who was it?" someone asked.

"Oh, I wouldn't say," Dr. Needleman said. "She'd chosen me over more experienced celebrity psychiatrists because I was 'sincere' and 'available.' Indeed, I not only helped her finesse her physicals for the entertainment doctors but was available to her at any hour, even, at one point, curtailing a vacation to oversee one of her crises."

"You can't do that with a borderline patient," Dr. Nathanson said.

"Of course not," Dr. Needleman said, "but I was so young. The second I tried to draw a line, she fired me and moved on to the next chump."

"That's not Ruth," Trevor said.

"I have to go to the bathroom," a woman said.

"Me too."

And then, at the garden doors, with her rifle, the terrorist. Or HT.

Trevor stood at attention, as if awaiting critique of his scene at an acting workshop.

"You," the HT boomed, crooking her finger at him like the Ghost of Christmas Past, "are a real asshole. Are you kidding? You think I'd do all this for someone I've never even met? You think I'm some garden-variety stalker?"

Trevor looked surprised, and a touch hurt.

"Not to mention your show's a joke. SWAT just bursts through the door, like it's a birthday party and they're all yelling 'Surprise!' When they cover down at all, they cover down all wrong. Plus everyone has miracle revolvers that hold, like, sixty shots. And point them sideways like gangsters." She demonstrated with a parodic *Scarface* move—the hostages yelping and ducking as she aimed. "Like that would hit anything, ever."

Helen made her way toward the doors. By now everyone understood that to go anywhere took a while: each seated person needing to stand to let you pass, like when you leave a movie theater seat during a climactic scene.

"Hi," Helen said, with an odd sideways glance.

Before Helen could speak, Mary's baby awoke and began to cry. Mary and Jake conferred in whispers. Alas, the diaper bag—with the baby's bottle—was in the kitchen.

"So I have nothing for him?" Mary hissed in amazement. "No bottle? No clean diapers?"

"I wasn't really expecting to be locked in here," Jake reminded her.

The HT's shoulders shook a bit, as if she were giggling. Enjoying their discomfort.

Helen made a twinkly face that indicated controlled mirth.

"I'm really impressed with your planning," Helen said confidentially, angling herself toward the glass of the French doors so she didn't have to talk quite as loud. "You've obviously really thought this out. You researched SWAT, huh? To know how they were likely to react?"

"Didn't need to."

"Oh?"

"God was on my side," the woman said. "God provided." This she said in a southern preacher voice, drawing out the *aw* in *Gawd* and shaking her head as if to make her jowls shiver, if she had preacher jowls. Then, looking heavenward, *"Elhamdulillah!"* Because of the mask, it wasn't entirely possible to tell if she was joking. Helen could see without looking at them that the shrinks were blinking out DSM codes. If Allah told the woman to do this, or Elvis, if she were schizophrenic, there would be no reasoning with her.

"They don't call it SWAT anyhow," the woman added. "They call it tac. For tactical team."

"I didn't know that," Helen said softly. "I keep wondering if you had a plan B. Because this would not have worked in the garden."

"Why not? In the garden, it would all have been faster."

"These people sure can talk. They could talk all night."

The HT said, "I'm surprised no one's shown up yet. Your neighbors don't object to a little gunplay in the yard?"

"You know," Helen said, "you did so much work getting this set up. Something really awful must have happened to you."

The woman said nothing.

"You must have been really hurt," Helen continued, "to be pushed to this."

The woman said, with conviction, "You have no idea."

"I know I don't. But I really want to."

Jake pushed himself close to the door and said loudly, "Why not come in and tell us all about it?"

Helen said, "Be quiet, Jake."

"Have a seat," Jake said. "Take off that hot, sticky, uncomfortable mask."

Helen: "Shut *up*, Jake."

"Right on," the terrorist said, with a sort of Black Panther power-to-the-people fist pump that, again, might have been ironic, and might not have been.

As if she'd momentarily forgotten about the bomb, the HT crouched with her back to the door and, leaning the rifle against her body, fiddled with the contraption, adjusting the angle of a wire. The back of her wedding dress, which they had certainly seen before but had not concentrated on, had Victorian buttons down it—a phalanx of tiny satin-covered buttons joined with tiny loops. Someone had to have gotten her into that dress. Because the dress was strapless, the top buttons were right in that spot between the shoulder blades that is almost impossible to reach.

When she straightened up and turned to face the crowd, she looked surprised to see them, or pretended to look surprised. Then genuine surprise as a helicopter appeared overhead, as sometimes happened—a news crew getting an aerial view of a fire, or people being medevaced to hospitals. But from the HT's gestures of uncontained excitement, it seemed that she assumed the helicopter was for her. She aimed the rifle upward, and shot at it. Shot again.

Was the helicopter low enough to see someone on the ground, especially through all of the trees? Helen suspected not. Probably they couldn't even hear the bullets over the noise of the engine.

If the HT had turned to face the great room, she could have watched the hostages through the glass, as if they were an ant farm, as they screamed and writhed. But she didn't turn around. She ran after the helicopter, as if she could reach it. Then simply vanished out of the hostages' line of sight.

When she was gone, Miranda said, with conviction, "She's an actor."

"Could be," someone agreed. "This is quite a performance."

"Or a cop," Billips Sr. said. "She said 'cover down.' The way she held the rifle"—and he demonstrated, twisting hand over fist. "She's had some training."

"Or she's an actor who wants to play a cop," Trevor said.

"Or military?" Billips Sr. added.

"Or a cop who wants to be an actor," Trevor said. "A crazy lady cop. Did you recognize her guns?"

Before Billips Sr. could answer, the women who had needed to go to the bathroom interrupted to make it known that they now really, really had to go to the bathroom.

*T*he event to this point had taken just under an hour, longer than some of the guests had gone without checking their cell phones for years. An hour is short for a flight, long to be closed in an elevator stalled between floors or to bleed in an ER waiting room before you're even asked for proof of insurance. The room was tight and hot, but it wasn't a cattle car. To have ancestors die horrible deaths in the camps, only to meet your own end in a suburban house because of some random lunatic's pathological jealousy: it was unthinkable. Most found it hard to believe they could be trapped much longer. She had fired the rifle outside. Someone would have heard. Even without that, some late guest would find the front door locked, ring the bell. Then, stumped, walk around back. Someone would have heard the gunfire. Someone who couldn't attend would have sent a gift. They'd be saved by the FedEx man!

In any case, the women would not be holding it in.

Tess and her Doctors Without Borders cohorts now relocated Wailing Amy, moved the couch forward, away from the wall, and created a space where you could crouch to relieve yourself a little more privately, especially if they cordoned off the couch somehow. Gabe got the bedpan they'd found in the TV cabinet earlier and collected the couple of remaining tissues in men's pockets. The bride asked her mother if the afghan she kept on the couch was stowed in the room. Providentially, it had just been shoved into the cabinet with the DVD player. They could hold it up as a curtain. A group of men formed a blockade with their backs to the couch, sealing it off from view with the blanket.

The most desperate woman went in first, blushing and apologizing. You couldn't see her, but you could certainly hear her.

"Someone ought to sing," a guest offered, over the noise of the woman's prodigious stream.

By the third woman, you could hear not only the stream itself but the noise of the stream hitting—or missing—the existing accumulation. You could also smell it. The smell was not a big deal for the Doctors Without Borders people, many of whom had been in makeshift rooms in which cholera patients slept in beds with holes cut in them and buckets underneath. But for the rest of the guests, the smell called them back to the gravity of their situation.

Now Sylvia Needleman proclaimed that she had to go but was not willing to go behind the couch. Sylvia had been a long-lashed, plump-lipped stunner, heavily courted by a progression of successful men before she and Ira fell desperately in love. Ira and Sylvia had only last month celebrated their fiftieth wedding anniversary.

Women and children first into the lifeboats. But what about the geriatrics?

There followed a quick, desperate inventory among the elderly guests about their physical ailments and needs. Hip replacements, bypasses. Helen Burns's mother, who was probably the oldest at eighty-eight, was still alarmingly sharp. Unlike many deaf older people, who tend to withdraw into isolation, Agnes Burns had been a widow for a long time. She seemed both comfortable with her solitude and grateful for, rather than demanding of, outside attention. Socially, Aggy Burns was twinkly and chipper. She wore her derring-do expression now, although her good cheer seemed to be wilting a bit. Helen, who found her heart slayed every time she picked up her mother at the independent-living facility and found the woman waiting for her in the lobby with lipstick on, in a prim, ancient dress, hands folded in her lap—sympathy, and maybe a touch of fear as well, since Helen herself had lived alone for even longer now and would shockingly soon have to pack light for her own reduced possibilities—tried to beam regular reassuring expressions that her mother quietly acknowledged and lobbed back, efficient as birdcalls.

And Sal, Helen noticed, was providing the same service for her mother-in-law. Sal had taken the chair vacated by Delbert Billips Sr., who had been standing and at attention since their situation began, and had her arm around her mother-in-law's shoulders, occasionally whispering to her. Helen hadn't even paid enough attention to the old lady to get much sense of her. But it was clear from the way the woman's head followed her husband as he paced that they would have been the long-married couple on the *Titanic* who folded down the sheets and got into bed together tenderly to await the end.

Helen Burns's father had died of a massive coronary at age fifty-nine, the age Helen herself was now. What better way to go than a heart attack? Though not at fifty-nine. That he died taking the trash to the curb might seem ignoble, but better that than the bomb.

At this point, any movement in the room got everyone's attention, as it does when someone stands to leave a classroom mid-lecture. But Tess in particular looked puzzled as to why Mara Lowell was bent over to whisper in her mother's ear. Mara and Helen conferred as the last person finished up behind the pee couch.

Mara moved to the lectern. "I want to say something," Mara announced. "I'm not going to tell my story, because it's irrelevant. Some of you here know it anyway. But I just want to share some stuff with her about how she must be feeling."

*M*ara and Ben met at a book party, at a powerful editor's loft, and slept together that night. The ambition at the party was so viscous that everyone seemed to be rutting. A novelist with famous hair, shoe-polish black with a white swath in it, had spent quite a while chatting Mara up, angling toward her Byronically on a couch, rattling the ice in his bourbon like a snake charmer. Then his wife arrived. The wife was a well-known photographer. She wore a retro black dress and her hair was much shorter than her husband's, a seriously good haircut, surrounding her face like a subtle turn of phrase. But on this score, at least, Mara had it all over the wife. Her own russet ringlets were a thing to behold, whether she wore her hair casually but artfully clipped, as she did that night, or tumbling down her back in its Pre-Raphaelite splendor. The novelist sighed to signal his disappointment, breathed "Farewell" in the brogue that seemed to have gotten more pronounced, not less so, from his decades in New York, and went to greet his wife, leaving Mara to look around at the loft. He didn't ask for Mara's phone number or even her last name.

At that moment Ben appeared by her side. "You think you feel like an idiot, think how she feels," he said.

"Why would I feel like an idiot?"

"*Womanizer*. What a strange word. It sounds so mechanical. Which I guess it is. You're much better off with me."

Mara studied him, cat-eyed. "Why?"

"Let's see. Because I'm about half a century younger? Because I don't have deep lines around my mouth like a marionette? He looks like Howdy Doody. Plus I can actually keep it up. In fact, I will bet you hard money on hardness. Not that, taking you to bed, that would be so hard for anyone. In fact, every male in this room is *haaarrrd*"— this delivered in the famous novelist's rolling brogue—"just looking at you."

This didn't impress her. It was merely a statement of fact. Mara never entered a room without turning every head, male and female, in lust or envy. Of course, in the city you were rarely the only gorgeous woman in the room. Even at this party, Mara had been running GPS on the competition—had identified the sisterhood of knockouts and locked in their coordinates so that she could work a different beat. One sharp-edged, adamantly braless woman with short white-blond hair that she'd somehow managed to gather into runty pigtails, kind of like a robotic milkmaid, Mara found particularly vexing.

"What's your name, anyhow?" she asked mildly.

"Ben Kramer. You haven't heard of me. Yet. But when we're married and telling the story of our first meeting to our kids, you can tell them how the lowly publicist was flinging herself at the notoriously faithless has-been, risking genital warts or worse, when the novelist of the future rescued you."

"The novelist of the future, huh? Sounds like a world's fair exhibit."

"Are you too drunk to fuck?"

"How did you know I was a publicist?"

"God, you've got great legs. It's taking all my self-control not to kneel at your feet and pull up your skirt and go down on you right now. Though I guess in that posture I'd be going up."

"When we're married and telling the story of our first meeting to our kids, do I have to tell them what a foul mouth you have?"

"Let's go. Let's go, let's go, I can't wait anymore, let's go—what's your name?"

"Mara. You shouldn't propose to people whose names you don't know as a come-on. That's just plain tacky."

"I would marry you right now if the office were open. You are the One, Mara. Come on, hurry up."

She went home with him that night. Ben mainly impressed her as a boy, strange as one of those hypoallergenic, hairless cats. The older men she'd been sleeping with had hair on their backs and arms. She'd grown used to their graying fur, even grown to like petting it. Ben didn't even have hair on his balls.

She didn't come, but then she rarely did the first time, or even the second or third. There wasn't anything wrong with Ben's technique, although its worshipful aspects—his oral sex ablutions vaguely Muslim—kind of irritated her, and made her self-conscious. For whatever reasons of psychology or anatomy, she fared best doggy-style. Not that him reaching around from the back with the "helping hand" wasn't appreciated. A couple of weeks later, things were going gangbusters when her hair, which she'd forgotten to tie back, got in the way. Ben didn't tenderly brush it aside in one of his typical "Praise Mara" moves. He grabbed a chunk of her hair and pulled, rearing back. He bronco-rode her, holding her mane like a rein. The rest of her hair appeared to be caught on something—was it possible he was kneeling on it? Her "Ow" and "Oh," at that moment, were not terribly well delineated. She was startled to find herself coming with him; in her experience, mutual orgasm was mostly the stuff of (male) fiction. She could count on, well, part of one hand the number of times in her life it had happened and never like that, so forceful a storm out of nowhere.

Never again quite like that with Ben, either, although she kept hoping. She even tried bringing it up once: "Remember that time you were about to come and pulled my hair?" Bringing it up was a mistake, because his response ("You liked that, did you, you wicked wench?") was so predictable, and then he trotted out a bunch of asinine role-playing stuff, like spanking her.

They dated for a little under a year. She was taken off guard, but not devastated, when he suggested they stop seeing each other. She assumed he'd find some plain Jewish doctor or lawyer who could support his writing habit. Imagine her surprise when it turned out he'd left her for, and very quickly married, the very shiksa, Norwegian or something, whom Mara had pinpointed as the competition, at the party where Ben and Mara met for the first time.

Imagine her surprise when both Ben Kramer's literary career skyrocketed and his blond bombshell made a name for herself as a designer and "fashion icon." When they had children. When they got the Brooklyn brownstone. But before and worse than all that, imagine her outrage when that time in bed, which she often replayed while masturbating, appeared as a scene of romantic exploit in one of his novels, over-the-top as something from a Victorian bodice ripper, except, it being Ben, of course ironic, and her hair was cruelly, publicly mocked.

The novel's hero is an evolutionary biologist. During sex, he's thinking about the aquatic ape theory. Despite very little fossil evidence, some evolutionary biologists believe that dolphins and whales went to land, then had second thoughts and dived back in, which is why humans are the only primate species that is hairless as a walrus or manatee. *When she came, hair wild and matted around her face, she looked like an ape. He knew long, luxurious hair was supposed to appeal to men, healthy hair proving the womb reproduction-worthy, but to him it was a little too—hirsute. So he grabbed a hank of it, partly to prevent her grunt-squeal of pleasure from sounding quite so much like that of the Goeldi monkey of South America, whose hair is used, mostly, as a threat display . . .*

Mara could never understand why everyone was so impressed by this passage. She could get the exact same information on Wikipedia.

He didn't even go to the trouble to change her hair's color, or uncurl it.

Humiliation about this novel drove her into therapy. She was almost thirty, still unmarried, and now known far and wide as Ben Kramer's great hairy ape, his rite of passage before evolving toward his slick, smooth Swedish dolphin. Mara made ugly noises when she came.

"At least he says you come," a friend said, by way of reassurance. "He could have said you were a frigid bitch."

Said another, "No one reads novels anyway. I mean, it's not like he's Stephen King."

At the very least, Mara felt she had to do something radically different with her hair, but chopping it off would seem like she was aping Little Miss Swiss, and it felt criminal to change the color.

Eventually none of Mara's friends would talk to her about Ben Kramer anymore, and she had begun to feel like her therapist, Helen Burns, was bored with the topic as well. Mara was really making an effort to come to terms with the roots of her fixation. Her father and all those older men, obviously. But her therapist tended to ignore Mara's efforts at self-analysis and say things like "Maybe he just wasn't the one for you" and "Your hair is very nice" (!!).

Mara often wondered if Helen was smart enough. Ben Kramer saw a real psychoanalyst he didn't call by his first name. Ben Kramer kept a dream journal. Mara had Googled Ben's psychiatrist and looked up a couple of his articles.

"Maybe it was just their time," Helen said.

Ben and Britte met at a party. Or, more accurately, failed to meet at a party. Both arrived alone, and both left with someone else. They met again, later, at another party. Still he didn't hit on her; by then he and Mara were a couple. Their first dates weren't even dates, but coffee after workouts that happened to be at the same time at the neighborhood gym. He didn't even know he was drawn to her until he dreamed about them having sex, a dream so richly specific that he felt as if he'd already done the deed.

In the dream, they were in love. She wasn't so much the corporeal Britte—with the charming accent, and the one sideways-leaning eyetooth, and the dainty ruby nose stud—as a pure presence, and so was he. It was as if their souls were fucking.

Ben tried to make that line he'd written in his journal—*it was as if our souls were fucking*—sound heartfelt rather than ironic. He failed. He didn't even believe in souls. But in the dream he felt that he had been seen by her in a way no one had ever seen him before. What struck him was that what happened between them was *private.* That it couldn't be said because giving voice to it was contrary to the very nature of the feeling, which couldn't even be expressed in words but only through touch, which as a language was more like music than words, all pitch and pressure and pause, rhythm and echo.

This was all something of a revelation to him. He loved the sex scenes in his novel, but they certainly weren't love scenes, probably because he had never been in love. How else could you explain why he never showed Mara the whole novel? (Well, there was also the stuff about her hair.)

Thinking about Britte so much, so intently, made him shy. When he saw her at the gym, chugging away on the elliptical trainer, she almost seemed to have a halo around her. That was partly her hair. It was ridiculously blond and cut supershort—weird after Mara— except she was fond of gathering up pieces of it that stood straight up randomly here and there, stumpy as the frills on top of the toothpicks that hold club sandwiches together. She was as stylized as Japanese anime, except Scandinavian. She was small-breasted but you could tell she wasn't one of those tedious women who had an issue about it. She carried her breasts with a kind of pert pride.

You were in my dream. The former Ben would have said this to her. *I have to warn you, it's pretty smutty.* But he couldn't do it. More and more he was beginning to feel like he wasn't in love with a real woman at all but a legendary character, Lizzie Bennett or Anna Karenina. And at the same time she was more real than anyone.

"Benjamin, I must tell you something."

Starbucks. A million Starbucks, only one Britte. Small table, mid-morning.

"Benjamin, I had a dream about you."

He could have stood up and kissed her. Certainly, after all the dry runs of his proclamation, he should have come up with something to say. But he was silent. He must have smiled, because she

smiled back. He offered his hand on the table, palm up. She put her
hand on top of it.

Ben and Britte. B&B. How fucking romantic is that?

We met in a dream.

Mara knew this much about Ben and Britte's courtship because his
e-mail password was a straightforward combination of his childhood
dog's name and his birthday. Birthdays, street addresses, pet names—
she had gathered the information over time, and then was able to hit
it within, say, a dozen tries. So she had access to his e-mail. When
they broke up she gave him back the key to his apartment. But she
had made a copy. Since he didn't have a job (except for his writing), it
was hard to be sure that he wasn't at home, and with caller ID, one
could no longer make hang-up calls. But he did go three times a week
to the gym where he met Britte, and also taught a weekly adjunct
writing workshop. Once she had his schedule down, she left work for
a "dentist's appointment," went to his apartment, felt blessed that his
laptop was there, and installed software for a program that accessed
his computer files remotely.

She had not informed her therapist that she had committed a
criminal act, nor did she report that she could now read Ben's diary,
which he kept on his computer. So she knew that among the things
Ben loved about Britte was how she said his name. "Benjamin," Britte
always called him, which made him feel like a Mossad chieftain. She
was also privy to his often-failed attempts to transform his love for
Britte into art:

> Something about her orgasms reminds me of one of those
> Dutch master still lifes with the dead pheasant hanging up-
> side down. She comes with her pleasure finely etched like
> that, every brushstroke visible

At the time of the diary spying, Mara had been rereading all of the
great scorned women of literature, starting with Sylvia Plath. Mara

had worshipped the poet in college and still had her well-worn college copy of *Ariel*, the white cover smudged and yellowing (if they'd known it was going to be a classic, they should have chosen a color that hid dirt better). Sylvia Plath and Ted Hughes had also met at a party, where they shared a mythical first kiss. Ted, macho as a matador, had ripped off Sylvia's headband and in return she did not nibble at but bit his ear, hard enough to draw blood. They married at once, and proceeded to make each other deeply miserable. After some years of distracting procreation and parenthood, he left her for someone else, and her great talent was cut short by a man who had the distinction of being married to not one but two women who committed suicide.

Then there was the French poet Louise Colet, Gustave Flaubert's girlfriend. Louise, the model for Emma in *Madame Bovary*, had been insultingly portrayed in that novel in a way that made Mara's own cameo in Ben's novel look like an adoring funeral oration. She was an older woman; maybe they don't have the concept of cougars in France, where women are allowed to continue to be attractive as they age. Louise and her boy toy (still living with his mama) were so hot and heavy at the beginning of their commuting relationship that Gus had kept one of her jeweled slippers with him while she was away, to scratch and sniff and—well, one does not want to contemplate what else. But then Louise got whiny about commitment, he loped off to explore the great syphilis-bestowing mysteries of the whores of the Orient, and then, after she frantically banged on his door repeatedly one night in an attempt to get what heartbroken women everywhere are still calling "closure," he penned what may well be the nastiest kiss-off letter in the proud history of kiss-off letters.

> Madame: I was told that you took the trouble to come here and see me three times last evening.
>
> I was not in. And, fearing that your persistence might provoke me to humiliate you, wisdom leads me to warn you that *I shall never be in.*
>
> I have the honor of saluting you.
>
> G.F.

Then he burned all of her letters.

She kept his, however.

A dream Mara had about Ben: walking in Brooklyn, she happens upon him at a cafe table writing in his notebook as he often did, hunched over his pad to concentrate in the way she knew so well. She feels a stab of love for his pale, thin fingers, his familiar handwriting. He doesn't see her. Somehow she's behind him now, peering down to read what he has written, and to her delighted surprise it is all about her. How he made a mistake, can he have another chance? He has mailed her a letter revealing this, not an e-mail but an old-fashioned letter with a stamp. She's holding the precious letter in her hands by a gas lamp, maybe, and she feels the rush of fulfillment and joy that an Austen heroine does, when she finally gets her man.

Actually, she *is* an Austen heroine.

She seems to be in a long dress with an empire waist, her hair in a tight bun, a couple of artful curls framing her face in the golden light. And she knows this because—she isn't really herself. She's Jane Austen! Or herself as Austen! Somehow she is actually *writing herself.*

She didn't want Ben. She wanted to *be* Ben!

Mara quit therapy. She didn't think Helen had much more to say to her. Helen had encouraged her plan to plumb her creative side and shared her jubilation when she was accepted into an M.F.A. program for fiction writing.

In the workshop, a couple of the (male) writers dismissed her subjects as chick lit. At first she roused herself to feminist indignation. But then she decided she would be quite content to join the pantheon of scorned women who had laughed all the way to the bank.

Shortly after she began writing in earnest, she met Zach, who had just begun work at a law office in her building.

People always tell you, it happens when you least expect it.

The first time she saw him, he had just removed his helmet and was trying to maneuver his partly deconstructed bicycle into the elevator.

The other patrons glared: Were bicycles even allowed in the elevator? The logistics of the ride had him backing her into the corner. He turned to give her an apologetic smile.

He was a wide guy. Not football-player wide, and not fat, but solid. His hair was still wet from the shower. She could smell his shampoo.

The couple of other riders got off, leaving them alone. Her floor came first. He swiftly steered the bike out, to let her pass.

And that is how they met.

She wasn't aware of much more at the time than noticing the clip or whatever it was called he used to hold up the pant leg of his suit, and thinking it was cute. Nerdy, but cute. Later, though—after it turned out Zach did pro bono work for Gabriel's nonprofit, after they were seeing each other—that elevator ride would become, in memory, a kind of Regency-era dance to do Jane Austen proud, and she found she could remember absolutely everything about it, even the catch in his voice as he said "Have a good one."

She could understand, now, what Ben had felt for Britte. Ben hadn't felt it for her. But Zach did. You didn't have to glorify it as fate. They just fit.

Mara was astonished to find herself involved enough with Zach and her writing that she didn't know when Ben Kramer changed his Internet provider and password. She could still follow his activities online. For large periods, however, she not only did not check but did not even note to herself that she hadn't checked.

Not only she had changed. The culture had. It might be impossible to long for anyone who daily updated their blog and Facebook page. Facebook, Twitter, and blogs have killed romance. For romance you need teasing distances, mystery.

Because Mara and Zach often biked in the park on weekends, and because it was hard to fit all her hair into a helmet, she cut off about a foot and a half of it and donated it to cancer patients.

Zach claimed to like the new blunt bob, but also confessed to missing the messy mass of her old hair, which made her look somehow romantic, old-fashioned. She felt exactly the same way herself. It sure was easier to wash, and there were moments, making love, when the lilt of the hair near her ear echoed the whole new ease and lightness she felt with this man, the same way his very bones—the heft of him, his silent solidity—made her feel liquid and lithe. Other times, she just didn't quite feel like herself. But as anyone can tell you, the thing about hair is, it always grows back.

All my life," Mara told the crowd, and, presumably, the hostage taker, "I have been longing for a man. In memory they're not a lineup, more like a collage of fragments. Chins and hands. Mouths, hairlines. The things I mourned! The things I thought I couldn't live without! The men always left. They never called. And I never learned. I spent years waiting by phones, manically pressing the refresh button on computers like one of those caged lab monkeys addicted to nicotine.

"It's not like I didn't scold myself, 'Suck it up.' 'Get over it.' 'He's just not that into you.' It's like that old Zen paradox: 'I will not think of you. But to think that I will not think of you is to still think of you.' And because we can't control ourselves, we get to feel bad from both ends: having failed at romantic love and having the stupidity, the lack of self-control, to dwell on it.

"All of which is to say, I feel your pain.

"I don't want to tell you, 'Be patient. Your prince will come.' Why make it so mystical? My prince turned out to be a lawyer in an elevator. I also don't want to say, 'Love yourself more, and then, whether he comes or not, you won't care.' Well, that was also true for me. People who used to recommend distraction to me, including my therapist, made me so angry. But then I was in school, and really having to struggle to find time to write, and then sending work out, which has a real pissing-into-the-wind feel about it, the ultimate failed blind date. Then one chapter got accepted into a literary magazine, and just like they tell you it will happen, I'm now in a position to shop for agents. And because I was focused on that, I wasn't as needy this time. Although I have to confess that for a while I was starting to do the same thing with agents that I'd done all those years with men—locked into e-mail, hyperventilating.

"But then"—here a grateful, private exchange of glances with Zach, who wore the expression, half-proud, half-embarrassed, that boyfriends do in romantic comedies when their uptight significant others get drunk enough at the club to lurch to the stage to perform karaoke—"Zach would kind of reel me back in. And we'd just take a bike ride and pick up Indian or something. One thing they always tell you that turns out to be true: exercise is good. Releases endorphins. Same chemical as breast-feeding and orgasm. Another thing: spicy food. Serves as a stimulant or something.

"It's kind of interesting that when things are good, they're good in all these interconnected ways. Good sex makes you hungry, gives you energy for exercise, which makes you feel sexier and burns off the calories, which makes you feel like having sex. Depressed, you eat badly, have no energy, feel fat. Not surprising that success breeds success, and failure, failure.

"Turns out all you have to do is get one thing right, and then the other things are more likely to line up like baby ducks and just follow the one thing across the road. It's not too late, no matter how far you've sunk."

*M*ara didn't look at Ben once as she spoke.

It was true. She was really over him!

Helen Burns felt, foremost, pride. Mara had been a patient for less than two years. While many of her patients drifted away without a graduation ceremony, in the last sessions, one of her favorite questions was "Why do you think you were able to find this new happiness?" The patients almost never mentioned her as a catalyst. Even cross-legged on her couch, where they'd spent so many hours, they thought they'd done it themselves. She didn't find this insulting. On the contrary, she saw it as proof of success: that she had led them without being coercive.

The following thoughts occurred to Helen almost simultaneously as Mara finished her pep talk.

One was that the hostage taker would not appreciate the gesture of sisterly sympathy from another wronged woman. It was likely to make her very angry. And Mara's happy ending with Zach would seem like one-upmanship. Upwomanship.

The second thought was an uncharacteristic stab of self-pity. The dramatic, difficult Mara Lowell could find love, but generous, easygoing Helen Burns was still alone twenty-four years after her divorce? Unsurprisingly, Helen had failed to collide with a future mate weeding in her garden. Though for a while she'd held out a quixotic hope for dog parks.

Truth is, as a divorcée, she'd never had the heart for the series of auditions that her female patients endured with men, repeatedly.

Though she knew she was wrong, she believed that finding love should be like it was for Tess and Gabe, immediate and intense. Tess was so much like her, too. Solid or stolid, depending on whether you wanted to embrace or dismiss. But then Tess had fallen in love in Africa. Maybe if you were a quiet, pale dirty blond like Helen or Tess, you had to go that far, thrust yourself that much outside your comfort zone, to stand out. Once more, it came back to Helen's primal failure: staying in this town, in this house.

In all of these years, she'd had only one serious suitor. He was the brother of a woman with a kid on Simon's Little League team, new to the area and attending his nephew's baseball practice. He wasn't divorced, wasn't a widower, hadn't been out of action in federal prison, but was just, by sundry twists of fate involving relocations, single. Available. He'd been as grateful to find Helen as she was to collide with him. But she'd declined to follow him after his next work transfer to Phoenix (her kids were in school, her kids deserved to see their father regularly), and the long-distance romance had petered out as they mostly do.

Helen had already put down two dogs and would outlive this one, too. She would die alone. Not even a close girlfriend at this wedding to share her joy: her best friend dead in a car crash, her two other good ones tied up with their own family obligations on what she had known all along was a cursed day on the calendar. Would either of them get Maynard out of the kennel and give him a home if she died today? Would her sister? Probably not. Maynard would be put down. The dog, too, would die alone.

This poor-me moment came to her as a flash of her younger self in Phoenix with her lover at a special dinner at the Arizona Biltmore. Their faces aglow. The hotel about exactly the color of her golden retriever. And then Jake hadn't *really* seen his kids anyway. She should've moved to Phoenix, and let Jake and the kids have the long-distance romance! Offered sun and sky, she'd chosen dirty snow.

By the time she realized all of this, her lover had married. And by then, in her late forties, Helen had crossed the line that no woman even realizes is there until she's on the other side of it, where no man will ever look at her again with lust, maybe even just with interest, unless he needs a nursemaid to change his colostomy bag. Not the superpower kind of invisibility. The unhappy kind where, in dreams, no one can hear you scream.

But Helen shook off this line of thought because not only was it unproductive, but she needed to concentrate on what was perfectly obvious now:

Just as Mara had obviously been spying on Ben, the hostage taker had been spying on whoever had offended her. Whoever had offended her had to know Helen's address and the date of this wedding enough in advance to plan, which meant that the object of her affection had to be either a wedding guest, the lover of a wedding guest, or someone connected by profession to the wedding itself.

That could include the caterers.

Helen turned to study the caterers. Scowling and sweaty, they looked totally miserable, but then, so did everyone in the room.

The male caterer was a balding fireplug, heavily tattooed if you could take the fact that he had neck ink as a sign that he had ink everywhere beneath the long-sleeved chef's jacket, with more hair on his knuckles than on his head. Slightly simian. Helen tried to divine if he was unfaithful to his wife. As a therapist, you're supposed to be able to scan voice, eyes, gesture. If you're a good therapist you can do this on the fly. You can read defensiveness, vulnerability, brittleness. You recognize, too, the relaxed postures, the open and steady gazes that mean people love, are loved, and know they're loved. Except if you're a child or a pregnant or nursing woman, it's hard to look like that if you're not getting laid. It's hard to do it without the serotonin flushing your system, though running helps. She surveyed the rest of the crowd for those who had good marriages; for those conversely who might be inclined to stray.

The good marriages did not call a lot of attention to themselves but gave off a quiet hum. Delbert Billips Jr. and Salome, who had held hands almost throughout the entire siege. Delbert Billips Sr. and his silent wife; Helen could see, now, that even though he barely looked at her as he tried to manage the crowd, he always angled his body so she could see him, be reassured by him. The bride and groom, of course. The pulse of raw affection Helen felt for that girl—well, maybe proud parenthood was as good as sex. Tess and Gabriel no longer stood together; Gabriel was translating or mediating between the Africans and his American friends, and Tess had gravitated to her stepmother, to help her with Theo, who was flipping out. Sarah Barrett and Matt. Sarah made a lot of comments about her age and fading looks, your cue to loudly protest that she still looked great. The younger husband clearly invigorated her. She was actually more like Jake than she'd ever want to hear, except unlike Jake she cared about her kids and stepkids. It made a difference, cut through the somewhat petulant self-regard that was a standard feature of physicians, male or female.

And the bad relationships?

Helen didn't count the actor and actress, who would break up at the first sign of trouble. You hardly needed to be clairvoyant to predict that. As she surveyed the crew, the couple that jumped out at Helen as doomed was not the cranky caterers, who seemed like ordinarily unhappy married people who had the extra pressure of working together. It wasn't Jake and Mary. It was the novelist Ben Kramer and—what was the wife's name? Brigitte? No. Helen should know, given how much she'd had to hear about her from Mara.

Helen had noted, earlier, how delighted Ben seemed by the whole notion of a hostage event at a wedding. Clearly the wife had noted it, too. Her expression was closed, sour.

Mara wasn't the HT. But Ben Kramer could have slept with another unstable woman. Some aspiring writer—one who didn't have the benefit of two years of therapy with Dr. Burns—would be a good candidate for crazy as a loon. Didn't Ben say he was from New Jersey? Maybe a local ex.

Helen did all these calculations quickly, trying to tune out her husband's voice. He'd been grandstanding.

"She won't want to hear any of that," Dr. Jake Nathanson told Mara. "She doesn't want to share the stage. This isn't a chick flick."

"I concur," said Dr. Gold.

"She might get a kick out of being ringmaster here for a while and forcing us to air our dirty laundry," Jake continued, "but soon she's going to get tired of us."

"*I'm* sure tired of us," one of Gabriel's friends said.

The hostage taker did not appear at the door to comment on Mara's offering, and Helen entreated herself: Concentrate. Who, other than the caterers, would know where and when this wedding was to occur?

The printer of the wedding invitations—but that firm was in New York.

The florist. The caterers' staff.

Helen did a quick accounting of the caterers' crew. The hired hands had thrown in their lot with the brave boys, who were now gathered around the room's high windows and staring at them as a dog will stare at a leash on a hook. Scanning the faces and posture of the catering kids, Helen saw only fear and a trace of indignation, that they should be roped into this kind of danger for minimum wage.

"A narcissist especially," Jake said, "would not want to share the limelight."

The other shrinks nodded their agreement.

"Narcissists," Jake explained, "are very easily hurt. They're so into themselves, they find it almost impossible to believe someone could not admire them."

"Jake!" Helen said sharply. To shut him up. Was he that stupid? Almost in synchronicity, Amy, on her couch, stood.

"You guys are all such assholes!" she said. "I already *told* you. It has nothing to do with any of you."

But no one could understand anything else because of her sobbing, and then, almost immediately, warning yells from several of the young men near the windows, who thought they heard something and wanted Amy to shut up so they could track the sound.

Everyone was sick of Amy, almost as sick of her as of the ADHD boy and Theo. And exasperation with her crying gave everyone in the room license to sound out. As Helen tried to sidle her way to the couch, there was a thump from the second floor of the house, and what sounded like repeated bangs with the butt of the rifle or some other sharp object, the rhythm threateningly manic, which seemed to raise the pitch of Amy's cries, not stifle her, and, along with her louder cries, louder admonitions from the trackers of the overhead sound, so that they very quickly formed a kind of chorus of yell and counteryell punctuated by Asperger's moan and baby cry duet, and then the African men got into the act: they and the young white men now joined together to get in Amy's face, as if the vigilante mass of them would terrify her into silence.

Amazingly, it worked.

Helen pushed her way past the men and, trying to think quickly, asked them if they wouldn't mind holding up the "curtain" again around the narrow, makeshift bathroom space carved out behind the couch. They complied and, as Helen said, "Amy, please, come with me," Amy, stunned, just followed. Helen tried to face her away from the piss pot. "Amy," she said, leaning into the girl and hating herself for a beat for the cheap trick of repeating the name so much, "tell me quickly. What's going on? Don't cry. Please talk quietly so it's just you and me," and here is what she learned.

$\mathcal{A}$my had an ex-boyfriend whose persistence had gravitated into harassment before becoming criminal. At first it had been kind of charming. Or at least not alarming. Amy had felt both sorry for him and interested in sounding the depth of his attachment to her, whether she would find herself swayed. So he wasn't wrong to insist that she'd led him on when he first did the things that suitors in movies do to win back their beloveds: the barrage of calls and letters, the flowers. No woman twenty years old has been sent enough velvety, just-opening red roses to be indifferent to them.

But then it got old.

She had to be firm with him—mean, almost.

If she told him, Don't be here when my classes end, don't be here when I get off work, I'm blocking your calls and mail, he would just cheerfully carry on. Even her silence was charged for him.

He began to follow her when she went on dates. She didn't know right away that he was following her, probably because she'd been so emphatic she didn't see how he could hold out any hope, and for a while it was different guys, no one she was serious about. She didn't even know the first time he keyed her date's car while they were in the restaurant. It was a city neighborhood. Anyone could have keyed the car. Likewise the date whose rear window he busted out. Because you don't want to be paranoid. True, they didn't take the radio, but perhaps they had been scared off.

Then, about three months later, another date's car was keyed. And on the second date with the same man, a man she thought she might really like, they came out of a movie to find one of his tires slashed. Only then did it occur to her that her ex could be following her, could be dangerous.

Amy and Steve were in the parking lot in the local mall. They kissed for the first time leaning against his car, waiting for AAA. She remembered everything about that first kiss: Steve's look of steady concern as she told him about Kevin; how he said, "I don't want you to think I'm the kind of guy who doesn't know how to use a jack, but . . . I don't know how to use a jack"; how he leaned against the car and pulled her to him. "I can see why someone would not want to lose you. But." The fear that Kevin might have been watching them from somewhere, like a sniper. The newness of Steve, the sense of being safe with him. "Next time"—Steve hoarsely, into her mouth, exploratory first kisses—"let's take your car." Not caring who saw them, their motions anyhow fit for public view, his hand barely moving on the small of her back.

Kevin was smart. He was surprisingly disciplined for a crazy person. He didn't steadily escalate the threats; they came unexpectedly, with hiatuses impossible to quantify; and random reinforcement, Amy's abnormal-psych professor said, was the very worst way to learn something. Steve and Amy would have almost forgotten about him when there would be a rock through Steve's windshield, a condom full of paint thrown at his apartment door.

To call or not to call for "Please, leave us alone"? That was the question. Amy steadfastly refused further contact. Restraining orders were evidently hard to get and almost impossible to enforce, although her father, who was concerned and had a friend in the police department, tried. The police officer she'd seen with her father was the one who advised her to say absolutely nothing. Even if they paid for a private detective and proved that Kevin was responsible for the damage, it wasn't as if he'd directly hurt or threatened Amy herself, so the sentence would be light and would probably be read as a provocation, even as an encouragement. Likewise any warning—from her father, from the cops. It would more likely ratchet things up than defuse them.

In the movies, her new boyfriend would have issued a final warning to the old one, then the two men would fight it out. But Steve, the man who didn't know how to use a jack, wasn't going to get into any fisticuffs. Instead, to her astonishment, Steve grew to believe that this was somehow Amy's fault, some signal she had failed to give her ex, some faint but audible encouragement. Like the rape victim, she'd asked for it!

Their relationship lasted ten months. Just as it was impossible to prove that Kevin was responsible for the acts of vandalism, it couldn't be proven that he had chased away a man she really loved.

She didn't want to see anyone else. She was afraid to see anyone else. She was afraid a lot. Along with her sadness about the breakup, she felt jumpy all the time. She expected Kevin in the car next to hers, or behind hers, at every red light. The two men had nearly identical silver imports, so it was almost funny, or would have been if she had any sense of humor left: Old Boyfriend's Car syndrome, amplified exponentially. When the phone rang she'd bounce along a curve of disappointment and fear—that it might be Steve, that it might be Kevin. The fact that Kevin hadn't called her, hadn't returned to any of his old shenanigans (the single red rose through the handle of her car door, the card propped under her windshield wiper with a single question mark), somehow made it worse.

During this period, the caterers' office was broken into not once but twice. Both times Amy told them about Kevin, and both times she waited for the other shoe to drop. It never did.

She couldn't concentrate in school and wound up having to withdraw from two of her courses. When her lease ran out, she gave up her one-bedroom apartment and moved in with another girl she'd met at her part-time job at the catering company. Going back to having a roommate, to dealing with a roommate's music and boyfriends, felt like moving backwards, but really, she couldn't sleep alone in an apartment.

The only health insurance she had was through school and those were the school counselors. They were useless. They just gave PowerPoint workshops about study skills and handling stress. A psychiatric consultant came to campus once a month to hand out antidepressants as if they were Halloween candy, or free condoms in a nightclub. Her father had offered to pay for real therapy, but she knew his situation and couldn't accept that from him.

Her father did something else for her, though. They instituted a system. Amy called or texted her father three times a day: first thing when she woke up, between 3:00 and 4:00 p.m. depending on her class schedule, and lastly before she went to bed. If he didn't hear from her by midnight, he called or texted her.

Every day.

They weren't elaborate exchanges. Sometimes nothing more than an "OK" or "xo, A" and he'd send back a "Nite honey." If she'd been seeing someone, a midnight phone call from her father might be annoying. But she wasn't seeing anyone, and she found it reassuring that her father would never permit her limp body, throat slit, to be undiscovered for days, giving Kevin ample time to move to Buenos Aires. True, with a roommate that wasn't likely anyway, but her roommate often worked late at her bartending gig, and then more often than not hooked up with some guy and went to his place.

Her father knew from her morning text that she had a catering assignment today. So he would not be alarmed that he hadn't heard from her at the midday checkpoint. But he would spring into action if she did not call by midnight. If she did not call by midnight, he would call the police, and he would know where to send them because she'd told him the address, as she always did. At least they knew that much. If they could hang in there for another six hours or so, her father would save them all.

*I*n retrospect, Helen wouldn't remember which parts of this information she would acquire later, when she would grow to know Amy much better, and which she got right there, in the urinal tent. Probably little of it on the spot, although she would remember being curious about the lack of mention of a mother. (The mother was dead.) She also found herself moved by the father's passionate vigilance, the way Amy's face seemed to soften each time she said "Dad." Another wave of stress-induced regret: Why couldn't Helen's children have had a father like that? Or a grandfather—why did her own fine father have to die so young?

"But, Amy," Helen said, calling herself back to the task at hand, "that isn't Kevin, right? Because that's a woman, right?"

Amy had a theory. Maybe Kevin had stopped calling her because he'd actually met someone else. If he had gotten someone else to see him, the woman would have to be as crazy as he was. Maybe she'd found out about Amy and was as jealous of Amy as Kevin had been of Steve.

"I know it sounds far-fetched," Amy apologized.

Helen shook her head to mean *Not at all*. "So let's follow it through," she said. "Does he know where you work?"

Of course.

"Have you shared this story with anyone else at the caterers'?"

Her roommate, plus Matt-and-Cyndi—and the police—when the caterers' office was broken into.

"Anything else I should know about the catering company? Might someone be after them for something?"

Only, Amy said, that Matt, the caterer, was a total sleazebag. He hit on all the girls. His wife would go out with a tray, or cross the room to the oven, and he'd begin to flirt with whoever was plating right next to him. And if that girl brushed him off, as forcefully as she could without getting fired, he just moved on to the next girl.

"Does anyone take him up on the offer?" Helen asked, trying to swallow her own triumphant feeling at having already considered this possibility.

"Are you kidding?" Amy said. But, she added, he was, in his own disgusting way, as persistent as Kevin. He would try the same girl night after night, firm in the belief that at any minute his hairy ears would become irresistible. He'd finger your nose ring and ask you if you had one on your belly button, too, or he'd grab your hand to compliment your manicure, then turn your palm over as if he were going to read it and just start stroking your life line while you tried to keep from hurling. And of course, since the work wasn't all that reliable or high-paying, there was a fair amount of turnover/fresh girls. Amy got the feeling that business being off had made things even more tense between Matt and Cyndi.

"So do you think there's any chance the woman could have anything to do with Matt? That he should be the one apologizing?"

The face Amy made for contemplating the possibility that someone would have sex with the caterer, never mind be so into him they'd stage a hostage event, was appropriate for breaking down the door of a lunatic suspected of animal hoarding and being confronted by the stench of feces and stacked cat and dog corpses. But she conceded that it was possible.

Amy and Helen were able to talk behind the blanket without being heard because, in the room beyond the barricade, an argument was ongoing, between, as best Helen could determine while trying to pay attention to Amy, Delbert Sr. and the young men who wanted to stage some kind of breakout. The argument gave the two women cover for five minutes or so. But eventually someone called, "Hey in there, piss or get off the pot," and Helen led her charge out, Amy considerably calmer now for having been distracted and engaged.

When they emerged, Tess was wearing a reproachful expression that Helen hadn't seen on the girl's face since she was maybe nine years old.

The bride's lip trembled. She tightened her jaw to keep tears from spilling. She didn't look directly at Helen, but Helen knew what the face meant. It meant: *Why are you spending all this time comforting the hired help and not your daughter, who is the bride?* It meant: *How the hell do you know Mara Lowell?* Plus: *What did you do to Dad, to make him leave?* Also: *Make the fake bride go away! Why did you invite her here to begin with!*

Always, everything, forever the mother's fault.

And Helen was willing to take the heat, like a commander in chief assuming full responsibility for bad behavior by his troops in distant lands.

"All better now?" Tess said to Amy, in an uncharacteristically sarcastic tone.

Helen tried to get to Tess. Her most serious job was to comfort her stoical daughter. But the events that happened next forced her to change direction.

*T*he intercom system crackled, then made a bleating noise, like the one on tests of emergency broadcast systems.

Helen and Delbert Sr. had both approached the intercom. The button to turn it on and off from that room had been removed. If the HT had gone to this much trouble, presumably there was a nanny cam somewhere in the room as well. Presumably she was watching. Maybe it was behind the intercom. They hadn't thought to take it apart.

"It would be so nice to talk to you directly," Jake said. He, too, had approached the intercom.

"Please be quiet, Jake," Helen said.

"We've been waiting a long time to hear from you," Jake continued, all hale and hearty. "Who cares about all these other people? You're the one who matters."

"Shut *up*, Jake."

"Yeah," the HT said, "shut up, Jake."

Helen felt a surge of such raw annoyance with her ex-husband that her tone now was entirely unfeigned. "Can you believe I was married to him?" Helen said, making an exasperated face for the camera, if there was a camera. "Can you believe he's a psychiatrist?"

"You're kidding," the HT said.

"I'm actually a very good psychiatrist," Jake said. "You can talk to me. Have you ever been in therapy before?"

"Dad!" the bride said, sharply. "Let Mom—"

"He walked out on me," Helen said, "when the kids were really little."

"That must have been rough," the HT said.

"It was. But then Sarah—" Helen continued, "that's the mom of Theo, who's talking—walked out on him, so there's justice in the world."

"So that's his third wife?" the HT asked. "The blond with the baby?"

She *was* watching them from somewhere.

Helen jumped as her ex-husband jabbed her in her ribs, to alert her that she shouldn't be talking about herself to an armed psychopath. As if Helen didn't know it was not the most standard conversational proscription—but the HT wasn't a standard subject. It seemed to be working, as a method of building rapport.

"Three women would marry him!" the HT observed, musingly.

"It sure is easier for men," Helen agreed, and then (Enough about me, what about you?): "I'm impressed you pulled all this together. I'm personally so bad at that kind of thing. Computers, TV remotes. I hate to be the kind of woman who has to 'ask the man to take care of it.' Especially since, in my case, there is no man to ask."

"Yeah," the HT said. "At a certain point, you just need to take things into your own hands."

"Exactly. So did you have training in all this stuff, or did you just figure it out yourself?"

"Little of both."

"And it seems like you're artistic, too. The getup! It's wild. Not just the technical skills."

Taking the HT's silence as agreement, Helen went on, "That makes it even rarer. You need to be creative and also—"

"True." The HT. Proudly. "But that's kind of what film work is."

Film! Didn't mean she was actually in the business, though; among schizophrenics, Hollywood success was one of the most common delusions. Helen held up a warning hand to Jake down low, where he'd poked her, to keep him from forking off on this tangent.

"So you fixed the intercom yourself, too?" Helen asked.

"Yes, I did. Well, sort of fixed. It's permanently 'on' here."

"Well, thanks! All I can say"—Helen, continuing, her head pressed almost to the intercom to concentrate and to be heard over the commotion behind her in the room—"is that someone like you, as capable as you, must have been pushed really, really hard to get to this point."

No answer from the other side.

"I mean, where else would he find someone like you? The guy must have been a total . . ."

Prick? Asshole? Talk in slang, Helen reminded herself, not professional jargon, but she cursed so rarely that the words, coming out of her mouth, would make her sound like Theo. False and robotic. *I got you. Yeah, that's bad.* Keep reassuring her. But not too obviously. Not like a shrink. Put her in touch with her strengths. Get her to the point where you can reason with her. She has taken on a persona that she's not altogether comfortable with. Separate her from the persona. Gently peel her away from it.

"You hate him, I know," Helen said. "But . . . it's so complicated . . ."

Again, no answer. Hard to read what her silence meant, without a face. "To be treated like that . . ."

The HT said, "Exactly."

Exact was exactly what this line of questioning wasn't. But Helen paused to note where they'd gotten. Their hostage taker was a single woman with a background in film, and the man who ditched her was not in the room at all. If he'd been in the room, the HT would have called him out by now. Helen also knew, suddenly and forcefully, that this had nothing to do with any of them.

She would later scold herself that it took her so long to figure this out—that they were all strangers to the woman; that their deaths, if they died, would be as completely arbitrary as those of any gunned-down patrons of a bank or Burger King. But, in her own defense, randomness is so counterintuitive. It's almost impossible to believe someone would threaten you who had never met you, didn't want your money or disapprove of your uniform. A whole branch of psychology, terror management theory, discusses how people deal with the threat of random violence by taking it personally: figuring out how they, themselves, could never be in the crosshairs.

At that moment—just as they were finally getting somewhere, just as Helen had an opening to ask why them, why her house—a violent crash.

Idris Deby, hoisted up by Souleymane and Ngarta, had broken one of the high transom windows behind the couch. What he had used to break it was unclear—not his fist. A bookend from the TV shelf, maybe.

Helen was probably the only person in the room not watching this happen. Helen and, it appeared, the HT, because if she had a nanny cam, she would have stopped it before now. It's not like the man—very dark, very tall and thin, barefoot, with enormous feet— was hard to spot.

Most of the guests just screamed. But some tried to jockey closer to the window to be next in line to leave. Idris, still held up by his ankles, did a tippy-toed one-armed push-up on the ledge and, in one dramatic gesture, swept the remaining glass off the window with his other hand. The ankle holders gave a high orchestrated push, and the second-story man began to try to turn his head to fit it through the window while holding himself up with all his strength on one bent arm.

Concurrently, a noise from the other side of the room. Using the butt of her rifle, the HT had pushed or hammered the intercom grille from the other side, in the dining room, and now also banged out the one leading into their room. They would now have a clear view past dangling wires and Sheetrock into the dining room, except what they saw, through the grille, was the rifle.

Helen, who had crouched and covered her face, looked up to see a split second of the HT's own head, unmasked for the first time, framed in the grille behind the rifle. A round face, slightly freckled.

The HT now surveyed the room and shot one bullet upward at the ceiling.

Clearly not trying to kill anyone.

Except that someone had been hit. A male wailed.

Delbert Billings Jr., the groom's father, had taken the bullet.

He collapsed forward into his wife's arms as his father yelled "Clear!" and grabbed his son, commandeering enough floor space for the wounded man to be stretched out.

Theo stood for a one-man chorus of Asperger's opera, cataloging the amount of blood. More surprisingly, as Simon, like all the other parents, gripped his children more tightly, his daughter Rosalind was trying to break loose from her father's arms and edge closer— ambulance-chasing flower girl.

The bride and groom headed toward Delbert Jr. at once, the crowd parting for them like rows of corn in a breeze. As Gabe walked, he simultaneously shed his jacket and tie and was now ripping off his white shirt to stanch his father's blood. Several of his friends did likewise, another managing to quickly deliver the blanket from the urinal tent, handing it forward as you'd pass sandbags at a hurricane barricade.

Gabe, Tess, several of their Doctors Without Borders colleagues, and Dr. Sarah Barrett now gathered to help Delbert Sr. get the blanket flat on the floor and the victim on the blanket. Salome kneeled. To Sal, the front of her dress already Pollocked with blood, the whole scene happened in grainy slow motion. The bullet had hit right above the boutonniere on Del's lapel—right above it and not below it, which would have been his heart. In surreal close-up, she saw the white rose and its spray of baby's breath now dripping blood. The blood darker than she'd imagine gushing blood to be, a crusty maroon, and thick, like the chocolate coating on a dipped ice cream cone. Another shirt ripped open, and if there was a hole in the man, who could see it for all the blood? Delbert Sr. quickly rolled his son over to look at his bloody back.

Delbert Sr. gingerly touched the area. "Not hollow-point, good," he said to Dr. Barrett, who nodded. "Press," he instructed Gabriel, and Gabriel pressed his white shirt into his father's shoulder.

Because there was so much screaming, they couldn't hear the HT leave the dining room. But some did notice there was no longer a face framed there. Several people pressed their heads up against the little exposed square, like the door in prisons wardens open to talk, and began to yell *help*. You could barely hear that, either.

Those closest to the window watched the man struggling to fit through it. The windows had not been designed to be bigger there, or lower, because they would have a view only of the neighbor's asphalt driveway leading to their garage, and the trash cans on the side of the neighbor's house. The window was meant to reveal only a discreet rectangle of light and sky. The man's face was bloody from the remaining shattered glass, but he had the sense to keep his eyes closed. He had to position his head sideways to squeeze it through, and it was hard to get the angle right when he barely had a hold on the window, but once he did, the men below gave his feet a final tremulous thrust and his shoulders fit through, too. His arms squeezed tight to his body and shimmied, like a swimming sperm, and then he was out to his waist.

A thump, even over the screams, as he landed. It was a sizable drop to the driveway—eleven, twelve feet.

But if he was injured, he wasn't injured badly. They knew this when some of the wedding guests closest to the bomb-rigged patio doors jubilantly pointed to the backyard. Past the tables, Idris sprinted across the garden, the soles of his feet flashing light, visible as a deer's tail.

A cheer went up, and then the excitement of knowing that their ordeal had to be over, close to over.

Tess and Gabe were not surprised that it was Idris Deby who managed to escape, and felt immediately more confident—Idris would know just what to do.

But where was the HT?

She wasn't chasing the escaped man with the rifle.

If she was in the driveway, they couldn't see her. She'd need a ladder to reach the window and seal it off. Unless she drove off and left them there.

Bloody blanket, blood on the floor, a series of white shirts turned red. The blood seemed redder on the shirts than on Del's naked flesh. A groom naked from the waist up. A phalanx of bare-chested young men, like the chorus at one of those male strip shows. How much blood could a person lose?

Souleymane, Ngarta, and several of Gabriel's male friends were heatedly discussing who would be next through the window. But then there was the thunderclap of another rifle shot—through the ceiling again, in the far corner of the room. Sheetrock raining down near the caterer and his wife.

And soon the HT was back at the intercom grille with her rifle and her gas mask back in position, slightly askew.

"That was very. Very." Hyperventilating. "Stupid."

And then she was gone again.

"Keep pressing," Delbert Sr. told his grandson. "Just keep applying the pressure."

Del's eyes had been locked on Sal's since he was shot.

"Is your life flashing before your eyes?" she whispered. Trying to keep it light.

"Know what I'm thinking about?" he asked.

She shook her head no through tears—what?

"Dim sum," he said, chuckling through gritted teeth.

If he died, her husband was going to go remembering their first date.

"Love you, too, dumpling," Sal said.

At which point she passed out. Already kneeling—coincidentally the very best position in which to faint.

$\mathscr{S}$al and Del fell in love standing on line at the office cafeteria the day they met. Their names were twins, and they were grabbing identical tuna salad sandwiches to eat at their desks.

Delbert was not a flirt. His demeanor was earnest enough to imply a subtle self-parody. He turned to Salome in line so cautiously that his neck might have been in a neck brace.

"Del," he offered.

"Sal."

"New?"

"Yup. You?"

"Yup."

All of this delivered staccato, as if they were neighbors on an assembly line. Then they both reached for the same sandwich, so that they could later tell people that they held hands for the first time ten seconds after they met.

"Be my guest." (His hand removed to make a gesture of offering.)

"No, you be my guest." (Her supplicating hand, ditto.)

At which point they both laughed, and a disembodied hand came from behind the aluminum serving rack to shove more sandwiches in, so they could both have tuna, with no further wrangling.

Salome's theory about "love at first sight": it's really hindsight, memorializing. You take everything you've learned about the other and layer it over the primordial meeting, so that the scene feels as dense, rich, and complicated in flavor as a good reduction sauce.

What's so touching is that the younger selves who fell in love stay clear, and uncrushed, under the weight of all that superimposed knowledge.

Decades later, though they were still together, she could still miss that Del. She could miss the self that Del loved.

The next day, Sal looked up from her computer to find him there. His shirt chambray, in a deep bright blue that always made her happy.

"May I, Salome, take you to lunch?"

His shirt freshly pressed, still creased. Unwrapping the relationship like a man's shirt from the dry cleaner's, pin by pin. If she said, now, *Chambray*. What a nice word," even that could pass as interesting.

He took her for dim sum. He didn't ask if that was something she'd want for lunch, as opposed to, say, a Caesar salad. As it happened, she loved dim sum. Around them as they talked, at huge round tables, huge Chinese families evaded the workday to be together. Toddlers toddled, adorably, toward the live lobsters in the tank. Sal felt safe in the intensity of her listening. Her fingers around the chopsticks were jaunty and confident.

Under all the cheerful chatter of the very long lunch, both studying each other, knowing.

At the newspaper parking lot, Del seemed to be having trouble locking his car door. When he straightened up he looked across the roof of the car and said, solemnly, "I think we should start seeing each other." Not a question, or even a suggestion, but an announcement, as from Management.

Offer on the table. His hands on the roof of the car. Salome had already had time, at lunch, to note the knuckles on those hands, the strong nails. The world obliging with appropriate visuals: crack of police siren passing and then the October wind, until then a fine crisp whisper, cracking a whip of her own hair into her mouth, so she had to remove it as she smiled.

The smile must have been adequate answer, because he came around to her side of the car and stood directly in front of her, exactly as far from pressing against her as she had been from mouthing "Okay," and then just put the side of his head against the side of her head, brushed his mouth against her ear: "Busy after?"

The words carrying a gust of lunch garlic—Chinese food smells surrounding both of them, no doubt, in a cloud—along with Irish Spring soap and under that, a Del-smell, indescribable but certainly identifiable, that she was already listing toward, wanting to wrap herself in like a dumpling.

They were twenty-six. Old enough to have dropped a half-dozen children and dropped dead in many cultures, but whenever Sal scrolled through the montage of early days her refrain would always be a mournful *So young!* Here they are drinking at a bar after work. If Sal indulged in hard liquor now, she would go straight to sleep with a migraine and wake up with a hangover, but then she was always sitting around smoky bars drinking bourbon after bourbon. She took them neat. And on an empty stomach to boot—or maybe not quite empty, since the dim sum lingered, which is why they decided to forgo dinner. Forget the hangover; it would probably take her a week to digest dim sum now. But they drank neat bourbon and ate handfuls of free peanuts from the bar. Their whole courtship like an ad for antacids.

Del's forearms, exposed by rolled shirtsleeves, totally hairless and so sculpturally beautiful that Sal, at the bar, was experiencing some difficulty not just reaching for them. In another example of their spooky synchronicity, Del said, hoarsely, "This," and then with a forefinger traced the profile of her biceps, taut without gym or effort in the way of the young: "Nice."

Sal's and Del's knees just out of reach on neighboring bar stools, and it is this point, when you're certain a relationship is going to happen, that the surprise of how is most delicious.

What happened is that they leaned forward to hold each other's wrists, almost as you would in that child's game where you swing each other around as dizzyingly fast as you can. Then went on to catalog all the parts that were accessible, and reasonably public: hand, arm, knee, thigh. Del, grave as an FDA inspector, approving each part, serially. Nice. Nice. And it was. Sal almost moaning "Oh!" under the noise of the bar.

Hightailed out of there for a first kiss that could now carry the bar smoke and burning wood—people starting fires, barely cold enough yet for that but people do start them, in fall; urgent enough that they didn't even wait for Del's car but just took the first relatively private wall to lean against yet even with the support both of them almost staggering, drunk with the weight of the relationship and also, probably, drunk.

Race, it should be mentioned, did not come up.

Did Salome notice the man was black? Uh, *yup* (as a cartoonish copy editor at the paper liked to say, when confirming something self-evident). But race was by no means the pull quote. It is true that she had never slept with a black man before, but back at his place, bedroom dark, contours haloed by light from the open bathroom door, color was not an issue. Smell was. Those hickory overtones, so Sal felt like a log on the fire, waiting to ignite. *Licked by flame*, uh-yup. Texture, too. The rest of Del's body, like his arms, surprisingly hairless, his chest smooth as a swimmer's, all that tense sinew of his calves and back.

The day after the first night she spent with Del was a Friday, and neither had an article closing. Then it was the weekend. Her apartment contained no pet to feed and, although this was pre–e-mail, there were no letters on the dating crises of ex–college roommates she was hungering to fetch from her mailbox; she could live a day without her utility and college loan bills. So on Friday they stayed in, and on Saturday it rained, ferociously, turning colder, so they stayed in again, mostly naked. Of the available options for renters' heating—too cold or too hot—Del's apartment fell into the latter category, so the radiators were scalding and you needed to leave the windows open. Later, Sal would occasionally confront one of the zoned thermostats in her house, technological marvels so complicated you'd need to be an astronaut or a Talmudic scholar to decipher them, and be nostalgic for the days when all that a change in temperature called for was to snuggle winningly in one of Del's shirts, not too close to the open window.

Was not young love very much like being a renter? So easy for Salome to miss being that unencumbered now. That their weekend felt like camping out was really no triumph of Zen concentration. Their whole lives were like camping out. Later, encumbered by children and the stuff that comes with children, the life of juggling the stroller and diaper bag given over to even more complicated encumbrances, aging parents and home equity loans and the endless parade of stupid issues at work, their younger days would seem like a bower. Back then it was all teeth-gritting onward-ho.

But maybe that isn't fair. Because weren't their personalities—their *issues*, the stuff that could ruin the marriage if they let it—already hardening like mobsters' concrete around their feet? Del making breakfast (eggs and sausage) or lunch (BLTs—for a man who balked at any racial stereotyping he sure went heavy on the smoked pork products). Sal naked except for his shirt. "I love rain like this," she tells him. "Don't you love it when it rains this hard and you're safe inside? Reminds me of being a kid, I guess," to which he responds, "Guess you weren't a kid anywhere with hurricanes," which is true, she was not, but was that not their whole future in a nutshell? Delbert and his military father's inflexible *way of doing things*, even a BLT requiring a system, whereas Salome was a slob, or thoughtless. *Lazy.* Not willing or able to think things through.

It is true she could be pretty happy sitting at the table after sex, hungry but about to be fed, watching the rain hit the window, thinking nothing at all. Tomatoes and plums ripening in a bowl. Several kinds of jam. In the freezer, meat pieces frozen individually for flash defrosting.

"For a bachelor," Sal noted, "you keep quite a larder."

" 'Bachelor,' " he scoffed. "All the men I know can cook."

"I'm not much of a cook myself," she confessed. "Though I have learned to do a 'quick,' 'simple' pasta. I mean I can fry up some garlic along with whatever's left in the refrigerator—like three asparagus spears or the part of the zucchini that doesn't have mold—and toss it into some noodles."

"Pasta's overrated," Del informed her. "I only eat carbohydrates before basketball. For working out I aim for straight protein. It metabolizes better. Just a plain chicken breast or a piece of red meat."

"You count bacon as 'meat'?"

Him serving her the sandwich, now, on grown-up plates. "Oh no," he informs her, "this is a sweet and salty treat for my sweet and salty treat." Did he actually say that? Did she actually find it witty? But maybe the line delivered in the context, which she would not forget: how easily and unaffectedly she lounged, flushed, in his open shirt, the window steaming up from the heat of the pan; how he put the plate down and then just brushed the shirt aside, so he could brush one nipple upward, a rough flick, making her eyes close; the line said right into her mouth, *sweet, salty*, God the man could kiss, cook and kiss, what more could you want?

Dim sum. Bacon and eggs. BLTs (such ripe tomatoes for October!) swilled down with beer so thick you could float toy boats in it. The menu for their early courtship sure was heavy. But they must have been burning off the calories. Salome herself provided the lightness, the feeling of air and grace. In sex as in much else at the beginning, Del made her feel fleet and shimmering. As if he were the air traffic controller helping her land. Her on top, eyes open for just long enough to ascertain he was watching her the whole time, what a sense of security in that, like a child being tucked in for bed, but also, because he was so pleased, he made her feel a bit spectacular, a planetarium or something supersonic, a Concorde of responsiveness. When he came he always tried to bury his head—in the pillow, in her spine—as if hiding from the sensation. She found it very touching.

She still did.

They always advise you to put your head between your knees when you feel faint. Because Salome Billips was already kneeling, in posture for prayer, her head just slumped forward, then the whole unstable mass of her body fell to the side. As Tess, already crouching at the scene, reoriented herself to cradle Sal's head, Delbert Jr. tried to get up, to help his wife, and Delbert Sr. and the groom had to hold him down. But his howls of pain at the movement woke Sal. When her eyes snapped open, she saw only the blood. She turned her head into the bride's lap and puked.

Concurrently, Dr. Ira Needleman began to wave his arms and cry for help.

His wife, the diabetic, had also swooned.

Dr. Sarah Barrett now went to the moaning, muttering Sylvia Needleman and tried to gauge her condition.

"She's getting dehydrated," Sarah said.

Near the couch, half a dozen of the younger guests argued about who would go next out the window. Some men contended that their wives should go out first—women first, oldest rule in the book—but others believed that they could run faster to get help.

Souleymane, one of the two remaining African men, claimed that since this was their idea and their broken window, they should go. Ngarta agreed, but also ratified the women-first idea, proposing his wife, Acta, as the next person to exit, especially since she was smaller and would fit through the window more easily. Acta stood by his side, waiting to be lifted out.

On this point, Souleymane and Ngarta disagreed heatedly in French. Delbert Sr. left his son with Sal and crossed the room to try to break up the fight.

By the time he arrived, the pitch of the hysteria had changed once again. The HT was at the window, clearly on a ladder hauled from the garage, with her drill and some stray piece of wood, which she was now attaching to the side of the house, across the broken window.

"That's it," Amy proclaimed, joyfully.

Indeed, it was hard to believe that a woman on a ladder in a gas mask with a rifle would not precipitate a call to the police by someone.

Now they could hear the ladder being dragged across concrete, and here was the HT, at the other window, with another piece of ragged wood.

"It's like a Renaissance painting in here," Ben Kramer said to his wife, loudly enough to be overheard by others. "All these separate three-ring circuses of activity. You know how those paintings had events from different times in the character's life played out in them? Here's the saint in his childhood over this hill, and here by the stream is the saint being burned at the stake? That's so cool. I love that. I wonder how you could get that affect of simultanety in fiction."

His *fiction* turned into a cry as one of the young men socked him in the face.

"What the fuck!" Ben shouted, cupping his bleeding nose as he realized that the man who had hit him was Zach Whitehead, Mara Lowell's current beau.

Mara looked surprised, then pleased. Several of Gabe's other friends hooted or made approving noises, but one was jumping up and down, waving his arms as if to stop a vehicle while hitchhiking.

"That's my bass!" he yelled.

It was true. The HT seemed to have smashed his bass, which had been in the dining room waiting to be taken outside for the musical portion of the event. Several strings still dangled.

Simon was working to contain his daughter, who was wiggling

toward Ben Kramer and his bloody nose, as excited by it as she'd be in an open fire hydrant on a hot day. He'd been crouching to surround his children since the first gunshot, his hands on the tops of their heads as if his hands could protect them from anything, the muscles in his thighs cramped and stinging. Simon's two sons reacted with video-game pleasure to the punch itself, doing their head bobs of pow, pow, but then quickly got distracted by the mourning musician. Rosalind, on the other hand, was going to be either a surgeon when she grew up or a serial killer. Simon thought, A surgeon. He felt a flush of pride in her curiosity, which hopefully Haddonfield wouldn't destroy, and realized that his bond was now not with the young lovers at this wedding but with the parents. He would take a bullet for these kids. No question. Under his hands, every strand of their ludicrously blond hair was alive, tender, frangible.

"I can't believe it," said the musician whose bass was now the window barricade, his voice cracking from the outrage.

"That can't be very strong," a Rambo boy said. "We could bust through that."

"And get shot? No, thanks."

But the HT wasn't waiting for them outside. She was already back in the house. Helen could see that, through the intercom hole: see clear past the dining room, which was not that large, to a visible sliver of the kitchen, where the HT stood at the island, in profile, without her gas mask.

The novelist had mentioned paintings. Helen's view of the HT through the intercom hole was a little like a Vermeer: a long shot through a series of rooms at the end of which you saw a woman bent over something, privately. Sewing, reading. Even though the light wasn't so good, the HT's reddish hair glinted like a memory. And although it was too far away to see her expression, her posture was both tired and triumphant.

Helen watched the HT empty the hat full of guests' cell phones onto the kitchen counter. Choose one. Then, Kabuki-dramatic, punch in three numbers—911.

She didn't say anything. She just put the phone down on the counter and stared at it, arms crossed.

Finally she picked up the phone. "Oh! I'm so sorry," she said, in such an exaggerated stage voice that Helen could hear. "The phone was in my purse and I guess it got bumped. Nothing's wrong," and then she pointed her rifle at Helen's freezer door, and shot.

Then hung up the phone. Put one finger, musingly, in the hole the bullet had left.

"I need a diaper," Mary said, to no one in particular and unnecessarily, since everyone could smell that.

"I only have two left," the other woman with the baby said, "but I'll share."

"And he needs to eat," Mary said.

"I could express some milk, if we could find something to put it in."

"There's nothing," Mary said helplessly.

"I think it's broken," Ben said. "You broke my fucking nose. I mean: Why?"

Helen caught the colonel's eye across the room, awaiting instructions.

Delbert Sr. put two fingers in his mouth for an impressively prolonged Bronx cheer.

"Pull it together, people! We have a man down here and a woman in bad shape, too. This time is critical. I repeat: *critical*. We're near the end now, but everyone has to calm down."

"How long, do you think?" someone asked.

"I don't know. A half hour or so. We can do that, right? Sit here quietly and not lose any lives."

Unfortunately, Delbert Sr. had quieted them down a minute too late for them to hear the doorbell or the subsequent knock on the door. Not that they could have done anything about the doorbell in any case, but maybe it would have given them a shot of hope, or caution.

In the sudden silence, everyone listened to Mary's baby cry. The other mother gave Mary one of her remaining diapers, the diaper pad, and a wipe. The two women exchanged a look to acknowledge their bond. No one wanted to die, but no one else had infants. No one else's death would have as wrenching a consequence. Wordlessly, people cleared a space for Mary to lay the baby down. Louis's shit, in the diaper, was the color of baby shit, that brown veering toward puce that can be found nowhere else in nature and that you forget about after you're done with babies. With care and love, Mary folded the single wipe to get maximum usage on the baby's behind. Those who knew Mary knew that she was a very nervous woman, and couldn't help admiring how she tried to keep her movements smooth, so as not to upset Louis, not to transfer to the baby her own fierce desperation. You could see him calm down from the clean diaper, from his mother's performance of serenity. If he died this minute, he would die at peace.

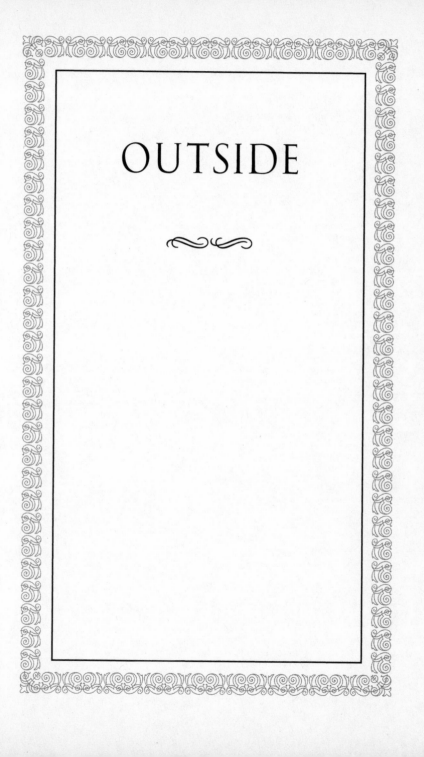

OUTSIDE

*I*dris Deby ran through Helen's yard, past a waterfall and fish pond on the neighboring property, and, blocked by a fence, onto the golf course. He was barefoot and his hands and face were bleeding. When two men rounded a hill with their golf equipment, Idris let out a call and waved his arms. They just stared at him, or in his general direction. He called again. They conferred briefly, then retreated more quickly than they'd come.

No doubt there would be someone in the white building on the golf course, but it was too far away. Idris reversed direction, into the first yard that wasn't fenced off from the course.

A small, naked child sat alone in a baby pool, beating up one rubber duck with another rubber duck. Idris assumed that a caregiver was close at hand, because this was exceedingly dangerous. A young child could drown in even an inch of water. "Little girl, where is your mother?" he asked, aiming for mildness, although he was alarmed for the child. The girl looked at him for a split second of welcome before she began to cry.

Now the mother rushed out the patio doors, took in the tall black man with huge bare feet and a white shirt splotched with blood, and screamed.

"Please call the police—" But she had already snatched the child from the pool and run back into her house, shrieking the whole time.

The neighbor next door came out to investigate, then immediately shrank back inside. Idris crossed to her yard and stood by the open patio doors to call her. "Madame," he said. "Madame, I need to use your phone." He took a step into the coolness of a room with a plush rug, freshly vacuumed. He could see the phone in the kitchen, and was heading toward it when, from elsewhere, the woman of the house warned, "Get out of here or my husband will kill you."

Idris took that seriously.

"Please call the police," he called as he left.

Except when he was in the field in Africa, Idris had lived most of his life in Paris. He also knew London well. But he had little experience with the United States, certainly not with its suburbs. Perhaps they'd never seen a black person here before. More likely, he determined, they didn't expect to see a black man in this neighborhood unless he was carrying a paint roller or a rake. For a second he considered acquiring such a tool as a semaphore of subservience, but then he figured that, with the blood, it would seem more like a weapon.

So he returned to the golf course. The white building had a black man in uniform at a desk in the entrance.

"Sir," Idris said, "please dial the police. There is an armed woman, and a hostage situation, at a house over that hill."

"What?" the man said.

Idris repeated himself. The man at the desk said, "I'm sorry. I can't understand you."

Idris's English was the King's English, French-accented but impeccable.

"The police," Idris enunciated. "Call the police."

There followed a startlingly inefficient phone call to 911. The security guard communicated that a man at the Tavistock Country Club seemed to be in distress, then handed Idris the phone to let him explain the problem. The dispatch operator seemed quite insistent, however, that Idris provide an address. Idris explained that he had gotten a ride from the hotel and did not have the invitation, but he could lead them directly to the house from the golf course.

"Slow down, sir. What is your name?"

"Idris Deby."

"Can you spell that?"

B in French is *bay*, *d* is *day*, and a non–English-speaker is certainly not going to utter the phrase "D as in Debbie."

"Debbie? What is your last name, ma'am?"

Not Debbie. *Deby.* My first name is Idris. No, not Iris! The man at the desk eyed him with the curiosity due an immense African cross-dresser or transvestite.

Idris was quite familiar with bureaucratic red tape and incompetence. It did not occur to him that he was being kept on the phone this long intentionally, by a dispatcher who, more on-the-ball than usual, had thought to connect Idris's call with the two other calls that had come to report the intruder and a third, suspicious cell-phone call traced to the same street: a hang-up, with gunfire.

Haddonfield had only two officers on duty on weekends, and one of the officers was quite nearby—across the street from Helen Burns's house, in fact, on a call from what the officers called a frequent flyer. Some of the people who regularly called the police were mid-divorce and prone to vicious arguments. But many Haddonfieldians, especially the crotchety old-timers, called because a neighbor's trash was put out a day too early or uncovered, children were playing hockey on the street, a kid's lemonade stand was attracting flies. The police had to respond respectfully to every call no matter how petty the grievance, but really, some of these people needed to be shipped off to Afghanistan, get a taste of real problems. Or Camden, which was closer.

The neighbor had not seen the woman in the gas mask out his window or heard the rifle shot from the backyard. Amazing how often people ignore gunshots, thinking they're a car backfiring, or construction noise, or, in this neighbor's case, an offensively loud wedding band tuning up. He had called the police because a parked car was blocking his driveway.

The officer who responded to the call knew that there was a wedding on the street, because the homeowner had called as required by borough ordinance. He saw that a vehicle was indeed protruding into the driveway. However, it was not in any sense blocking the frequent flyer's egress. The officer volunteered to help maneuver the owner's car out of the garage so as not to interrupt the wedding. But the offended citizen, arms crossed in his driveway, said that he wasn't leaving now. As a taxpayer, he should be able to leave his own house at will.

So the officer trudged up to ring Helen's doorbell. Knocked. Got no answer.

If the car had *really* been blocking the driveway, the officer might have walked around the back of the house and seen the hostages. Or the side and seen the broken window. But for this codger? He just went back to inform the homeowner that, unfortunately, there was nothing else he could do right at this minute.

"Aren't you going to ticket the car?" the old man demanded.

The officer was beginning to write the ticket as the call came in that there had been an attempted burglary or abduction, three doors down.

The other officer responding had already called the supervisor, who had called for backup. Then an alert that, bizarrely, the suspect was on the phone with 911 at the country club. Turning himself in? The supervisor now called for mutual aid from neighboring towns, to round up all officers who, on a Saturday in summer, weren't Boogie Boarding, fishing, at a casino blackjack table, or at Home Depot, stacking wood with a borrowed truck for the deck repair project that, the wife pointed out, they'd put off long enough.

Within minutes, the two officers and a detective met in the parking lot and entered the club with weapons drawn for *Hands up!*

Idris dropped the phone to comply.

Before the suspect had time to fully turn around, the men had pushed him against the desk to pat him down.

Idris pointed out in his best deferential African checkpoint tone that *he* had called *them*. Pleadingly, he explained again about the hostages and the bomb.

"Sure, buddy."

Officers kept showing up, each with an expression so startled he could have been caught in a lunchtime tryst. One of the officers was black, and Idris found himself addressing the black man, unaware of how off-putting the officer would find that; bad guys regularly tried to form a special brotherly bond with him.

Once more they demanded an address. Once more he said that he did not have it but could lead them there. They asked him for ID. His passport was in the safe at the hotel.

The cops eyed him skeptically.

Would it have been better, or worse, if he had been in African garb? At least they would have believed he was from out of town and not an African American criminal.

"Where are your shoes?" one cop asked.

He told them about the men holding him up to the window, how it seemed easier for them to push him, and easier for him to fit through, if he was barefoot.

Most of the time, bad guys jumped out high windows because the homeowner had returned. But no one would rob a house on a street with that many cars. Any idiot could tell there was a party. Of course, many criminals were idiots.

"Look," Idris said. "Handcuff me. Let me take you. It's just over there."

Nice of him to bestow permission for the arrest. "Where you from?" one cop asked.

"France!"

The cops exchanged a look.

"I was just there," one cop told the other, "and I didn't see anything."

"Did you see the broken window off the driveway?" Idris demanded. "Did you go around to the back patio doors and see the bomb?"

After radio consultation with their supervisor, the police agreed to drive by the house again. They handcuffed Idris and put him into the back of a squad car.

Back at Helen's, the squad cars landed like a flock of crows. The neighbor came out of his house.

"Are you going to tow the car now?" he asked excitedly.

They barked at him to go back inside.

Two officers crouch-walked around the side of the house. Sure enough, the window was broken, two windows roughly boarded up, shattered glass below. More cautiously, they went around to the back. Sidling along the house, they didn't get close enough, or at the right angle, to see the hostages. But they did see that there was a contraption attached to the patio doors.

From the front of the house, gunfire.

From inside the house, in the room with the bomb, screaming.

One officer, watching the house, saw a quick flash of a woman in a gas mask, with what looked like a rifle, in an upstairs window. They covered down behind the car and, through a bullhorn, requested her presence at the front of the house with her hands up. When no response was forthcoming, they called the police chief to call the tactical team before they shoved Idris down on the backseat and barked, "Lay low."

$\mathcal{B}$ut how low could he lay? From an upstairs window, the squad car was the easiest possible target. The first to escape to safety, Idris might well be the first to die.

No stranger to gunfire, Idris knew how to be still in a confined space, how to reduce mental clutter, too—cut out the background noise of panic, so he could track essential sounds. He maneuvered onto the floor behind the passenger seat, arms over his head, and remained there for the interminable amount of time it took the SWAT team members to arrive. After an even longer wait, they whisked him up the street, where he would be interrogated by a series of uniformed men, first by a detective in a different car, then in the trailer that served as headquarters for Command.

Because of the bomb, they needed to consider that they were dealing with a terrorist, and could not dismiss the possibility that the barefoot, bloody black man was some kind of accomplice, although he claimed to be an employee of Doctors Without Borders.

"What kind of doctor are you?" Idris's interlocutors asked.

They clearly didn't know much about Doctors Without Borders, which insiders sometimes jokingly called Doctors Without Doctors.

"I am not a medical doctor. I am what they call a logistician. I help to organize the relief efforts in a given location."

"Are you a Muslim?" (Except the questioner said it "moslin" like a fabric, somewhere between muslin and poplin.)

"I am a Christian, sir."

"Are there any Muslims in there?"

"I believe there is one man, from Mali."

"Do you know his name?"

"I do not, but I assure you the hostage taker is an American woman."

"What does she want?"

"An apology," Idris said.

"From who?"

Idris indicated that he had no clue, but sincerely doubted her grievances were political or nationalistic. He believed she had been disappointed in love.

"By the groom?"

"No. Someone else. She had us trying to guess."

The specificity of his answers must have convinced them that he was in fact an escaped hostage, and useful. Or they were just too busy to remove him.

If Helen Burns had an instinct for zeroing in on people quickly and accurately, Idris Deby had a similar talent for psyching out organizational structures, even—maybe especially—under pressure, on unfamiliar terrain. Soon he was alert and engaged, trying to figure out how all the moving parts of their response fit together.

Despite having seen his share of movie shoot-outs, much of the process surprised him, starting with how exasperatingly slow it was. Only three or four American cities, Idris was to learn, have dedicated strike forces. For an event requiring SWAT intervention, the men have to be rounded up. When they receive their text pages, they bolt. Still, it takes an hour just to assemble the team and equipment: the big RV, the communications van, and the air-conditioned bus where the tactical team waited—the men they called "the stack," who would breach the house, should that prove necessary.

The RV for Command had bank after bank of computers; phones with separate channels for the hostage, the negotiators, and the tactical team; and a huge high-definition TV split into four screens. On those screens, they watched the first team members to arrive evacuate the neighbors directly across the street—the old-timers none too happy about it—and get snipers positioned in the upstairs windows. They cleared out all the houses on the street whose residents weren't already at the beach. Then the incident commander, the SWAT commander, a bomb expert, and Idris watched two scouts in camera helmets, as fleet as men can be in full armor and gas masks, attach small cameras in various positions with views of the house to function as what they called "eyes on."

All this, too, took time. Concurrently, other team members organized all of the information they had gathered about the house. Tax maps, Google map aerials. They were lucky: the homeowners had applied for a permit to build a family-room addition, so they had details about setbacks and window and door placement in the room where the hostages were being held. With the maps of Helen's great room in hand, that part of the team began to do tabletop plans for how they'd breach the house, should negotiations fail.

Around the back of the house, the scouts reported that they couldn't safely get close enough to the bomb. So they returned to Command and sent the robot, a gray box on wheels with a camera which could go over any terrain and was covered with Kevlar, bulletproof.

The robot's camera got a close-up of the bomb and then, panning behind it, the dense crowd of hostages.

When they first saw the robot, some hostages began to scream, but some now waved with two hands in arcs, as shipwrecked people would try to gesture to a distant ship. Command now got a pan shot of crying babies, a black man bleeding on the ground, a fainting old lady on a couch, a woman flapping a broken wrist, a teenaged boy whipping his head from side to side and clutching his hair—"What's wrong with him?" the incident commander asked Idris.

"Something," Idris said, unhelpfully.

The bomb expert studied the enlargements and said the photos were inconclusive. Clearly it was an IED or HME. (Like the psychiatrists at the house, these people had their own thicket of code words and acronyms.) Idris had told them about the black box on the HT's arm. Bottles were involved, and they guessed fertilizer and household cleaners. There didn't seem to be enough wires. But why go to all that trouble for a fake?

One hostage negotiator was already in the trailer with Command. Others waited in a van. The communication van patched through a cell-phone call to the house's hardwired line so the negotiator could begin.

The woman who answered said, cheerfully, "May I help you?"

They looked at Idris to confirm that this was their woman's voice. He nodded.

"Ma'am," the negotiator said, "this is Lieutenant Mike Ramis of the Camden County Crisis Unit. I'm here to listen. First, are you all right?"

"I'm swell." She sounded it, too—upbeat, cordial. Manic. No doubt soon to be screaming or crying.

"Good." Calm, serious, unthreatening. "Can I ask what you'd like me to call you?"

"No," the woman said. "I want a woman negotiator."

The county had twenty or more negotiators available. They could speak Spanish to you like a native of your own Spanish-speaking homeland. They could send someone to speak Vietnamese to you, or Arabic. They had one of everything: a Puerto Rican, a black, a woman. Only one woman, though, and she was out of town. On a suicide threat the year before, their one woman had been on vacation. Perhaps they should get more women. For that job, they'd imported a negotiator from Atlantic County, but meanwhile, if the HT wanted a woman, they would have to use a female member of the Haddonfield police force—of which there was also only one. They sent for her from the outer perimeter, where she was stationed to do crowd control.

"While we're waiting for her," Mike asked the HT, "can you just try to sketch out for me what's going on?"

An upstairs bedroom window cracked. Snipers at the ready. No head visible; the HT must have been ducking. What emerged was not a weapon but a paper airplane.

They were not going to send men to fetch it, even covered by snipers. They sent the robot.

The woman on the phone giggled as the robot dug its retractable arm into the bushes. "That bot isn't very anthropomorphic, is it?"

"Pardon me?"

"I mean, it's just a box."

"Oh. The robot? Yes. Can you see it from where you are?"

"Boys with toys! I expected it to be . . . cuter."

The airplane was made out of thick cream paper—good résumé bond. In ornate calligraphy, as on a wedding invitation, the unfolded airplane said:

911. What's your emergency?

Their question exactly.

"She mentioned SWAT to us at one point," Idris told the men. "Might she know someone on the police force?"

The men said that anyone could research SWAT equipment online. "The actor believed the hostage taker was herself a policewoman."

"What actor?"

"I don't remember his name. He's from a police show."

On the robot's footage, Idris identified Trevor Hunter, and the men paused to make the face that people always make when in the presence of a famous but not terribly consequential personage: a smirk with eyes atwinkle.

The female sergeant from the Haddonfield police force arrived and sat between two negotiators in the command unit to get a crash course about active listening, calming techniques, and paraphrasing. The negotiators obviously did not expect an untrained street cop to get all this in three minutes, so on big pads, they supplied her with her lines, starting with "Hello. I hear you prefer a female negotiator. I'm Sergeant Heather Nolan from—"

"Heather?" the HT said. "The cop?"

Heather looked to the negotiators for guidance, abashed. One held up the pad with her answer. Then they both looked at Idris, who had predicted this.

"Yes. Do we know each other?"

"I recognize your squeaky little voice. I don't want you."

Because Heather had to pause to wait for her response, the HT had time to add: "You're not a negotiator."

"That's true," Heather said, improvising as her coaches nodded. "We're getting someone for you. In the meantime, do you want to talk to me, or do you want to go back to Mike?"

"I want a real female negotiator!"

Now another paper airplane.

"Fetch!" the HT said, as the stalwart robot made a return trip.

This airplane had a photograph. It was the famous one from the papers a while back, of a Muslim woman about to be subjected to the barbaric ritual of death by stoning, although, in this context, they had to do a double take to figure that out. The victim is buried upright to her neck, unable to move her arms to protect herself from the blows, only her head in the hijab protruding. A newspaper photograph enlarged and photocopied onto the same cream-colored bond—except another, non-Arabic-looking face has been imported in, not seamlessly Photoshopped but crudely cut-and-pasted. Below, in the same fancy calligraphy:

Do you think you're so much better?

Tucked inside of that paper airplane was a baby paper airplane, smaller, on thinner paper. The HT had clearly done some aerodynamic test flights. On that origami plane she had handwritten a note, much of it rendered hard to read by the tiny lettering and the creases of the folds. The commander handed that to the negotiator to decipher and showed the photo to Heather. "Look familiar to you?" he asked her.

Heather said no.

"Did you see her face?" the commander asked Idris. "Or was she in the gas mask the whole time?"

"She wore the gas mask. With sunglasses. Like that."

The men shook their heads. She was probably under the impression that the groom should be hers, or some groom, and decided not to hold her peace, or piece. What this had to do with Heather was unclear. Heather had no memory of any standout female arrests, although they were doing a database search for female shoplifting, weapons, and DUI charges.

To the negotiators, it was beginning to look like suicide by cop. In their experience, the perpetrators of suicide by cop were exclusively men—too macho to admit to being that depressed, but not macho enough to noose themselves and jump off the chair. The women suicides wrote long letters detailing their grievances. They gobbled fistfuls of pills, then got in bed in pretty dresses. But the men wanted to go out in slow motion, alone against the multitudes, their heads thrown back like St. Sebastian tied to the tree and shot with arrows or like the climax of any number of Sylvester Stallone movies. They wanted to be martyrs. What is suicide by cop but suicide bombing, American-style?

The negotiator now read aloud from the airplane missive.

> On TV there are guys who are good sports about letting their wives be porn stars, or call girls. But in the real world, in this day and age, men are still celebrated for sexual profligacy whereas women are degraded and devalued. In Iran, in Afghanistan, in large swaths of Africa, a man can take multiple wives yet a woman, if she is even suspected of adultery, can be brutally put to death. PIGS!

"Does she mean male chauvinist pig, or cop pig?" Heather asked the negotiator.

"So, what?" the incident commander asked. "She's a feminist?"

A pissed-off feminist with a big vocabulary who had now brought the Middle East into the mix. They had to take that seriously. The

HT could be protesting American military intervention. Haddon-field was not the most likely target for terrorism, but perhaps it was a target of convenience. They now involved the Joint Terrorism Task Force, to see if there was any credible chatter about Jersey jihad.

Heather whipped her head from one real negotiator to the other as both frantically wrote, in tag team: *Are there any causalities, ma'am? Can we get the injured people out? That's really important. Remember, the charges could be just aggravated assault . . . we're sure you had a good reason . . .*

But the HT no longer seemed to be answering.

"I am quite sure," Idris told them, "that this whole Iran burqa thing is—how do you say . . . *faux problème . . .*"

"What do you mean?"

"False problem," he said, frustrated, because he could not come up with the English idiom *red herring.*

The men in command looked at Idris briefly, then seemed to decide, without discussion, that he had nothing more to tell them, and sent for someone to take him to the Haddonfield police station.

Idris was disappointed. It seemed unfair to remove him now, when they were so close. It had been interesting in the van. Far less interesting in the tiny holding cell with cement block walls where they shoved him next, in case they had further questions.

The SWAT commander had been staring at the first paper airplane, muttering to himself as he tried to free associate. 911. Call 911. Emergency.

"Dispatch?" he mused. "Someone in Dispatch?"

Heather said: "Oh. My. God." And covered her mouth with her hand to stanch audibility, though she was no longer on the HT's channel.

"What?" they asked.

The snipers stationed in the house across the street called their attention to the live feed. They could see the HT in the upstairs bathroom, facing the wall, probably a bathroom mirror. Her gas mask was off and the curtains were not drawn. At one point, she seemed to turn toward the window and smile, almost as if she were posing for the feed, or the snipers.

"You know her? What?" the commander prodded.

"It's Crystal," Heather said definitively. "The psycho from the gym."

It went this way sometimes, if you were lucky: you had nothing for a long time, and suddenly you had almost everything. Like tearing apart your house looking for your car keys, then discovering they're in your coat pocket.

By the time the female negotiator arrived, having been thoroughly briefed en route, they had already sent for the HT's personnel file from the county, initiated contact with the perpetrator's mother, begun a search for her father, and sent for the man who was, evidently, responsible for this mess.

"Crystal," the new negotiator said. "I hear you want a female negotiator."

"At last!" the HT said. "Congratulations. It sure took you long enough. And you are?"

"Alison Jenkins from the Burlington County—"

"I don't want you. I want a different female negotiator."

The new negotiator gave the old one a *Say what?* look, then responded to the HT, "Just give me a chance, okay? Now that we know who you are, it would help a lot if you told us what you want. We'll try hard to oblige."

"If you know who I am, you know what I want."

"We're getting him for you," the negotiator said.

"And her?"

"Now, on that one, you've lost us."

"Ask Van," the HT said.

Oh, they would. But in the meantime, would Crystal mind just filling her in on what had driven her to this act? Just give us a sense. He must have been unbelievably mean to you, the negotiator said, and their hostage taker, voice wavering, admitted that was true.

*B*ecause the cops were such unimaginative sexists, they'd assume the hostage taker was some lovelorn lowlife. They got domestic calls all the time from those women: wild-haired, mascara raccoon-smeared, cursing in their bathrobes. But Crystal was elegant and educated. She had an M.F.A. in film with a specialty in sound. Their biggest surprise, she believed, would be when they discovered she was Haddonfield born and bred, and the cruel man who had forced her to this act was one of their own. When they saw her without the gas mask, they'd know that she was not just smart but beautiful enough that, just from her carriage and voice, the hostages had no trouble believing she was an actress.

In fact, she had always acted. Some of the Haddonfield hostages might even recognize her, from school plays. She was only four years older than the bride, two years older than the bride's brother, though in high school, those were light-years. And by high school, she didn't get the leads anymore, because casting was just a popularity contest, no different than prom queen. So she gravitated toward stage crew, where she tended to be the only girl. No spotlights or applause, but it was fun hanging out with the guys in the rafters with the pulleys and lights, and at the sound booth. By college the sound crew felt not like outsiders but like members of their own little tree house club.

Crystal got her undergraduate degree and M.F.A. in film in Los Angeles, then began to work in the industry. Despite her share of dating dilemmas—the spurts of solitary despair that any single woman in her twenties endures—those years were the happiest of her life. Her future felt like one of those overhead shots of palm trees on a long boulevard, full of possibility and freedom. She'd interned for a company that had Academy Award nominations for animation sound effects, and they hired her to stay afterward, or rather Paul, one of the co-partners, did. Mummies, musketeers, superheroes: they all needed whooshes, crashes, broken glass, the moan of doors slowly opened and the creak of floors under tiptoes.

She wasn't exactly the first intern whom Paul had fucked. Later she'd learn that the whole outfit sniggered about his "Friday lunches" with fresh new prospects. When he threw her over for the makeup person whom he eventually married, she was understandably upset. When he "let her go," one friend thought she had grounds for a sexual harassment suit, but the lawyer with whom she consulted felt that it would be hard to make the case.

Then, before she could find other work, a strike. The whole business disabled, not permanently, but for long enough that she had to move back home.

If she was depressed being without Paul in L.A., she felt much more hopeless once reinstalled in her childhood bedroom in Haddonfield with her chain-smoking, mean, bitterly divorced mother and her mother's yappy dachshund. Unlike in L.A., where everyone was young, there were no people her age in New Jersey. Everyone she knew from school was gone. Understandable—people got out at the first possible moment.

Every Fourth of July, Haddonfield hosted fireworks at the high school. In the bleachers with her mother, surrounded by wild toddlers, she felt her spirits sink. She was the only attractive single person in the entire town—maybe the only single person, except for a couple of kids home from college for the summer and the handful of tragically damaged middle-aged men, retarded or autistic, still living with long-suffering elderly parents. There was no film work in Philadelphia and she'd had no luck getting even an interview in New York. Her mother suggested that she teach. When she noted that she had no certification, her mother said, "Well, get it." When she said that would take years, her mother said, "Well, substitute teach." As if the hourly pay would net her much more than a couple of hoagies.

She was churning on all of this with despair as the police chief commanded the microphone to welcome them to the event. The mike crackled, then went dead. Instinctively, Crystal made her way down from the bleachers to help with the equipment. A cop muscled in to keep her off the field. She explained that she was a professional. He countered that they had their own professionals.

The cop was good-looking, rugged in a relaxed rather than preening sort of way. He had no wedding ring. She beamed her approval in the slightly self-parodic, hey-there-sailor way she'd learned in Sound.

Turns out there *were* single people in Haddonfield, and they were all armed.

She briefly considered becoming a cop herself, but one of the men—the very first night at a bar, where she was invited by that cop and some of his cop friends—suggested something more efficient than the long haul of police academy: emergency dispatch. It seemed like the perfect blend of her skills in sound technology with her new-found interest in law enforcement. Her application from initial test through interviews, fingerprinting, background checks, and training took three months. She got an apartment, hugely relieved to be away from her mother and starting some kind of life.

Dispatch had its own kind of reality-show drama. A lot of the emergency calls were from people who thought 911 was 411 and called to get the phone number of a pizza parlor. Most of the phone calls about shootings or drug overdoses got referred to Camden. Still, there were heart attacks, car accidents. Unlike some of her colleagues who drawled "Nine-one-one, what's your emergency?" with all the pep of someone slipping into a coma, she took each call as if it mattered.

The dispatch room was not the cheeriest workplace, as cut off from the rest of the world as a submarine. The men were mostly ill-groomed and middle-aged. To hang out with officers, she participated in all the police fund-raisers. And every once in a while, an officer would come through to get a tour and get introduced to everyone. She always dressed well, even on the job. Luckily for her, she joined Dispatch right after they discontinued the uniform policy, for cost savings.

She didn't meet Evan there, though. She met him at the shooting range. She'd bought a gun, and thought she should learn how to use it.

The first thing he said to her, taking a step back and waving his hands: "Laser rule!"

You should never point even an unloaded gun. Certainly not at someone's crotch.

His voice in such a fine register, bass saxophone with a stir of gravel. Crystal was pretty much in love the second she heard him speak.

She'd always loved his voice. The way men were breast men or leg men, the way women first saw hands or pecs, Crystal was drawn to a voice with texture, complexity, gravitas. Later, longing for him, it would be his voice she conjured in the dark.

Evan, who went by Van, was at the range because he was one of the elite Camden County police officers who had qualified for the SWAT team. Normal officers, who in an entire career might fire once or twice, had to qualify with a weapon only twice a year, but the team had to qualify monthly. "You're SWAT or you're not," the guys liked to say.

At the range, Van taught her about anticipation. This was when you pushed your weapon down and out, told your weapon to fire rather than letting it fire naturally. He stood behind her to guide her arms, the way men in old movies helped women with their golf swings. "There you go," he said, almost into her neck, and, if she wasn't mistaken, moved his hands just slightly so one finger of one hand was almost in her armpit.

Talk about anticipation: from that touch, she knew they would become lovers.

Van wasn't that tall, but he was quite a specimen. Zero percent body fat. There was something coiled in him, a ferocious readiness.

His personality was as blunt and precise as his fade haircut. It went without saying that he was a man's man—all the cops were—and didn't go in for anything romantic, like foreplay. That night, before they made love, he'd sat on the edge of the bed in his stark apartment and commanded her to undress. Then said, "C'mere." Oddly she felt not taken advantage of but taken in, accepted, as if all the nonsense from the years of dating had been stripped away.

He did something unusual that first time. "Long legs," he said, and reached out to grab both of her knees so hard that she almost lost her balance. Held the pressure for a second. Before she knew it he was out of his pants and they were going at it, which might have offended a different kind of woman, but she was more than ready for him.

"Nothing like the right tool for the job," she said to him after, which he found enormously funny. She loved to make him laugh.

Sex with him was like SWAT itself: speed, surprise, and violence of action.

But after sex, he'd sometimes do these lovely, musing, exploratory things to her body. Like follow the faint freckles on her chest with two fingers as if he were leapfrogging from one rock to the next in a stream. Or slowly, lightly circle her belly button in one direction until, abruptly, he'd go the other way. She'd close her eyes and dreamily ask him a question, because once he got talking he'd get distracted and just keep doing whatever he was doing with his hand.

One thing about her, she knew how to listen. She would have made a good shrink. Once a month, the tactical team ran simulations. She loved to hear about them. Most school hostage situations, for example, happen in auditoriums, so the *door-kickers* would go to a school to practice how they'd enter. The tactics were a precise ballet. The *point man* went first. They'd *double stack* (two at a time) to clear the hallways. One guy would face backward with his rifle (which they called a *long gun*), while one squatted to open the door. Then, *here comes the squeeze*, when they were all lined up crouching and the rear guy would touch or tug on the team member in front of him to let him know it was time. When you came out of a room you *looked for work.* But *just because you have a guy posted up doesn't mean your ass is bulletproof.*

Once Van took her for a drive in a tricked-out Dodge Durango on loan from the tac team. They pulled over on a secluded stretch of road so they could have sex on the backseat; in the husky postcoital voice she loved, he said doing so made him feel all nostalgic. He praised her on her flexibility in a tight space and it was true, it *was* like being a kid, all the weird angles she'd enjoyed in sound booths, except that Van was considerably less tentative than those boys.

The sound guys felt like ancient history and the other cops, though she didn't know it at the time and had agonized about each relationship that didn't go anywhere, had just been warm-up.

She bought him a pair of super-lightweight insulated boots, not for his birthday, just to be nice, because he bemoaned how hot his feet got during drills. The boots fit, but he told her she shouldn't have, sounding like he meant it.

"I just wanted to. It's not like I'm asking you to reciprocate," she said, and he just stared at her.

As a surprise, she cooked up a storm for a game night he was hosting at his apartment. It's not like she made coq au vin. It was beer-commercial food: tacos, good dips for the chips, pigs in blankets.

"Pigs in blankets?" Van said incredulously, when she delivered the food.

She felt a sense of failure so profound that she had to fight back tears. This happened to her occasionally and inexplicably, about little things.

Van said, "You have to leave."

"I'll just lurk in the kitchen," she said, pulling herself together, "like a happy hausfrau, and help you clean up after everyone goes."

"Crystal, you've got to go. *Now.*"

"Can't I just stay and say hi to everyone? Why not?"

"Look. Just get the fuck out."

Just that week, she'd gotten an e-mail from a friend in L.A.

alerting her about a sound studio that might be hiring. She didn't pursue the lead, because she wanted to make things work with Van. Besides, Dispatch was a good, solid gig. In her spare time, with what she'd learned from her involvement with the police, maybe she could write a screenplay. She had never pushed Van, had never, not once, uttered the line "When will I see you again?" She didn't e-mail or text him a lot, either. When he was off work, the last thing he wanted was to hang out at a computer. He wasn't on Facebook—Facebook, he said, was to stalkers the way stagnant water was to mosquitoes.

She joined the gym where he worked out. This made him furious. It's not a girly gym, there are no step classes, he almost spat. She retorted that it was a free country and he said fine, then it was the *only* place he'd see her. Voice shaking, she promised to go back to her own gym.

But she didn't. She was familiar with his rotation of shifts. Their work schedules were currently not in sync at all, which made it easier to go to the gym when he wouldn't be there, but harder to find a time to see him. He canceled a couple of dates, then he failed to return her calls.

After she hadn't seen him at all for the longest month of her life, it became clear that he was seeing someone else, and she thought she knew who it was.

There was a female cop on the Haddonfield force named Heather who worked out at the gym. Heather was a tiny woman with a tiny, high-pitched voice, a cutesy cop doll with big blue eyes and bright blond hair. It was hard to imagine her doing police work until you saw her in the weight room. She did timed cross-training: 100 pull-ups, 100 push-ups, 100 sit-ups, 100 squats. Heather had been encouraged to try out for the SWAT team, and she was now training to qualify. Her fellow officers egged her on: "All day, now! Come on, push through!" She ran on the treadmill in a forty-pound vest.

Crystal began to detest Heather so much that she was thrilled when the midget failed the PT portion of her SWAT tryout. The dummy carry did her in. She had to drag a 250-pound man backward twenty feet. She tried to drag him by his vest, then his belt, but then his belt broke. She would train more, and try again. "I saw a winner," one of the guys assured her. "You didn't make the time, but you didn't quit. You dragged him across that finish line."

It wasn't Van who confronted her but Heather herself.

"You have something to say to me?" Heather asked her, in the women's locker room.

"What?"

"Why are you staring at me all the time?"

"I'm not."

"Uh-huh. I get this sometimes from dykes. To get it straight: I'm straight."

"Oh!" Crystal said. "Oh, no. Me too. I'm Van's girlfriend. Or at least was, until *you* . . ."

"Van? You mean Evan McCormick?" Heather almost snorted. "His 'girlfriend'? Yeah. Right. Just so you know," and she thrust her left hand into Crystal's face and wiggled the fingers. A smallish diamond flashed. Crystal had never seen the ring before, but maybe Heather didn't wear it when she worked out, or maybe it was hidden beneath the fingerless weightlifting gloves.

"So what?" Crystal said defiantly. "Since when did that stop anyone?"

"Wow. You *are* a nut job. Listen, be a cop hopper if you get off on it. I love the guys like brothers but they're mostly pigs. No thanks. And 'Van'"—again the miniature pony eked out her whinnying laugh.

"What about him? Do you know something?"

Heather just shook her head. "Just stop staring at me, okay? You're skeeving me out."

Shortly thereafter, Van left a message on her voice mail.

"You don't take a hint, do you? Don't know what you think we had, but it's over. Can I make it any more clear than that? No e-mails,

no phone calls, don't drop by, it's over. We're done. I mean it. Another thing. Get out of my gym. I don't want to see you there and I
don't want any of my friends telling me they've seen you there.
Thanks for the memories, over and out, now fuck off."

She played the message repeatedly, stabbed in the heart each
time. As she reviewed their relationship, from their instant attraction
at the shooting range to the debacle of game night, she began to itch.
It was as if her skin itself were crying out for him. And at night the
itching got worse. She would lie in bed and sob and scratch, her
whole groin area on fire with itching.

Eventually she went to the doctor, and he informed her that she
had scabies, microscopic mites that live beneath your skin. They like
to hang out and lay eggs at the warmest parts of your body. Your
armpits, in between your fingers and toes, your pubic area. Bugs that
wake up at night to party: what a going-away present! But the doctor
said that scabies was not a venereal disease; you could get them from
sex, but also from sweaty gym equipment that had not been wiped
down in between users. As well as the medicated cream, he also gave
her, at her request, a prescription for sleeping pills.

As she washed all her sheets and clothes in hot water, she tried to
cleanse her mind of Van by hating him. The Neanderthal was as
communicative as a tree stump, didn't really converse at all unless
the topic was law enforcement. She wasn't even going to tell him about
the scabies. She hoped his skin got scratched raw and he infected
half the skanks in New Jersey. She should have pursued that job in
L.A. Why should she even want him?

Except she did.

The longing came back, and so did the itch. When she returned
to the doctor for more sleeping pills, he refused to give her any and
suggested Benadryl. He said it was normal for some itching to persist
for a couple of weeks after treatment, but to be on the safe side, she
should cut her nails short, since eggs could hide there, wash everything again, and repeat the treatment. He also gave her a referral for
a psychiatrist, should she want to speak about the breakup that had
upset her so much she couldn't sleep.

"Do they live inside the body?" she asked the doctor.

He looked puzzled. "You mean can they burrow in *through* the skin, to the internal organs?"

"No. I mean . . ."

"Like, vaginally?" He chortled for a second, then tried to compose himself. "Oh, no. Not to worry. Perish the thought!"

She wished she could. Her dreams were full of the most appalling insects. Vaginal, rectal. They weren't microscopic. Some had scrunched little faces, their expressions menacing as gargoyles'. *Do not use this medication internally*, the insert on the scabies cream warned, but after some of these dreams she was tempted to douche with it.

She took a lot of pride in her nails. Having to cut them off was a last straw. Puffy-eyed from crying, out of shape (no way was she going to get reinfected by public gym equipment), sleep-deprived, and without her French manicure, she fell into a despair so profound that she did make an appointment with the psychiatrist. At least she could get another prescription for sleeping pills.

Tearfully, she told the balding Jewish psychiatrist about Van, Heather, and the scabies. She told him that Van had definitely been seeing someone, and she needed to know who because she wasn't going to be able to bury their relationship until she got the autopsy. Otherwise, it was as if their relationship—indeed, Crystal herself—had been buried alive.

Furthermore, she told him, when she tried to force herself to stop thinking about Van by focusing on the larger issues of the world instead, she got even more upset. She was angry about the wars in Afghanistan and Iraq. She was haunted by war rape, sex slaves, and eight-year-olds forced into marriage with abusive, toothless old men. In Afghanistan, a husband or father felt perfectly within his rights to cut off the nose of his property should she "dishonor" him. Crystal was still tortured by images of the maimed girl photographed in *Newsweek* trying to hide her nose in her burqa, could not begin to comprehend such violence, did not understand how to continue living in a world that harbored such violence. Did the men do this only when they were casting the women off, to mark them as valueless? Or would they continue to fuck the women, leering right into the caverns in the middle of their faces, proud to see evidence of their own righteous anger? Crystal once dreamed, horrifically, of a demonic Van teasing the ragged nose hole of a Muslim woman with his cock. With dreams like this, it was hard to see the point of sleeping.

The psychiatrist listened with a poker face punctuated by flashes of alarm. He asked her if she thought about hurting herself and she said yes. She said she was sleeping and eating very poorly. She was afraid to go to the gym, equally afraid of getting fat and unattractive. He didn't say, "Oh, come on, you're a knockout." Maybe they weren't allowed to say that, but he could have reassured her with his eyes.

Trite as a movie psychiatrist, he inquired about her father. Crystal watched slot machine fruit click into a match in his eyes as she informed him that her father had walked out on the family when she was little, and was not in touch at all. "What does he do?" the shrink asked. He was an ex-marine now involved, she thought, in some kind of contract work in the Middle East. At this thrilling news the shrink looked like he was restraining himself from jumping up and down in his chair like an orangutan.

Did he think she was an idiot? Yes, she was drawn to strong men. Who wasn't? Yes, her father knew how to discharge a weapon, but so did most men who weren't Jewish shrinks.

When Crystal asked for sleeping pills, he claimed to have something better, and wrote her a prescription for Abilify.

He said that therapy could help her but it would take some time, and this pill would smooth things out in the meanwhile and allow her to concentrate on feeling better. Don't go home and look it up on the computer and get all upset, he warned. This drug is effective for many conditions and most of the side effects never show up.

Crystal was too shocked to ask him for a diagnosis. She went home, Googled Abilify, saw it was used to treat bipolar depression and paranoid schizophrenia, scanned the long scroll of possible side effects, and got all upset.

She didn't fill the prescription and she didn't return to the psychiatrist, who had the nerve to mail her a bill for the missed appointment.

She did, however, return to the gym.

She went right before they closed, and marched into the empty men's
locker room. She put on rubber gloves to install, on the underside of
the changing bench, an acoustical contact microphone that she'd
bought from an online spy store. She installed one in the women's
locker room, too, and a third under a bench in the weight room.

In movies, the surveillance people had vans full of high-end
equipment, slide controls that when you adjusted them up or down
greeted you with a handy "whee-oooh" noise like a theremin, dial
upon dial on dashboards from the starship *Enterprise*. Crystal had
sound skills, but recording conversations over the noise of clinking
weights; the men's histrionic grunts and groans; the gym's awful
piped-in music; and showers, hand dryers, flushing toilets, and slam-
ming locker doors in the changing area did not go well. The tapes
took forever to listen to, and no one seemed to say anything worth
hearing. The only thing of interest was this, between two women in
the changing room who were confident they were alone:

"Yeah, I know. What *is* their fascination with it?"

"Maybe just that it's hard to get."

"Think it's, like, latent homosexuality?"

"Nah. [Unintelligible] said [unintelligible—laughter]."

"I could definitely do without."

"Oh, I kind of like it. Once in a blue moon in the right
mood and with enough lube."

"I'd rather [unintelligible—more laughter—slammed
locker door]."

Crystal couldn't tell from the voices if Heather was one of the
women. No matter how many times she replayed the tape, she
couldn't make out the most critical line, who said what about whom,

but she was hounded by the suspicion that they were talking about her and Van.

That's when she gave up trying to get to the bottom of things herself and decided to hire a private investigator.

Or tried to. The first two she consulted declined the assignment.

"The guy broke it off," the first detective said. "You don't need a PI to figure out where he's at with you. Plus he's a cop. On SWAT. Who you suspect might be messing around with a married cop? And you want me to infiltrate a cop gym to get the lowdown on his sex life? Think I'll pass."

The second detective said, "I can tell you if he has any lawsuits against him or a stash in the Cayman Islands, not like you're entitled to any of his assets, and frankly these days you could do a record search yourself. You ask me, you ought to just move on."

The third detective was a nice-looking woman. Before she stumbled into the private investigation racket, she'd gotten an M.A. in English literature. Because of her own divorce, she was considerably more sympathetic to Crystal's sense of frantic loss.

The weeks during which the PI was on the case were Crystal's best in a long time. She didn't itch at all. She just waited for closure. On the job, she was both looking forward to and dreading the moment when the rotation of 911 calls and dispatchers put her on with Van, and she was able to keep her voice flat, utterly unengaged, with just a soupçon of disdain. But amazingly and in defiance of the odds, that never happened.

She went to the investigator's office with excitement. Later, she would ask herself what she had possibly expected to hear.

"Which do you want first," the PI asked, "the bad news or the other bad news?"

Van McCormick was well-known in the local cop world as a skirt chaser. Not, according to some of the ladies, the hardest-working officer in the sack, although he had "a nice nightstick." The PI said that it was easy to extract this information from the badge bunnies at the bar. Crystal asked what "badge bunny" meant. The PI expressed surprise that Crystal had never heard the term, and explained that certain women were, like Crystal herself, really drawn to men in uniform. The PI had interviewed five cop groupies who said they'd had relations with Van during the period in which he was seeing Crystal. They said he liked to pretzel a girl up in the backseat of the SWAT car and dribble a little manhood on the seats, like a dog marking.

Crystal herself was familiar to the badge bunnies. They remembered the night she showed up at the bar all bright-eyed and bushy-tailed and acted like she was the only girl in the place. Shortly thereafter, she got a job in Dispatch, so she had an "in" that the other women didn't, actually got to interact with the guys during their workdays, when they were all focused and soulful. The cops knew she had a screw loose but kept screwing her anyway.

Crystal began to cry.

The PI handed her a tissue. "I'm giving it to you straight," the PI said, "because there's really no way to sugarcoat it. You know, many of the cops really are decent guys. They marry and have families. But you're not going to get those guys like this."

Sobbing too hard to talk, Crystal managed to say, "Like what? I'm not promiscuous! In my whole life, eight guys. It's libel!"

"Not really. More like gossip."

"How am I going to get on the phone with them now? How can I even do my job?"

"Oh, I forgot to tell you one compliment. The guys evidently do think that you're a very competent dispatcher."

The PI said that her master's thesis had been on Henry James, and asked Crystal if she'd ever read *Portrait of a Lady*. Crystal had not. The PI said that the moment when Isabella Archer discovers that she's been duped is a wonderfully accurate account of how it feels to be a woman betrayed. Coincidentally, the PI had been working on her thesis at the very time that she found out her husband was sleeping with one of her oldest friends and quietly stealing money from her. All of that coming together was what got her into her current line of work. If only Isabella had paid someone to do a background check on Osmond before she tied the knot!

Crystal found herself becoming so impatient and irritated that she stopped crying. Why did women always assume you wanted to hear the story of their lives? Crystal had attended one book club meeting hosted by a coworker at Dispatch and had not returned for this very reason. Manicurists were the worst. Being forced to smile and nod through their detailed, dramatic narratives was, literally, like watching paint dry. The best thing that ever happened for American womanhood was when all the manicurists became Vietnamese, and couldn't speak enough English to bother you.

The whole time she spoke, the PI played with a stack of color photographs that she'd put on the table. "Good, you're calm," she said. "These are your money shots," and she picked the pile up and began to put the photographs down on the table serially, like tarot cards.

Van with a woman. The woman—not Heather—wore glasses and a dark suit. Van opening the car door for her in daylight. Leaning toward her in a restaurant, both of their faces intense, serious. After lunch? A handshake! But then: nighttime now, a fancier restaurant on some kind of pier with twinkling lights in Philly. And . . . a shot of a closed apartment door.

"Sorry about that. Technological difficulties. I missed the goodnight kiss. You'll have to take my word for it: there was one. And then: he's in!"

The woman in the photographs was, of all things, a negotiator. She and Van had met while handling an incident together. The Camden team's only female negotiator was on vacation, so they'd imported this woman from Atlantic County.

But, Crystal objected, the tac guys don't like the negotiators. They think they're snobs. And the negotiators think the tac guys are gorillas.

The PI said, brightly, "True." But she noted that police were most often attracted to others who understood the pressures of their work: Firemen. EMTs. Air traffic controllers.

The last picture: the woman holding hands with a little girl. "It's really interesting to me," the PI mused, "how often the Don Juans go for the single mothers when they retire their horndog jerseys. What can it mean? That no one was ever tender with them, probably."

Crystal felt dizzy. The PI had just uttered the negotiator's name when her client stood suddenly and bolted from the office so fast that she didn't even take the photographs, or get the bill. Not the first time that had happened. "Hey, shoot the messenger," the PI joked to the empty chair.

The intensity of the humiliation was impossible to describe. Being burned at the stake would not be far off. Except at a certain point after unimaginable pain you would finally die. Crystal would never date another police officer. The entire police force of New Jersey was laughing at her. Everyone at Dispatch probably knew. People greeted her cordially enough, then probably sniggered and made hand-job gestures the minute her back was turned.

She did not get over it. She did not sleep more deeply. She did not cry less. She hated Van, but she still desperately missed him, too, so the candle of her burned from both ends: a mental image of him speeding in his car with one hand on the wheel would fill her with longing, and she would also want to crush the hand so he never drove again. And then she would imagine herself tenderly kissing the broken fingers.

The scabies were long gone, but shame still inflamed—shame and shame's evil twin, a white-hot fury that made her more empathetic with the young American men who, on TV, skulked off to join the Taliban. She wouldn't mind a wee bit o' jihad befalling Van Mc-Cormick. He was always very quiet, the neighbors say about these men. He didn't fit in, he didn't chitchat in the lunchroom. Crystal related to the losers' brooding loneliness, sympathized with their need to denounce not just the individuals who had caused their suffering but the entire nation. But the Taliban?

"Human rights are women's rights and women's rights are human rights." Crystal regretted, now, that she'd been one of the people who believed Hillary Clinton should have shown more backbone and kicked Bill out when he cheated on her. When Hillary ran for office, Crystal had felt a swell of feminist pride. Hillary had toughed it out, kept her dignity yet again when she lost to Obama, and now she was secretary of state. At some point, her husband would simply be too old for adultery. They would grow old and die together. They would not die alone.

On the news, woman after woman was publicly humiliated by her cheating jackass of a husband. Crystal did not feel a sisterly bond with these women, because they were *married*. They had children and joint property. They got book deals and told their stories to talk-show hosts. What did Crystal have?

Well, she had a job. She planned to keep it, even if she had to do twelve-hour shifts on two hours' sleep. She was determined not to be like those rough boys who slid off the American map and slouched toward Pakistan to be born again as suicide bombers. For some reason she'd found herself drawn to W. B. Yeats, having unearthed her undergrad copy of his *Collected Poems* at her mother's. Yeats had a lifelong unrequited crush on the Irish revolutionary Maud Gonne, and Crystal fashioned herself in the Gonne mold. She kept a stanza from the poem "Crazy Jane Talks with the Bishop" on a Post-it note near her laptop:

> A woman can be proud and stiff
> When on love intent;
> But Love has pitched his mansion in
> The place of excrement;
> For nothing can be sole or whole
> That has not been rent.

Crazy Jane wasn't really crazy. And neither was Crystal. Or at least that's what she told herself as more and more her fate with Van felt deeply intertwined with all the sadness and evil in the world. Did Crystal claim that Hillary Clinton came to her in a vision and commanded her to mow Van down in cold blood? No, she did not. Did General Petraeus personally tell Crystal that Van's face was now number one on that deck of Iraq's Most Wanted playing cards? No. As Yeats said (rather more eloquently), sometimes you have to go through bad shit to get to good shit. Her mission was to expose the rank sexism embedded in American culture that kept us from evolving into a real democracy. Only as a by-product of true equality could she exorcise Van and the way he had, both figuratively and literally, fucked her up the ass, the way America had fucked Iraq. In the process of delivering her feminist performance piece, she hoped to not only cleanse herself and gain catharsis—a kind of emotional enema—but recharge her artistic aspirations, since she was aware that she would certainly lose her job when it was over, if she lived.

In Crystal's apartment, her bed was made, her laundry folded and put away. Beside her computer were her last will and testament, done online through buildawill.com but properly notarized, leaving all her money to Women for Women International, which helped female war survivors; and the manuscript of her memoir, which was typed. She was not like those weirdos you see at the post office, feeding the lone Xerox machine quarters to copy endless piles of densely handwritten pages. That whole wild Unabomber act seemed distinctly male. Just because you could fire a gun did not mean you had to be a slob. On the other hand, you didn't want to obsessive-compulsively hospital-corner things, since that kind of military precision was yet another kind of guy act. No, she would handle things in a distinctly balanced *female* way, with humor and feeling.

She planned the event for five months. There was a lot to do, even more than for a real wedding but very similar activities, from selecting and "booking" a venue, if you could call it that, to choosing the dress and shoes, taking a self-defense class, and reading up on bomb-making.

The distraction of planning the event was what allowed Crystal to go on.

Yet what Yeats would call her "deep heart's core" was still a shrine to Van with a perpetual flame. She tried to keep the sense of catastrophic loss discrete, discreet, like a pilot light. But since her soul was as frail and dry as kindling, she was never far from being immolated. Sri Lanka, she had read in the paper, had the highest rates of attempted suicide in the world. People were always trying to set themselves on fire after marital fights. In truth, especially in the middle of the night when she wasn't working night shifts, half awake, wracked by visions in which Van and the petite brunette negotiator writhed entwined in sickening close-up, all teeth and tongue, the negotiator's moans so loud that the interrogator might as well be blasting them through loudspeakers in the prisoner's cell, death might be welcome.

INSIDE OUT

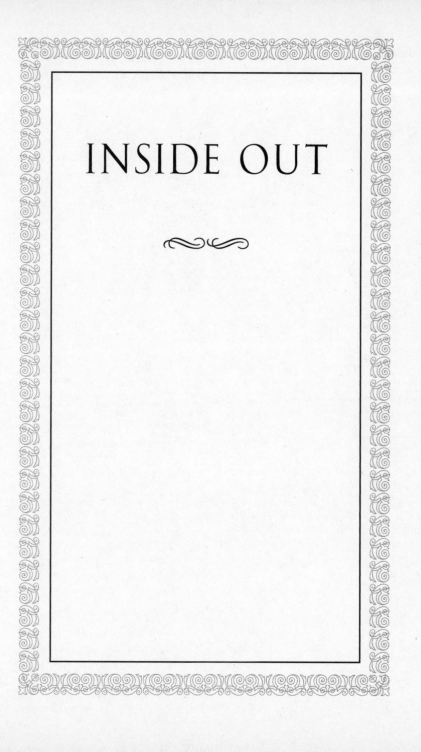

*O*nly Gabe knew: Tess might be pregnant.

Unless she was just late from the stress of planning the wedding. A couple of days too early for a pee stick, but her mother claimed she'd known both times almost immediately, if you paid attention to your body there were signs, your body hushed and somehow electrified, like the sky before snow. That pregnancy test kit was the wedding present that Tess was most looking forward to unwrapping.

Before she'd put on her dress today, Tess had stood before Gabe naked and asked what he thought. He touched one of her nipples with two fingers gingerly, as if testing the doneness of a steak, and declared that yes, her breasts did seem different, a different kind of swelling than before her period. He asked her if they felt sensitive.

"For you they do," she said. "In a good way."

Without discussion they'd made love in her childhood bedroom in a way that put them in mind of their first time, on a squeaky single bed in Mali: all slow and holy, eyes open, coming with the least possible noise.

Tess thought, This is the very best thing to do right before getting married. She was happy to sanctify her marriage with her lips all tumescent and her pheromones all loosey-goosey, glad to deliver a cocktail of congratulations to greet the embryo. They'd stayed wrapped around each other and smiling until her brother banged on the door and said, "Hear the thunder?" It was true, the storm seemed to be headed their way, so they threw their sweats on and began the big operation to start moving the wedding indoors, both grateful that they'd had the time alone to feel focused and blessed.

Tess had planned exactly the kind of wedding she wanted. Nice, but nothing too formal or fussy. It's not, as everyone assumed, because she eschewed opulence after the poverty of Africa. They make a huge deal about weddings in Africa. Much of that is business. Bride price, they call the dowry. And much to-do over the woman's virginity. Of course, you can always pay someone off to fake a maiden-head. In Mali they send a *magnonmakan*, a kind of sexpert, who offers instruction on how to please your man, it being the man's pleasure, of course, that is the chief, indeed the only, concern—the clitorecto-mies ensure that. The bride and groom stay in seclusion for a week. All of which is pretty meaningless if you're an American already living with your beloved.

For her the most important thing was that the wedding retain some quality of spontaneity. That was what she most loved about Gabe. His sister, Miranda, was the actress, but Miranda always worked from a script. Gabe improvised. When she first met him, she was joining Doctors Without Borders to train as a finco (financial coor-dinator), and Gabe, who had gotten there several months before, was in a dusty public square performing a mimed educational skit about condom use—AIDS being a big problem in Africa—using a wooden penis. The audience of Malians laughed and laughed. She loved that they didn't have a "real" wedding photographer who would produce stilted shots of them looking soulfully into each other's eyes, that "the band" hadn't rehearsed and was this wacky, wonderful combination of Eastern and Western instruments, bass and a xylophone that they'd rented for Souleymane. The thing about Gabe is that he could stop, anywhere, and just be.

So when Tess first saw the madwoman with the gun she'd thought: Okay. Bring it on. It certainly wasn't going to be a wedding that people forgot.

But if she was killed. If her maybe-baby was killed.

Dying babies had sent her home from Africa. There was much that Tess couldn't take. Most of all she couldn't take babies starving or dying of illnesses that were simply curable if the drugs were at hand. Gabe could have stayed, but she wasn't strong enough. They'd done only two missions, and neither was in a war zone. She felt shame about not being able to tough it out, but on the other hand, she knew she wanted to have children, and once MSF sunk its claws in you, you'd never get away. You'd never have a family. MSF was its own gnarled kind of priesthood. Look at Idris: the kindest man alive, and still single.

So she and Gabe had come back here and found a way to live where they could both still help people, and now she was pregnant, and as a punishment for being weak, for choosing American safety, she was going to die? In *Haddonfield*?

Silently, she began to cry.

The hostages were thirsty, hungry, sweaty, and exhausted. The room stank of piss and shit. They'd heard the bullhorn and sirens almost two hours ago, seen the remote-control robot at the doors, yet no one came for them. The HT was not gone, though; at unpredictable intervals, they still heard her stomping about or talking, presumably on the phone, presumably to a negotiator.

They'd been in the room for over four hours now, without food or water.

Delbert Billips Jr. wove in and out of consciousness. His wife had been assured that he would be all right. She sat on the floor, leaning against a wall, so he could have his head in her lap. They held hands. Every so often their fingers fluttered and adjusted. His bleeding had slowed down, but Gabe still knelt beside him, his shirt pressed lightly into the wound.

About Sylvia Needleman, the diabetic on the couch, they were less confident. And Dr. Ira Needleman was so distraught for his wife that he could not stop shaking, was himself at risk for a heart attack or stroke.

When Mary's baby began to cry again, his sonic squawk in some special ring of ear-torturing hell, she conferred with the breast-feeding mother. The two women's husbands stood gravely beside the women like their legal counsel, and all agreed that the breast-feeding woman should nurse the stranger's baby. She did not have AIDS or hepatitis; she did not even drink. They exchanged infants. The bride's second stepmother watched with a stricken expression as the stranger took the baby to her breast. Louis's eyes opened wide for a second, then he closed them, latched on, and sucked like a pro.

Watching the baby contentedly nurse, Tess finally lost it and began to sob.

People tried to give her a little space.

"What's taking them so long?" Tess demanded.

Gabe, bare-chested at his own wedding, was still kneeling to press his white shirt into his father's shoulder, and didn't see her right away. But her mother somehow did. That was okay. Tess wanted her mother anyway.

Helen took Tess's hand and, smiling a bit, wiped at the corner of her daughter's eyes with a pinky. As if smudged eyeliner were the biggest problem for a bride whose wedding dress was now a splatter art canvas of blood and vomit. But then Tess looked at her mother and somehow, because Helen was kind of psychic, Helen knew. She wrapped her arms around her daughter and let the bride sob.

"Oh, baby," she said.

*S*o she's going to mow down sixty hostages because McCormick gave her scabies?" the SWAT commander demanded. "Shouldn't she have gotten syphilis?"

"Syphilis you just take an antibiotic these days," the incident commander said.

"Herpes, then. Herpes is permanent."

"Or HIV."

"Did Van ever mention itching?"

"Gentlemen," the female negotiator chided. "Do you mind?"

This is why they needed a female negotiator. Although law enforcement is trained to avoid a gender bias toward aggression, the men couldn't help making certain assumptions about a female suspect. In sieges, women are more verbal. They accept, and inflict, more superficial wounds. They do not like wounds on their faces. And although being scorned in love was the motive for most male hostage takers as well, the police could not help but think even less of this woman, once they knew she'd gone to all this trouble for a guy. They couldn't get the right tone of sober respect for her efforts. They'd want to say, gruffly, "Come on. Settle down."

Alison, on the other hand, had managed to get the HT talking. Crystal had evidently written an entire book about how Van McCormick had mistreated and degraded her, chunks of which she had memorized. While at first the HT had claimed she would talk directly to Van McCormick and no one else, then wanted to let Van's girlfriend know face-to-face what kind of man she was exposing her young daughter to, the negotiator stressed to her how important it was to tell the top brass as well, if there had been infractions of professional ethics. The negotiator was particularly interested in how Crystal alighted on this particular wedding. It was a critical piece of information for assessing her psychological state, and thus the best way to deal with her.

The bomb-making, the Haddonfield stakeout, the arsenal, all required long-term planning, but her depression and anger seemed better suited to an impulsive act. By now the negotiator knew that the HT claimed to have done a stint in the film business. Many of the incongruities could be explained under the banner of bad art. The Virginia Tech sniper had been a poet. But what did the HT want? What could possibly satisfy her?

Crystal found Helen's house by calling caterers about a June wedding in Haddonfield, and asking for references in town. She didn't really want references. She just wanted to divine the location of a June wedding in Haddonfield, so Van would show up with SWAT. It had to be a private residence, because the churches and restaurants would have security systems, too many egresses, too many public-facing windows. Finding the site proved to be the most difficult part of her job. The prosperous people of Haddonfield were not drawn to home weddings. There were plenty of graduation parties in June, many of them catered. Crystal didn't want high school seniors as hostages, and furthermore, people wander in and out of graduation parties. She needed them to all sit down at the same time, so she could contain them. Plus, to properly present as the terrorist of love, she wanted to wear the wedding dress, which made no sense at a graduation party.

Matt and Cyndi's catering company was the one that couldn't accommodate her on one Saturday in June, when they already had a commitment in Haddonfield. To get Helen's address and the time of the event, Crystal had to break into the catering company office and study the big whiteboard calendar on their wall—no big deal, the building was not alarmed.

Crystal had clearly been certain that Van's tactical team would be called to the scene. To count on his presence was a bit foolhardy— not every team member showed up, especially in summer. She thought she could manipulate them. But if she really had inside information about how SWAT operated, it was a mistake to shoot so early. Did she honestly think they were going to send McCormick so she could give him a piece of her mind, or gun him down?

"Where is he? Why isn't he here yet?" Crystal demanded.

"We're getting him for you," the negotiator promised. "We're working on it. We have to find him first, though."

"You're lying," Crystal said. "Van is already there. You think I don't know he's the scout when you plant the cameras?"

"Generally," the negotiator lied. Van had been, as usual, one of the first men out. "But today we couldn't find him."

"Is he in May's Landing, with her?"

The negotiator murmured that she wasn't yet sure. She had been shocked to discover that a fellow New Jersey negotiator—a perfectly reasonable woman with whom she had bonded at many training sessions—was linked to this siege through the SWAT member with the legendary history of sexual conquests. Amanda had been located and would be en route as soon as she found a sitter.

"For him to just pick up women is one thing," Crystal said. "I know him. It's part of his 'fast-twitch conditioning.' It's about his 'performance.' It's all body with him. But Van in love? I deserve to know why, don't you think?"

The negotiator agreed. But Crystal knew the drill. If she wanted to be smart, she'd do some things to show good faith. She'd tell them more about the bomb. She'd send out some hostages: the kids, the injured, the elderly. Crystal confessed that there were some kids she'd love to ditch, but she couldn't do that because the door was boarded shut, and if she opened it they'd all get out. Hostages, the negotiator assured her, tended to be very cooperative. Especially when they were facing a loaded weapon. Crystal would stand at the door with her rifle, and once the kids left, she'd board the door back up. If she sent out the hostages, the negotiator said, Van would no doubt be there by the time she was done. How many hostages did Crystal feel comfortable letting go?

Crystal said she'd think about it. Mostly, she needed to talk to Van. Was that so much to ask? "It's not like I'm asking for a million dollars in cash and a private plane, or network airtime," she said, and the negotiator reassured her that she understood.

*V*an McCormick had been packing for a predawn departure when the page about the Haddonfield job arrived. He and some other guys had chartered a boat for some deep-sea fishing the next day. He wasn't entirely sorry to miss roasting for too long in too-hot sun with too much beer. Van had Irish skin (they ribbed him about the warrior paint of zinc oxide on his nose), and if he was going to get smashed, he preferred a neat single-malt Scotch. But he liked the ocean trips better than the ones in the brackish bay, and he pretty much had to go, because he didn't hunt. When the guys took their yearly pilgrimages to Maine or Canada, where the deer were better to strap to your roof than the scrawny dog-sized ones in the Pine Barrens, they'd say, "Afraid to take the week off, McCormick? Afraid your biceps will atrophy an eighth of an inch? Afraid you'll bench-press a half pound less?" And the cocksman would say no, he was after a different kind of prey, women who would deliver pleasures that the cop wives were incapable of even if the men spent every spare minute pussy-whipped into home repair projects—"Too bad you have to work so hard for it, McCormick. You troll for ground beef. I just go home and get filet mignon"—but in fact, he was afraid. He was military about his workout routine.

"I bet you were pretty strong back in the day," the young bucks at the gym would admit, as a backhanded compliment. The truth is, at forty-one, the ex–high-school wrestling champ was in the best shape of his life. The street cops didn't have to be in shape, because the only danger they faced was the threat of lawsuits from the doctors and lawyers of Haddonfield, when you caught their spoiled children breaking the law. You had to dot every i and cross every t, because the parents were in complete denial. A high school kid dispensing Adderall to middle schoolers would be stoned out of his mind, stinking of weed, with prescription drugs in a name other than his own on his person and a wad of bills, and smash his car into a tree driving drunk, and the mother would say, *My kid is straight. He did the D.A.R.E. program at school.*

So Van had made his peace with the jealousy of the street cops, always framed as mockery. His best friends were also SWAT. But as a career fornicator, Van's interest was, like his hair, thinning. Recently, as a young cop left a bar with a bimbo, another cop said, admiringly, "He's the new Van." As if Van himself was over the hill. Van had felt both uneasy about this and uneasy about his own uneasiness, puzzled by his oversensitivity when he thought he detected actual disrespect sheathed in the standard affectionate cop drubbing.

No one knew that he had been seeing Amanda, the Atlantic County negotiator, exclusively. Even to himself, he claimed he had just been too busy to dynamite fish for other action. As far as the men were concerned, he was the same old dog, the one they trash-talked for his fanatical devotion to keeping his reflexes sharp. The kind of guy who never goes anywhere for fear of missing the big call; who, for fun, turns off all his lights, takes his weapons apart, tosses the parts and ammo on the floor, and times himself reassembling in the dark.

Just as Van was getting off work Saturday afternoon, a present for him: a shiny black town car with New York plates.

Van was not one to run radar, but he did enjoy pulling over chauffeur-driven vehicles. There were often lines of coke being snorfled in the back. The drivers often had a few too many drinks while waiting for their charges to eat or gamble or screw. The passengers would cycle through a series of expressions, fast as one of those flip-books that makes a man ride a unicycle, as they realized that they'd been caught with women not their wives, and would have to grovel. Van would lean into the car and tauntingly linger on the woman first. Not once in his life had Van paid for sex, and he felt disdain for people who did, almost as strong as his contempt for rapists. That old, rich French Jew in the news—either he paid or raped the maid in the New York hotel; either way, he was a fucktard.

Most of the time he didn't bust people on 10-12s, although it took a lot of ethical restraint not to ruin the lives of teenagers on prom nights. Haddonfield had a zero tolerance policy about alcohol and drug use: one beer, one hit off a bong, and the student was barred from any extracurricular activities for the rest of his school career. So long, Ivy League admission and football scholarship.

This Saturday, as Van did his slo-mo cowboy walk up to the car, and the surprised driver handed over his license and registration, the tinted back window rolled down, and "Is there a problem, Officer?"—the line such a joke, it's a wonder it escapes anyone's mouth—asked the TV actor Trevor Hunter.

Cops during halftimes, or between rounds on poker nights, would often watch reruns of his wildly inaccurate cop show, and hoot in derision.

Or someone who looked exactly like Trevor Hunter.

And, beside him, a hot light-skinned black bitch.

Van hadn't seen any of her movies. They weren't his kind of movie. But she looked vaguely familiar.

When a cop leans into a car, the window is like a TV, except you look down. Missionary position. A cop peering down into a car produces an almost immediate sexual charge, even if the occupants aren't doing anything overtly sexual. It was Van's studied opinion that for anyone getting nasty in the backseat of a car with a driver, discovery is part of the kick, even if they don't admit it to themselves.

The hot black bitch wore a black dress, low-cut and tight. She sat the way a kid would, with one leg tucked up under her. She'd taken the shoe from that leg off. On the leg that hung down, the

other shoe dangled, a high-heeled sandal. She was bopping the foot up
and down in tune to whatever the driver had on the radio. From his
bird's-eye vantage, Van watched the bouncing of the foot slow, then
stop. The bitch was smooth. She didn't snap her legs together or pull
down the dress. Just stopped moving the foot. Van watched her watching him watch.

For him, generally, that would be a lock. He would have made contact, the woman would be ready to go, there would be no need for further discussion, mutual desire about as difficult as syncing a Bluetooth.

"License and registration, please," Van said to Trevor.

"Why?" Trevor demanded. "I'm not driving."

Van didn't dignify that with an answer. Just waited for the man
to comply.

When Van confirmed off the license that this was, indeed, Trevor
Hunter, he asked, "What are you doing in town?"

"Wedding," Trevor said.

"My brother," the woman said.

The woman pulled the wedding invitation from her purse, and
leaned over the actor to show it to Van.

Van went back to the squad car and ran the plates, slowly. He
Googled Trevor Hunter on his cell phone and got the name of the
actress. When he returned he walked up to her window, waited for
her to roll it down. After she did she looked away, flustered. That kind
of shyness could be a turn-on. Unlike the blue-light whores twirling
in their frilly thongs, Amanda would angle her body away as she
stripped down to plain white underwear. She had a sound of choked
surprise she made when he first touched her that got him every time.
Not that he wasn't used to pleasing women. But—

He noted with faint alarm that he was thinking about Amanda
rather than this famous actress.

"I'd better take you there," Van said gallantly and, to the driver,
"Follow me."

So he gave them a police escort to the wedding, complete with
flashing lights, before he went to the gym. Told some of the guys
there about it. They knew all about his town car hobby. "McCormick's

harassing the motoring public again," they taunted, with appropriate, mock-ominous sound effects—*"Alpha Four to Eighteen, Ten-Twelve"*—then they listened with pleasure to what a succulent little number the black woman was, up close. Several spread the word on the police radio about the presence of the celebrities in their borough, which was the first news that got picked up by the local stations, since the news stations, too, listened to police radio. In fact, because of Van, there were, conveniently, news crews trolling around town before anyone even knew there was a hostage situation. That Miranda and Trevor were among the hostages was the first news that got picked up nationally.

Now Van and the rest of the door-kickers waited on the bus for a signal from Command. They were not intimidated by the bomb. If the bad guy had a pressure button, they would shoot his nasal passages. Their hollow-point bullets would scatter the bottom part of his brain and slice the brain stem in half from the spinal cord. He would be dead before his knees hit the floor. However, a lot of terrorists overseas were using the pressure-release suicide switches, so now when they shot, the bomb would go off. If the bomb was big enough it would take them all and the hostages, too, but they would still drop him.

They knew it would probably not come to that. Most HTs are morons, easily manipulated. Once a negotiator asked an HT if he needed anything and he said, "Yeah. A six-pack of beer." You've got thirty men with rifles outside your door ready to take you down and you want to pause for a couple of beers? Guy like that, you throw a couple of pebbles at the back door and break in the front.

They were the last resort. It was all hurry up and wait—until they were summoned, when they had to be totally on. Not adrenaline management that most cops could handle. At least the marines, or Mossad, got to train full-time.

Van was in the required state of mind—mind off, reflexes totally on—when they radioed for him at Command.

•

He assumed it was some kind of spontaneous promotion, because he was the trusted right-hand man to Mark, the SWAT commander: some significant role in the takedown. Tomorrow they'd be drinking beer together on a boat. Instead, it was like being called to the principal's office in seventh grade.

In the RV, the incident commander and Mark didn't even offer him a seat. They pointed to a picture of Crystal on the feed. She was disheveled, her expression crazed, wearing a wedding dress that revealed a lot of heaving cleavage. "Know her?"

Van nodded yes, cautiously. "She's getting married?"

"She's not the bride," the IC said. "She's the HT. And she's here for you."

"No way," Van said.

"Yes way," the female negotiator said, as if this were a clever retort.

"This one's for you, bud," the IC said.

"You must be one fuck of a fuck," Mark said. His tone was jocular—but with an edge that Van wasn't used to hearing about his romantic exploits. Of course, it was probably for the older, married, paunchy IC's benefit, and for the female negotiator, who eyed him with a carefully neutral expression that barely hid her disapproval.

Once they gave Van a second to process that the siege had been staged for his benefit, this whole production and the lives of strangers threatened just so she could get the soulful goodbye he'd denied her, they asked him what Van could tell them about their HT. How long ago did he see her and how seriously?

"A while ago," Van said, and so casually that, he added, he didn't know her last name.

Because of the presence of the female negotiator, he couldn't talk about Crystal the way he would in a room of men. He remembered freckles. The freckles went right up to the aureoles of her cheerful tits, then stopped. He remembered a reddish bush and the noises she made when she came. If you blindfolded Van McCormick and played him tapes of all the women he had ever drilled, he believed he could match each orgasm with a body. The squeakers and the opera singers. The eye-before-the-storm ones who got quieter beforehand. He thought he was both passionate and scientific about sex. Almost . . . ornithological.

"You let her down easy," the IC asked, "or just hurl her off the cliff?"

Van admitted that she did seem to think they had more of a thing going than he did, but in his experience, that could happen with women.

"And how long have you been seeing Amanda?" the negotiator asked.

Without time to plot it out or totally swallow his surprise, Van demurred. He mumbled a vague answer.

"Do Amanda and Crystal know each other? Have they met?"

"Why don't you let me at her," Van offered. "I'm sure I can talk her down."

"Oh, it's you she wants all right," Mark said.

Van tried to reconstruct how he'd ended things with her. He assumed unceremoniously. Then he remembered. She'd joined his gym, which he took as a threatening invasion of privacy. An image of her all dolled up to slowly lift some minuscule dumbbells, examining herself in the mirror the whole time as if her abs were sculpted and glistening enough for an infomercial: now he couldn't recall if he saw this himself or if someone just told him. He felt he remembered waving off the taunts of the guys—*Is this the one, McCormick? You renting a tux?*

He never promised her anything. He was only in it for the tail, and if she said any different, she was a liar.

"Son," the IC said wearily, "you ought to stop driving the motor with the choke wide open."

And then they roughly banished him, saying they might call him back.

•

At the station, the first people he saw were two blond badge bunnies he'd screwed ages ago. "Hi, Van!" they twinkled in sync, waving. About one of these women, the main thing he remembered was that her fingernails always had entire little pictures painted on them, American flags or palm trees. Van had once joked that the women were so stupid, the entire contents of their brains could fit on their nails. About the other, there was a famous story.

At another PD, she had talked an officer into having sex with her in a detaining cell. She'd be quiet, she promised, she just couldn't wait, the officer in question was just too sizzling hot. Then she vamped it up for the hidden cameras, playing with her own boobs and throwing her head back to howl like a werewolf at the moon. The cameras weren't on, actually—they generally ran only when bad guys were in custody, so if a suspect claimed police brutality, it could be proven no one shoved a broom up his ass. But the story got around. Who told it to Van? Pete? Joey? Joey assumed it was apocryphal, but when the woman made the same proposition to him, he admitted he was spooked. He took it as a sign. Now Joey—who, if Van remembered correctly, had also done Crystal—was engaged to a nurse he didn't even kiss until their second date.

And here Joey was, suddenly.

"What are *they* doing here?" Van asked him.

Joey explained that the women had been alerted about the siege by the same police scanners that tipped off the news stations. They habitually listened to the scanners, to divine when the cops were getting off work and at which watering holes they might be found. The women had joined the crowd of spectators now assembled at the outer perimeter to pray, on camera, for the safety of the men in blue. Once SWAT learned that Crystal was their barricaded subject, the detectives had thought to interview the cop groupies; Joey, deputized to find them, had recognized them in the crowd and escorted them back to the PD. Although the women didn't know much about

Crystal, short of finding her stuck-up, they certainly weren't going to keep quiet about what they'd been asked, so they were detained at the station, "for their own safety."

Now Van himself was interrogated by a detective for any useful information about their HT. Who is in her life? A mother, a sister? Are they close? Does she have a pet? Is she on drugs? What kind of booze does she drink? What kind of weapons does she own? How good is her shot? What are her politics? Her religious beliefs? As if he would know! Is she depressed? Violent? Then, bizarrely: Did Van itch at all? Anywhere?

Obviously, he would no longer be part of the entry team for the largest SWAT event in Haddonfield history. He wondered if the men in the bus had already been told about Crystal. He wondered if Amanda already knew. Word would get around fast. He called her cell but got no answer.

It couldn't be the first time in his life that Van had gotten a woman's answering machine, that the woman wasn't waiting phone-side for his call. But Amanda's simple, old-fashioned ring tone, then her calm voice on her message, the voice he'd listened to her use to talk down an utterly psychotic suicidal subject six months before, seemed like a rebuke.

That's when he knew. Here was the mythical maturity that everyone warned was going to come over him when he hit forty.

He loved her.

*I*n Helen's great room, after the medical exigencies, the biggest problem was the children. They were desperately bored and whiny. They'd eaten their candy. They'd exhausted patty-cake and I spy. They'd made multiple trips to the curtained potty. "If she doesn't kill them," one hostage said, "I might."

Simon Burns found a stack of dusty board games in the cabinet under the TV and tried to engage his kids in Monopoly. His daughter got in the spirit. But his sons, raised on ever more lifelike video games, could not see the point of Monopoly. And the toddler with the torturous voice insisted joining the game. He kept upsetting the board, grabbing fistfuls of money. For a second Simon thought his older son was going to deck the gremlin. But then Miranda Mobley and Trevor Hunter sat cross-legged on the floor to join in, started making the tiny shoe game piece do a happy dance when they passed Go, doffing the little top hat, crying from behind prison bars, and all of the kids got much happier for the attention and distraction. Simon himself got happier, too. Even here, the actress had such grace about her, such a luminous combination of warmth and intensity.

Helen flushed with love for her son. Watching Simon with his children, she wondered whether his soon-to-be-ex-wife, if she were here now, would be able to see what a great father he was. He was all there, all in the moment, the hardest thing to be as a parent—to be, simply, present.

The Monopoly game was happening nearest to the family-room doors when they all heard the drill on the door.

After the expected screams, some assumed rescue, and gave a rejoicing cry. But Simon thought that a rescuer would have given them some warning. He stood, swept up his children, and tried to move them away from the door.

Now the HT stood before them at the open door, aiming the rifle.

She still wore the wedding dress with the ammo belt and the holster for the sawed-off shotgun, but not the gas mask or the veil. She was a tall woman, thirtyish, good-looking. Green eyes and high cheekbones. Slightly freckled.

"I'll take the kids," she said, "and anyone injured. And then I'm going to close the door back up. If anyone else tries to get through, they will be shot."

"Where are you taking them?" Simon asked.

"Out."

"We'll go with them," the ADHD toddler's mother said.

"No."

"How are the babies supposed to go on their own?" the nursing mother demanded.

"I'll take them."

"No," Mary Nathanson said.

"Come on. Chop-chop, before I change my mind. You," and she pointed to Simon's kids, "let's go, just go out and wait for me near the front door."

Simon just had time to touch his daughter's back before she and his two sons were gone.

Grief rose in him. Miranda took him around the shoulders and squeezed. The breezy lilac smell of her mixed with his terror. He couldn't believe how his children almost skipped out, oblivious to any danger. Absurdly, he flashed to the death of his childhood dog. His father had brought Simon along when they put the dog down, quite against Helen's vocal objections. Americans, Dr. Nathanson claimed, were too insulated from death. They didn't slaughter their own food, had never endured a war fought on their shores, and this had swaddled them from essential human understanding. Later, if there was a later, Simon would like to tell a woman he loved about stroking the dog's flank as the serum went in. If he were a method actor, all he'd have to do would be to think about that dog to bring himself to tears, and now the dead dog had grafted itself onto not only his parents' divorce, but perhaps the death of all three of his children.

Behind them, following his children, the squawking ADHD kid, his mother calling after him brokenheartedly, "Be a good boy, now!"

The two mothers came forward with their babies, buttressed by their husbands. The women and babies were crying; the husbands weren't. Although Jake Nathanson wore an expression that suggested his theoretical underpinnings had failed him.

The HT studied the babies appraisingly, the way you might consider a car trunk you were trying to pack. It was clear she couldn't juggle two babies and the rifle while also guarding the door against possible jailbreaks. "Just put them down there on the floor," she said, and she squatted twice to move them, one by one, outside, to the other side of the door.

Now Dr. Barrett presented her son, Theo.

"I'm not really a kid," Theo told the HT.

"He's eighteen," Sarah Barrett told the HT. "He has Asperger's syndrome."

"Eighteen and eight months," Theo said. "Closer to nineteen."

The HT said, "Off with you, Tin Man."

Theo asked his mother why the lady was calling him that.

"Go," Sarah Barrett enunciated. "Now. Theo. Go."

"Bye, Mom," Theo said. He had always been heartbreakingly obedient. He started to hug her, but the HT prodded him along with a gesture of the rifle.

Next Ira Needleman helped Sylvia to the door.

"I think you should take both of them," Sarah Barrett suggested to the HT. "He doesn't look too hot. Do you have high blood pressure?" she asked Ira, and when he nodded in the affirmative, the HT gestured for them both to leave. As Theo had, they stepped around the babies.

Helen watched as Sarah, who had been their chief medical responder through the siege—she knew as little about gunshot wounds as the gastroenterologist but was willing to put herself in the fray—rushed away from the door to collapse into the arms of her husband.

To Helen's astonishment, her mother, Agnes, had risen and hustled toward the door as well. It was hard to tell what the old woman understood. Sometimes she seemed to be in a cheerful fog; other times she seemed quite lucid. When Agnes arrived, she actually nodded and smiled, as if this were a reception line. The HT waved her through without so much as looking at her. Nor did Agnes look back at Helen, who felt awful about how little thought she had given to her mother.

Then Amy, holding up the injured hand for the HT's inspection. Amy gave a mournful glance back toward the remaining hostages.

Delbert Billips Jr. was the last to present himself, helped by his son and father. She told them to prop him by the front door and come right back. The HT took in his bloody shoulder and said, "Hey. Sorry about that." Delbert nodded faintly but did not look her in the face.

During these exchanges, Helen could see fatigue, but also determination and excitement, in the HT's expression. From her cheerful expectancy, and the fact that hostages were being released, Helen knew that negotiations were progressing.

Helen sidled up to the HT. She asked, in a confidential tone, "Is he here yet?"

The HT looked at her, surprised. "They say no."

Helen, with conviction: "I don't believe it."

"Me either. Why wouldn't he be?"

Helen: "Exactly."

Helen was close enough now to smell the HT's spicy perfume and hear the wedding dress rustle. She took in the spray-painted construction boots. Above the boots: Was the HT wearing *clown socks*? Yes! Helen got a glimpse of Ronald McDonald socks with big, blocky, horizontal red and white stripes, so as the HT swiveled with the rifle, when you spied the inch or two of ankle that used to be shocking on proper women in days of yore, the socks were what you saw. And on the HT's chest, glitter. Before she'd left in the morning and collected all her props—her cell-phone hat, her padlock, her rifle and handgun, her bomb, her strap-on bomb button—she'd put on these socks, and dusted herself with glitter powder.

The glitter gave Helen her idea. She couldn't have articulated what she understood but worked on instinct, the way a dog smells cancer.

Helen reminded the HT that they had the services of a professional photographer. Wouldn't it be a good idea to get some good portraits of her? Even with all she'd been through, Helen told the HT, she still looked great. But maybe she'd like to freshen up a bit. "Your lips," Helen said dolefully, "look a little chapped."

Helen hadn't consulted with Al about this plan, but assumed the war photographer would be game. Al, who had been shooting pictures of the hostage release, got closer to nod his concurrence.

In a small voice, Miranda said, "I can do your makeup if you like."

"No, Miranda," Sal Billips said.

The HT said she had to deal with the released hostages first. She'd get back to them, she promised, then slammed the door.

The front door to Helen's house opened just enough for Crystal to thrust the howling infants out, one by one. Each stopped crying, magically, the second he touched down. Perhaps the change in air temperature, or the interesting prickliness of the welcome mat. The babies just looked at the sky, sucked on their fists, and cycled their legs a bit, biblically. One of the babies cranked up the sound effects again when fully armored SWAT personnel crash-landed to fetch him and hand him over to the EMTs. The other baby just stared at the gas mask of his rescuer.

Three of the remaining children were related, and from town. They were handed over to Heather (always the girl cop, thus always her), who had been returned to deal with the restless crowd of spectators. On a hunch, Heather walked them all down to see if the mother was part of the crowd there.

Joan Nathanson had been weeping piteously at the barricade since news of the siege first got around. Her babies were in that house. Every other weekend, when she turned her children over to Simon, she felt wrenched. Now Joan's joyful reunion with her three photogenic children, the girl still sporting her flower girl headdress, in a group that included what anyone watching would assume was the father but was actually the man she had left the father for, was nationally broadcast.

So was Amy's emotional reunion with her father. He, too, had been drawn to the scene by the news reports. When he told one of the cops that a crazy ex had been stalking his daughter, and that she was in the house, they'd escorted him to the station to be interviewed for possible links to the catering company break-in that they'd learned about from Crystal. The detectives tried to detain him as well, but unlike the groupies, he seemed to know that they couldn't do this without cause or a protective custody warrant, so they released him with the warning that anything he mentioned about their questions, to anyone, would constitute obstruction of justice.

Amy held up her broken wrist for the news cameras and said, in a bravely wavering voice, that she did not plan to get any medical attention until she knew the fate of the other hostages. No one knew when the bomb was going to blow.

The press reacted with the expected excitement to the news of the bomb, until now kept from them.

In the RV, the nonplussed incident commander demanded, "Why am I watching our fucking hostages on TV talking to the press about bombs?"

The SWAT commander got on the radio to the hostage-escort officers to get an explanation for the mistake in egress. How in God's name had the press already gotten access to the hostages?

Nothing ever works exactly as planned at a hot scene. Of course they'd established separate areas for the press and the families of the hostages, but they'd corralled the two groups too close together. Now they established a different staging area where the released hostages could be debriefed. When they determined that the fourth kid's parents were both still inside, they sent Heather there with the squawking rug rat while they tried to rustle up a relative for him.

The detectives asked Amy if they could talk to her for a while. Her father accompanied her to the police station, and he was there when Amy's psycho ex arrived.

Kevin was a car mechanic. He had heard about the siege at work, but didn't know Amy was among the hostages. And then, suddenly, they came for him. They took him in his uniform, his name stitched on the pocket, his hands still covered with grease. When he passed

Amy's dad at the police station, the man boomed, "Fucker!" and arose from his chair as if to strike him. The father had to be restrained.

Crystal's mother was also taken to the station. She hadn't been watching the news. She seemed not distraught or worried but vaguely satisfied, as if this turn of events had confirmed some suspicion about her only child. She said that Crystal was moody, and had been a difficult child. She blamed much of the girl's emotional problems on her father, who left them when Crystal was five. Crystal was no longer living with her, and had barely visited. She noted that Crystal had always had trouble holding on to her men.

As a warm, trusting familial presence, the mother seemed not so useful. They did not plan to have the mother speak to the HT.

The psychiatrist they'd called in to consult believed that suicide by cop was indeed a real possibility, and deemed the HT's profile consistent with that of a stalker. Stalkers can hang on to their obsessions for years, even decades. The source, he said, was often a "grandiosely elaborated and distorted childhood abandonment fantasy." He encouraged them to find the HT's absent father.

The father, they learned, was in the employ of a private security company in Saudi Arabia. But this wasn't Waco, and they didn't have the budget for international private planes. They failed to get him on the phone.

The negotiator told Crystal that if she let more people out, by then they would be set up to let her talk to Van. He was on his way. Yes, it was taking him forever! Maybe beach traffic . . .

"Beach traffic?" Crystal said with contempt. "On a Saturday night?"

She announced that no one was going until Van talked to her personally, Van and Little Miss Negotiator. Word came through Communications to the entry team that she was losing patience. And then refusing to answer the phone.

The incident commander, begging into Helen's answering machine, had to play good cop to get her back on the line. For all her purported feminism, Crystal seemed delighted to finally be in touch with the real, male boss.

He let Crystal know that he personally was very interested in her story. Van could be subjected to a Psychological Fitness for Duty exam.

"You'll just cover for him," Crystal said.

"Not true," he assured her. Contrary to what Crystal might think, police culture had changed. Van would lose respect for disrespecting women. If Crystal cooperated, the extenuating circumstances would certainly be noted. Yes, Van was coming, but the detectives had to interview him first. While that was happening—well, Crystal had released twelve hostages. But was she sure all the other people were all right? Had they eaten? Did they have water? Did she think she could release some women?

They had finally found Van. He was on his way. As soon as the detectives finished with him, they would arrange a safe place for him and Crystal to talk. Obviously, they explained, that couldn't happen until they had the hostages—and, they did not add, had made at least a good-faith effort to keep her from blowing her own brains out.

Without Van, the door-kickers back in the bus had continued preparing. They did scenarios of their best entry method first on paper, then practiced on the street, marking their moves with kids' chalk. Doors were easiest, of course. SWAT could breach any door. They could break and rake any window. Their plan was to create a distraction at the opposite end of the house, away from the hostages. They'd throw flash bangs and do double entry—one team for the hostages, a team for her, and, if need be, a no-fail mission to take the bitch out.

At this point, the tactical team didn't know the identity of their barricaded subject. They only knew she was an armed woman in a wedding dress. Once they knew her sex, they referred to her as *bitch*. Other than their nickname for her, there was little foul language in the stack. There was little talk of any kind. It was almost dark outside now. As they sat on the rehab bus, their thought processes started to narrow. The HT no longer seemed human to them, certainly not female, but the thick black outline of the head and heart they'd be aiming for, the Coke-bottle shape on their practice targets. The negotiators would blather until dawn if they had their way, but SWAT had to be ready for the moment when they were told that they were going in and the bitch was going down. *It's Coke-bottle time. She's a Coke bottle.*

*W*ithout Theo, the children, and the babies, the hostages' room was blessedly calmer. The sun had set but the sky was still light. The HT poked her head through the intercom grate.

"Anyone else want to leave?" she asked. "I'll take five more people. You, and you—" Here she pointed to Helen, and Al. "I'll take you up on the photo op. And the makeup. Decide who's out. I'll be back in a minute."

The hostages conferred. No one challenged the idea of women first as too retro or sexist. The first four choices were easy: the two mothers of infants, the ADHD boy's valiant mom, Dr. Sarah Barrett. But the fifth? The tax attorney's wife had children at home with a sitter. Several other women did, too, including the novelist Ben Kramer's wife, Britte, and the Chadian woman, Acta Adoulaye. If numbers counted, Acta's husband, Ngarta, said, she had four children, but Souleymane Samake, the man from Mali, countered in fast and furious French that he had six children at home for whom he was the sole support. Mara Lowell again objected to the privileging of breeders. How about the groom's grandmother, Delbert Sr.'s wife? How about the remaining senior or seniorish citizens, like Dr. Myra Feldstein? For that matter, how about the bride?

"I'm not leaving without Gabe," Tess averred.

"I'll stay with Delbert," said Delbert Sr.'s wife, her first words all night.

To Helen's surprise, the military man didn't contradict his wife. Perhaps he knew it would be pointless.

"And I'll stay with Zach," Mara Lowell said.

"I'll stay with my children," Sal Billips said.

"I'll stay, too," Sarah Barrett said. "We should have a doctor here."

"And a makeup person," Miranda said, smiling a bit.

"And a photographer's assistant," Al's girlfriend, Alyssa, said.

Al said, *"Go."*

Now, after some clumping by their captor in her big white boots, the door to the family room opened.

They had become inured enough to the sight of the HT aiming a rifle that this time they did not scream. Ken and Rick, two of the jailbreak boys, exchanged a pointed look to note that they did not hear the drill, that they had not been barricaded since the last hostage release.

At the HT's feet, behind her, was one of the caterers' trays of food, and a shrink-wrapped pack of bottles of warm spring water from Helen's garage. And three bottles of champagne. "You," she said, pointing to Ken, "carry that in."

Everyone watched him as he complied.

"All right, who wants out? Line on up."

The hostages formed a queue such as kindergartners do to leave the classroom for recess. Except there were more than five. The HT laughed, waving them through with instructions for them to wait for her at the front door. As they noted her generous mood, several more women hustled forth.

Gone now: Mary Nathanson. The nursing mother, Allison Piccollo. The ADHD mother, Madison Matthews. Acta Adoulaye. Jennifer Needleman, the wife of the groom's second cousin. The shrink Myra Feldstein; the shrink Sam Gold's wife, Lucy; and the gastroenterologist Richard Silver's wife, Donna. Arden Thomas of the extremely small bladder. Maddie from MSF. Cyndi, the wife from the catering team, and the three other female waitstaff besides Amy. Reluctantly, pushed by the photographer, Alyssa Waters. Then Britte Jorgenson Kramer. And behind her, the only male, her husband, Ben Kramer.

"My nose is broken," the novelist said, in his own defense.

Alan had been quietly packing up his photographic equipment in the case. Wordlessly, he, Miranda Mobley, and Helen Burns followed the HT out of the room.

Once the door closed, it was finally, incontrovertibly dark. Simon found the light switch and fiddled with the dimmers.

"Why did Miranda have to go?" Sal asked her son.

"She'll be all right," Gabe reassured her. "She's curious. Boning up. Character study, in case she gets to play Loony Tunes in the film version."

"She's brave," Simon averred. "Have you noticed the women here have more balls than the men?"

The HT had not brought silverware, but the grilled chicken breasts, because they were cold now, unsauced, and a bit dry, were not too difficult to eat with just hands. With those hostages gone, there was enough to go around. Enough water, too. The room felt twice the size. They ate and drank quietly, with great relief.

"It won't be long now," Delbert Sr. said.

"Amen to that," Ken said, as he expertly popped the cork on a bottle of champagne. "Could anyone use a drink?"

Most of the hostages declined, preferring to keep their wits about them for what was to come. But Trevor Hunter was game for a swig. The young men began to pass around the bottle.

Lindsay and one of the Madisons, two of the single women still left in the room, joined the single men for a drink. The men scooched over so the women could squeeze between then, backs against the wall, legs straight before them. The women took off their high-heeled sandals, amazed that they hadn't done so before now. They flexed their feet, admired their wedding pedicures, and let their toes breathe. The Cava was perfectly chilled, the bottle dripping as if it had just been pulled from the ice.

Most of the hostages were not Doctors Without Borders people. But some were New Yorkers. All the New Yorkers carried a shadow of 9/11, a sense of both the horror of all the paper and people fluttering down in slow motion, and everyone's courage, the urban wartime bonhomie, like London during the air raids. The long lines of volunteers grimly sifting through buckets of debris. The men walking home over the Brooklyn Bridge with their briefcases, their hair covered in ash.

Thinking of ash, Tess got a flash of something she had once seen somewhere—the British Museum? The Met? A couple dead in a volcanic eruption, maybe Pompeii. Something—not the mummified Bog Man's magic peat, but a special quality of the spot where they fell, like one of those crevices in which, some impossible number of days later, a child was found alive after the earthquake in Haiti— preserved their bodies. When their remains were found, the bodies were entwined. Maybe they'd been asleep. But maybe they'd had a moment of consciousness to reach for each other as the debris engulfed them.

If asked to choose between prolonged and painful decline or sudden death, almost everyone would pick sudden death. But their situation, Tess thought, was the worst of both worlds: endlessly waiting for sudden death. At least she wasn't alone, though. She clung to Gabriel. If they were shot or blown up, they'd die together, and then she remembered: the molten-lava lovers might be resting in peace right across the Ben Franklin Bridge, at the University of Pennsylvania Museum of Archaeology and Anthropology.

Why think of such a thing right now? Tess chided herself. Except she was thinking about her beloved, too. After the honeymoon, if they lived and had a honeymoon, they could go and visit the volcano couple. Tess imagined herself hugely pregnant, peering into the mummy cases.

She leaned into Gabe's neck and whispered: "Let's get married."

*B*efore they could set up the photo shoot, a call came through. Helen, Miranda, and Al followed the HT to the kitchen so she could answer. On the counters, trays of food for sixty. Veggies and dip! Salmon! "Do you mind?" Al was bold enough to gesture to her, and when she nodded her consent, he and the actress started popping hors d'oeuvres into their mouths. They took turns bending their heads to the sink to swill down the food with tap water. Then dug into the salmon with their fingers.

For a while, Crystal would not answer the phone. Helen watched the HT's face. She looked like any scorned woman proudly declining contact.

Eventually Crystal said, to Helen, "You get it."

"Who are you? Are you all right? How is everyone else? Can I speak to her, please?" the negotiator asked Helen, but Crystal shook her head.

"Tell her Van would like to meet with her in person," the negotiator said. "He has finally arrived."

Helen passed this on, then reported back, "She says Van has to tell her this himself."

They called back. A man asked to have the phone passed to the woman, whom he called Crystal. That was the first time Helen had heard the HT's name. "Crystal," she said, "it's him," and from Crystal's joyous face—a kid's joy, broad and untrammeled—as she listened to the voice on the other end, Helen could tell she had finally been united with the object of her affection.

"Crystal," he said, loudly enough for Helen to hear. "They'll only give me a second. How are you?"

She didn't answer.

"We need to talk in person," he said. "And privately."

"What about Amanda?"

"I'm not concerned about her," Van said. "I'm thinking about you. When can I see you?"

Crystal informed him, blandly, that she'd let him know.

Which, like everything else so far, didn't make a lot of sense, if the conversation with Van was precisely what she'd been awaiting.

On the live feed, the team in the RV watched, mystified, as the foursome went back to the easy chair in the living room carrying the phone. An older woman, a man who must have been the wedding photographer, and what they thought was the famous actress whose presence in town they'd been alerted to were moving around a big chair and lighting equipment. The HT sat on the chair while the photographer took readings, made adjustments. Then the older woman and the actress began to fuss with her. The older woman brushed her hair. The actress crouched in front of the HT and applied makeup, some of it obtained by rummaging through what looked like a big trash bag full of women's purses that they dumped out on a couch.

The HT seemed to be interacting with her three attendants quite reasonably, even smiling at points, her rifle in her lap. The actress gave the HT stage makeup to be read from a distance. Eyeliner. Big, bold red lipstick.

They took pictures for a good long time. The HT in close-up, with and without the veil, pensive or provocative. The HT relaxing in the chair with her wedding dress hiked up to her knees to reveal striped socks and her big white boots on a hassock, her hand resting on top of the rifle as if it were a walking cane. The HT standing for a traditional wedding pose, with a bouquet of flowers that the older woman fetched from another room. The HT with her hands on her

ammo belt like a gunslinger. Then the HT aiming the rifle, in a posture that reminded those old enough to remember of Patty Hearst
during her stint with the Symbionese Liberation Army.

The photographer had asked her to remove the box on her arm
for the photos, and she'd complied. But after the shoot, she'd reat-
tached it. There was a blinking green button, like the one on a surge
protector strip, but, enlarging it on the TV screens, the bomb squad
could see no detonator. Perhaps the detonator was on her belt clip.

Crystal sat upright in her chair in her Cleopatra makeup, her arms
Sphinx-like on the arm rests. Miranda Mobley and Helen Burns at-
tended to her, like the Egyptian queen's handmaidens, while Alan
Smith continued to shoot. When she took the next phone call, the
HT's expression was so serious, she could have been the president
discussing troop withdrawal.

The HT had leaned her rifle up against an end table. It's true she
still had the shotgun on her belt, but would she really have reached
for it if they aimed the rifle? They could have disarmed her. But they
did not.

Listening to only one side of the conversation, Helen understood
much of what the negotiator said from the context. The negotiator's
voice wafted from the phone, and Helen was impressed with the
rhythm and pitch of her speech. The woman had found the exactly
right tone of calm, concerned respect to explain to Crystal why all the
hostages had to go first. Then Crystal and Van could talk—either
alone, or in front of witnesses, or both.

There was the matter of the bomb. Crystal now revealed that it
was a fake bomb, merely decorative, like one of those hollowed-out
books in which you can store jewelry to foil a robber. What did you
make it from? the negotiator asked. Crystal asked why it mattered.
They asked her about the flashing box on her arm and she said it was a
dummy, too, just a blinking light. Here, she said, as she walked into
the kitchen and showily stepped on the foot pedal that opened the lid

of Helen's trash can, dumped it in. Though the negotiator couldn't see that, in the kitchen.

There was a whole protocol of *how* Crystal had to leave the house. First off, she couldn't wear any clothes. She could hide a weapon in her clothes. Just her panties. How about her bra? Crystal said. The negotiator said she could hide a weapon in her bra. No one would see her, the negotiator promised, and they would be ready with a robe.

"Where is Van now?" Crystal asked.

In one of the vans, no pun intended, with the detectives.

And Amanda?

In another van, with other detectives.

Crystal said that the bra was nonnegotiable, and she was going to keep one of the women. They could have the actress, but she would keep the older lady. And her bra. Then she hung up, smiling, which Helen took to mean she'd anticipated the issue of nakedness.

"You get used to it," Miranda told her, meaning nudity. "After a while it doesn't faze you at all."

Crystal studied Miranda. "You're really pretty," she said.

"Thank you. You're quite beautiful yourself."

"And you," Crystal said to Helen. "You're really nice."

"Thanks," Helen said.

"She *is* nice, isn't she?" Miranda said.

"You ought to lock your doors in the future, though," Crystal said, and they all grinned.

"Ladies," Al said. "Group hug."

He lined them up for the most traditional of wedding photos, Crystal in the middle of the two women, one arm around each of them. To do this, he very quietly relieved her of her rifle, moving it out of the shot.

"Are you sure you like that guy?" Crystal asked Miranda. Meaning Trevor. "He seems quite full of himself."

"He's sweet when you get to know him."

"You can do better," Crystal averred.

Miranda gave Helen the subtlest of head-tilt inquiries to see if she should engage in some female bonding about how awful men can be, and Helen's small head shake to the negative back at her meant *Let it go.* Let the negotiator do the negotiating.

That's when Crystal noticed she no longer had her rifle.

"Think they'll let you keep your gun belt on with your underwear?" Miranda asked.

"That'd be a look," Crystal agreed.

And then she took off the bullet belt, laid it on the kitchen counter, and rubbed her hands together in a let's-get-this-show-on-the-road gesture.

That is how Helen, Miranda, and Alan disarmed the HT. Textbook hostage negotiation technique: distract, defuse.

Anticlimactic, but anticlimactic is exactly what you're after with a barricaded subject.

The release of the rest of the hostages would prove to be similarly undramatic.

Without their wives or girlfriends to grandstand for or be solicitous about, many of the men in the room had become withdrawn, sullen. The difference in the shrinks was most pronounced. They now seemed not middle-aged but downright elderly. With the women gone, the men were less embarrassed to urinate. The men's streams, like the hostage event to this point, went on and on, halting and sputtering, then starting up again.

The skinny bartender who had long ago thrown his lot in with the brave young men now revealed to them that he had read a lot of survivalist books. How to make water clean enough to drink, things you should have in a kit if there's a major breakdown of civilization. If there's an intruder in your house and you don't have a weapon, the bartender said, you can use a book for a chin jab and smash. The young men agreed in low tones that, whatever the old army guy said, they should be prepared to act. They went to the shelves to select the heaviest book that wasn't too large to wield under a chin. When Billips Sr. finally went to the bathroom, his first trip in their entire confinement, he stayed long enough for the bartender to faux-demonstrate.

With the HT occupied, Command sent men around the side of the house to get a throw phone to the remaining hostages through the shattered window glass. The hostages would soon get another call, and should exit with their hands in the air. They should not be alarmed by this instruction. It was pro forma.

The drinking party had made their way through two of the three bottles of champagne and were getting boisterously happy about their imminent rescue. They were about to pop the third when Gabe said, "Save that one for the ceremony."

*M*ali, Gabe told the remaining guests, is one of the poorest countries in the world. Average life expectancy is forty-five. There are eighteen thousand people for every doctor. But each year, on September 22, Malians celebrate their independence from France. One of the most beautiful traditions is the Malian Horsemen: the Sòmonò masquerade of Soden Mali la. A canoe floats down the Niger River and the troupe on board performs a masquerade for the joyful people lining the banks. They have horse puppets—wooden puppets on long rods. Simple, rugged, but strangely expressive. Gabe's company sold the puppets in the United States, and while they didn't expect to overtake Toys "R" Us, any American child who had a Malian rod puppet of a buffalo or lion in his bedroom had a talisman to keep all bogeymen away, not to mention giving his parents the satisfaction of feeding an African child rather than enslaving a Chinese one in a toy factory.

"Floating theater," Tess said. "So cool."

"Kind of like a mummer's parade," Gabe said, "but with water."

"That's what we wished our wedding could be like," Tess said. "Just take a ride down the river and let people know 'We're hitched,' the way Soden Lali Ia means 'We're free.'"

Tess and Gabe had already filled out the marriage license in front of a judge in the state of New York. This ceremony was just to "solemnize" things, although, if solemnity was the goal, they'd certainly chosen the wrong officiant. Their friend Kenny Schmidt was a cutup with a jock's booming voice. He'd already alerted everyone to the online provenance of his minister's license.

"I just wish my mother were here," Tess said.

"I'm here for you," Jake Nathanson said, his voice choking as he tried to load that line with its full implication.

Salome Billips approached the bride and groom, took one of each of their hands, and said with her eyes that she'd do her best to stand in, as motherly presence. Her eyes were already welling.

"If anyone else cries at weddings," Gabe warned, "just know, we're flat out of Kleenex. Have to use the backs of your hands."

"You want a shirt," someone asked the groom, "or are you going for the male stripper look?"

Everyone laughed a bit. They'd forgotten to notice that the groom was still bare-chested. For a while he'd worn his jacket, but it had gotten too hot. One of his friends quickly took off his jacket, unbuttoned his own shirt, and handed it over. Gabe thanked him.

"Too bad the photographer isn't here," someone noted.

"That's okay," Tess said. "We don't plan to get live footage of childbirth, either."

But then there was a very light knock on the door and Alan said, "It's me." He entered with his camera in one hand—and, oddly, the HT's rifle in the other. His flash equipment under one arm. He had what Tess and Gabe recognized as his war photography face on. Fear, excitement, focus.

"I only have a second," he said. "But I thought you might want a picture. Hold this," and he handed the rifle to the bartender.

The bartender held the rifle awkwardly, not quite sure what to do with it. Providentially, Colonel Billips Sr. was right behind him, and wordlessly took it.

Someone whistled a couple of bars of "Here Comes the Bride." Ngarta Adoulaye, a drummer (he had brought a traditional kodjo drum from Chad, to use as part of the wedding music ensemble and as a gift for the bride and groom), banged out a couple of bars of "La Tchadienne" on the wall behind him.

At this, both Tess and Gabe smiled. In the photos, the luminous couple would seem to be emerging from the darkness like saints, the faces of the people behind them shrouded, ghostly.

"I had a whole speech planned here," Ken said, and, as evidence, produced a folded square from his breast pocket. "But you'll be relieved to hear I don't think there's time for my speech. Tess, Gabe," Ken said, "so as not to belabor the point, with the power vested in me by universal ministries dot com, I now pronounce you man and wife. Or, so as not to be sexist, woman and husband. Tess, you may kiss the groom."

If you've been to enough weddings, the kiss varieties become codified. There's the lusty, we-don't-care-that-we-have-an-audience-we-can't-wait-until-later kiss. There's the gentle, bashful, let's-wait-until-we-draw-the-curtain-to-do-the-real-thing kiss, although these days the tentative pecks more often sequence into a deeper meeting of souls and tongues as the guests' roar of approval swells. Because isn't that the party line about marriage—that it will bring you both passion and tenderness? No one, getting wed, ever imagines that their union will deny them both and bury them, instead, in coldness and contempt. The guests applaud both from joy for the couple and relief at being released from the ceremony. They applaud the sweet myth that you can blend in as a good foot soldier of your culture, a homeowner and consumer and raiser of children, and still stand out as "your own person." They applaud the poignancy of living in time, of not knowing what will happen to you, not thinking about failure or grief or old age or death. Mostly they applaud the spectacle of hope itself.

Tess and Gabe kissed like people who had kissed before, and would kiss again. Like the bride and groom themselves, the kiss seemed sane, mature, also rather wistful, haunted by what both of them had witnessed, growing up, about the darker side of family life. The kiss of old souls. For the duration of that kiss, none of the remaining wedding guests entertained any thought that either could be with anyone but the other. That's all you can hope for, finally, and it's probably enough.

*A*lan went back into the hallway with his camera, and so quickly that it almost seemed like punctuation for the ceremony itself, without time to even open the last bottle of champagne, the hostages were instructed by throw phone to exit the room, hands up. Billips Sr. told them that oddly, he had the rifle now. What should he do with it? He was told to exit first, after thrusting out the weapon. The bartender positioned himself by the door, fully prepared to hit the HT under the chin with the dictionary should she enter shooting, but it was Miranda, not the HT, who opened the door for them, and Helen who was manning, or womanning, the front door, with Alan set up in the hallway to document the endgame. Which meant that no one was with the HT. She could presumably come from the kitchen with her shotgun.

The hostages didn't rush the door. When they got the phone call, those who were sitting stood and stretched. Many had been standing anyway, for the ceremony.

They had been there about exactly as long as they would have been there if there had been a wedding with drinks, dinner, cake, and dancing.

Tess and Gabe went last.

Contrary to instructions, each of them had only one hand in the air. The other hands, the ones between them, were joined.

$\mathcal{W}$hich left only Crystal and Helen.

Crystal still insisted on wearing the bra out of the house. She also insisted on keeping Helen. She wanted Helen to walk her out, and she wanted Van to be waiting for her within sight in the inner perimeter, not the outer perimeter. None of this was negotiable. They weren't going to let her use a hostage as a shield. She would get to see Van, but she had to be disarmed first. They didn't want her to hide the detonator in her bra. But as she pointed out to them, she could hide the detonator in her underwear. Look at Umar Farouk Abdulmutallab, the "Jockstrap Jihadist." Forget underwear; she could actually hide the detonator *in her vagina*.

They were displeased that she knew this. You could have a bomb in your rectum or vagina, with a short length of bridge wire protruding that could be detonated via a solid-pack electrical-type blasting cap. Some of the terrorists now were even experimenting with having detonators surgically implanted. Conceivably, she could have a detonator implanted in her breast—the wire coming out right through a hole in her nipple, as tiny and inconspicuous as the wick on a birthday candle.

More and more, they were thinking that there must be a collaborator on the outside. They were extremely interested in Kevin, the grease monkey suspected of the second break-in at the catering company.

Because of the power of the Terrorism Joint Task Force, they had immediate access to both Crystal's and Kevin's computers. It would take some time to scour the hard drives for bomb-making instructions, credit card bills for fertilizer or *The Anarchist's Cookbook*, catering company schedules, weddings, death by stoning. Meanwhile, the negotiator asked Crystal, apropos of nothing in particular, "What do you think of the war in Iraq?"

"I think it sucks," Crystal said. "Why?"

Indeed. Helen wondered: Was the negotiator stalling for time? She couldn't possibly think that this siege had anything to do with politics. Helen's opinion was that Crystal just really, really, really wanted to talk to Van.

And "Amanda." Crystal said Van's current girlfriend's name as if it were a piece of gristle stuck in her throat.

"Do you know Kevin Jackson?" the negotiator asked.

At the police station, detectives were giving Kevin a full body-cavity strip search to make sure he had no detonators, documenting it by camera to prove that the search had been done respectfully.

Crystal did not know the name. Why? Was that someone else Amanda was dating? Her ex-husband?

The more Crystal spoke about Amanda, the more agitated she got. Although the phone was cordless, she and Helen had stayed in the kitchen, with only occasional forays to the front of the house to make sure there wasn't any new activity on the street. At any point, Helen could have grabbed the bullet belt with the sawed-off shotgun on the counter. But she did not. Even if she knew how to use a gun, she couldn't shoot Crystal, or even threaten her. Crystal trusted her, which was why the gun was there to begin with.

It took a long time, but eventually a surrender procedure was agreed upon. Helen would crack the front door and throw out the remaining gun. Once that was fetched, Helen would leave. They would search her person. She would check that the arrangements the negotiator said had been made were in fact in place—see Van waiting in his van, and Amanda waiting in hers. She would call Crystal to confirm. Then Crystal would come out, in her underpants, but bare-breasted. The snipers at the front of the house would be the only

witnesses to her nakedness. She should understand there would be
snipers, and follow their commands exactly as delivered. They would
disable the cameras, so the surrender could not show up later on
YouTube.

And then, at last, she could talk to Van.

Amanda was secondary, but Amanda would be made to wait on
the scene as long as it took. And Crystal said it might take a good
long while. She had a lot to say.

The last thing Helen did before leaving the house was unbutton Crystal's dress in the back. That processional of small pearl buttons, each with its own silk loop.

"Still can't believe you managed to get yourself into this," she said, not meaning it metaphorically.

The eerie intimacy of it, Helen's hands on the woman's freckled back. Crystal shaking perceptibly, her shoulder blades drawn up and tense.

Crystal stepped out of the dress. It fell in a white puddle in the hallway. She still had on the spray-painted boots. She reached down to unlace the boots and took them off the way a child does, stepping on the backs. Then her striped socks, which she threw on top of the wedding dress with a parodic twirl of her arm, like a stripper.

Helen noted the clash of sexual messages. The burlesque brashness, and beneath that, childish innocence. Of course, innocence can be sexual, too. Whores dressed up as schoolgirls with pigtails.

Crystal in her bra and panties, spinning around for inspection.

Her undergarments were nothing special—not thongs, not transparent or lace, no bells or whistles. Clean, though. White. Her body great.

"I wish you luck," Helen said. "I hope you get what you need from this man. I really do."

Bright-eyed, Crystal nodded, then embraced the older woman shyly. "Thanks," she said.

"You'll be all right," Helen promised her. "I really believe that."

Crystal nodded agreement into Helen's neck.

When the reporters demanded, later, what she'd said in those last moments, Helen could honestly reveal, "Not much." She'd tried to pack meaning into the hug, though.

Before she left her own house, Helen was aware of the fact that behind her, Crystal had already taken off her bra and was standing in front of the door, her posture ramrod-straight as a soldier's.

*S*imon's ex-wife hadn't let his children stay at the barricade to find out if their father was all right. To the kids the whole scene seemed festive, like a block party, so they were disappointed. Joan and her boyfriend took them straight home. But she didn't make them go straight to bed. Once they were in their pajamas, she made them hot dogs, then hot buttered popcorn, and let them stay up to watch the hostage drama on TV. She couldn't stop crying or kissing them as they watched. Over and over, they watched themselves reunite, the children and their crying mother and her boyfriend in a football huddle, the cameras in a swooning tight shot on the flower girl with the bright blond ringlets.

Over the days that followed, Simon, too, would witness this footage repeatedly: his children running into the arms of their mother and her paramour. If he'd died in that room, his kids would have been fine with his replacement. Joan must have been very sorry, in fact, that he hadn't died.

There was no television coverage of Simon staggering out of the house.

He came out with Miranda and Trevor, and the police started to wave them down. They were taking their names on a clipboard, taking some of them to talk to the incident commander in the trailer, and then corralling the rest through someone's huge backyard, where ambulances were parked, and tents set up, as for a wedding except the tents had stretchers rather than tables and chairs.

Simon doubled over, breathing hard, then started to chokingly sob. An EMT approached him, put her hand on his arm, and asked if he was all right.

So did Miranda, but soon Miranda and Trevor were separated from him. They wanted to talk to Miranda at Command—not because she was famous, but because they knew she'd spent time with the HT.

Miranda and Trevor would split up in a different way shortly thereafter, when Trevor reunited with his last girlfriend. Trevor and Ruth would marry, then divorce, then get back together again—both, in between, having love affairs with other actors. Miranda was always warm to Simon when she saw him at family gatherings—at his grandmother's funeral, at Tess's baby shower, at the hospital after the birth of Tess and Gabe's baby girl—but she was always hot and heavy with some actor or director. Eventually she married one of them. Unlike Loony Tina, who would remain "loyal" to Trevor throughout the vicissitudes of his marriages to Ruth, Simon was not delusional. He didn't think that Miranda was going to fall in love with an ordinary Joe. Miranda and Trevor both declined to play themselves in the film version of the hostage story, which never got made—not because Miranda and Trevor declined to play themselves, but simply because most things don't get made. (For a while Helen Mirren had been on tap to play Helen Burns, which pleased the latter Helen deeply.)

It was almost seven hours until the hostages were released. Quite efficient, for a hostage siege. But the hostages not brought to the hospital had to spend more time—up to two hours, for some of them—giving their names and addresses, being "debriefed," having their pulses taken, and drinking little plastic cups of orange juice. For some of the hostages, this was a bridge too far. One of the old psychiatrists noted that after Auschwitz was liberated, the Jews didn't exactly get to go home, either. Most people didn't know this, he said: the Jews then spent almost two years in Russian camps. The conditions were much better. Nevertheless, they were still prisoners. The gastroenterologist said that he didn't think their fates were at all similar, since at some point tonight they would be released to sleep in their own beds, and that the real issue with the modern world, as physicians knew better than anyone except maybe cops, was that everything required far, far too much paperwork.

Tess and Gabe quickly noticed that their African friends weren't among the group of released hostages, and were concerned. Where had they gone?

When Souleymane, Ngarta, and Acta were released from the house and saw the legions of policemen and ambulances, the two African men buried their differences and came to an immediate agreement. They needed to get out of there. Ngarta took Acta's hand, bidding her with his eyes to follow. They joined the line of hostages marching toward the staging area and began to look for the best opportunity to peel off. In their brightly colored African costumes, they were hardly inconspicuous, but they hid behind a tree and, in the chaos, no one noticed, or pursued them, as they took a ragged course through backyards until they were well clear of the outer perimeter.

It was almost midnight when they reached Haddonfield's main drag. The drugstore was closed, and the Starbucks. It was a very clean ghost town. They stood there panting, wondering what to do next.

Luckily, a gang of teenagers on skateboards appeared in a tsunami of noise, and Ngarta, whose English was better, called them over. "Whoah," one kid said, rearing back, and another gasped, "Pee-you." The Africans did not smell good. Not only had they been hostages for a long time without deodorant, but they'd run the whole way from Helen's house. Another skateboarder asked, "Are you selling?"

"Pardon me?" Ngarta said.

"What you got?"

Ngarta had no idea what the kid was talking about, but he did beg a half-full Gatorade from him, and get detailed instructions on how to take the train back to Philadelphia.

They missed one train, trying to figure out how to use the ticket machines, and the next train took a long time to arrive. But eventually a train did come, and they made it back to the city, where, only blocks from their hotel, they were mugged.

The black mugger was nice to them when he realized they were just visiting the City of Brotherly Love and didn't speak much English. "Hey, man, sorry," he said, but he still took all of their money.

"How could you do this to us after what we've been through?" Acta demanded angrily—the first thing she had said since she greeted the bride and groom at four o'clock in the afternoon. But she said it in French, and the mugger only shrugged apologetically and trotted off into the night with their wrinkled bills.

Luckily, most of their money was safe at the hotel, as well as their passports. The hotel had the most amazing beds.

They all had a week in the United States, where they had never been, and none of them planned to let this turn of events ruin their trips. In New York, Souleymane got to see his wife's handiwork for sale in a fancy shop. He and the couple from Chad would become friends, going to the top of the Empire State Building together, and the torch of the Statue of Liberty, and a jazz concert at the Blue Note.

Simon would bump into the EMT he met that night a year later, at the hospital. He was keeping his father company while Mary Nathanson had a lump in her breast biopsied. He and Jake had gone outside for some air, and the EMT had just dropped someone off at the emergency room. He was amazed that she remembered him. They dated for a while. But Simon was slow to recover from his marriage. He might never recover. A fuck buddy was fine; it is difficult, however, to keep a relationship at that point of perfect equipoise between not staying overnight and joint assets.

Mary's lump was in fact cancer. She did not have the BRCA1 gene. She just had exceptionally lousy luck. If there ever was a woman you'd think would choose a lumpectomy and breast reconstruction, it was Mary Nathanson. But she had a small son she wanted to see grow up, and she chose radical mastectomy. She died anyway, at age thirty-seven. Any ill will her husband's previous families might have felt about Mary vanished in genuine sympathy for the poor woman and for Jake Nathanson: at age sixty-six, Jake now found himself the sole parent of a toddler.

He had been phasing out his psychiatric practice to be with Mary during her decline, and now retired entirely so he could spend more time with Louis. He did not attempt to seduce the succulent young Salvadoran and Russian nannies. Nor did he seem interested in the age-appropriate widows, some of them quite attractive and prosperous, who found ways to be introduced to him. He was like a character from Dickens. He grew a big white beard. Now that he didn't practice psychiatry anymore, he finally looked like a psychiatrist. At his beach house with Louis, taking long walks at low tide to look for shells; in the city, getting tickets in advance—thinking of this by himself, acquiring the tickets himself—to take the kid to Cirque du Soleil when it was in town. Inviting Simon's kids as well. To Dr. Sarah Barrett's delight, finding things to do with Theodore, too, and not just so Theo could babysit.

Jake also reengaged vigorously with his own psychoanalysis. His cherished analyst was long ago retired but saw Jake as a special favor. It seemed clear to Jake that he had never dealt with mortality at all, not the deaths of his parents—he had just used sex to avoid thinking about death—and had no tools to deal with his grief about losing Mary or his fear of dying himself, alone. Unfortunately, his psychiatrist was now ninety-five, and died. It was too late to get another analyst, just as it was too late to remarry.

There was only one woman he really wanted anyway, and that was Helen Burns.

Jake thought constantly about—obsessed about, really—what would have happened if he had stayed the course with his first wife.

To wish that he had done so would be to wish that he had never experienced the intensely spiritual and sensual times he had enjoyed with both Sarah and Mary, to further wish that Theodore didn't exist, or Louis, and he couldn't wish any of that. But now it seemed as if he had missed the big, easy river of his life and swum upstream, instead, on a series of secondary and tertiary streams. He just wanted to hightail it back to the main tributary. (Best he could do with the nautical metaphors; he wasn't much of a yachtsman.)

Unfortunately that boat, too, had sailed. For, after decades of singlehood, Helen, to everyone's deep surprise, was in a serious relationship, with a younger man—a relationship that began the night of the hostage drama.

While they waited for the hostages to be released, Amy had told her father how wonderful Helen had been, how Helen had drawn her into the tent and kept her calm, how Helen seemed to be the only person who had the touch to talk to the hostage taker and had probably kept them all alive.

When Helen was finally released from the house, she was brought directly to a car to talk to a detective. She did not see any of the other hostages—her children, or her mother. Crystal left the house almost immediately, so Helen would not see what followed—there were no TVs in this van—but hear every word and groan, along with a kind of play-by-play on one of the radio channels. It would be so long before she was released that she was sure that her family would have left already. Her mother had indeed been escorted home, but Gabe and Tess had waited for her. And Simon.

And Amy.

Amy and her father lied to an officer at the family staging area. Amy said she was missing her mother. It's not like the officer was going to demand a birth certificate. Somehow Amy and her father wheedled themselves closer to the inner perimeter, and Amy spotted Helen just as she was being led out of the van. Amy squeezed her head between two police officers standing sentry to call her over. The

officers told Amy to get back to the family staging area and told
Helen that no, she had to go to the hostage area now, but Amy had
time to say, "This is Helen. Helen, this is my dad."

Amy's father leaned over the barricade to shake Helen's hand.
"Thank you, thank you so much," he said, and reached over the barricade to embrace her.

Then, bizarrely, he kissed her.

Helen would later calculate that she had not been kissed on the
lips in over sixteen years. That just wasn't right. She was postmeno-
pausal. At her annual checkup, her ob-gyn had asked her, as he did
every year, if she had pain during intercourse, and as she did every
year, Helen had just laughed. Evidently she would have a rough time
if she ever attempted intercourse again, because the insertion of the
speculum had really hurt. The ob-gyn told her that her vagina was
closing up, from lack of use. He had always been a proponent of use
it or lose it, vis-à-vis vaginas. Like a rusty lock or a window painted
shut, she'd thought. "I have geriatric patients," he related confidentially, "I try to get even a pinky in there they howl from the pain."

All that night, Helen would muse to Harry once they were lovers,
and for years in her practice, she had listened to stories of how people
met. Those first electric moments made mythical: people freeze-
framed them, as if they could find there the whole truth of the relationships that unfolded. Helen was suspicious of the theory that
beginnings contained the DNA of the future. Sometimes, sure. But
people change. And people are inclined to overread as foreshadowing
things that are often just chance, not meaningful at all.

Still. That first kiss, with Harry.

Harry also had not kissed a woman in quite some time, and didn't
plan to kiss anyone then, and didn't know, would never know, what
made him do it. Maybe just celebration and relief. Soldiers in Paris
after D-day, leaning down from their tanks to gather their flowers
and hugs.

Like Helen, Harry had been a single parent. His focus had
been on keeping the boat of his life with his daughter afloat. Fiscally,

logistically. He was exactly the same number of years younger than Helen (four) that Sarah Barrett's second husband was younger than she. His old dog was exactly the same age as Helen's old dog, and the dogs got along as easily and companionably as their owners. Harry's wife had also died very young, also of breast cancer. He was kind to Jake Nathanson. Thanksgiving at Jake's house, the place lousy with his ex-wives, children, and grandchildren, his wives' current men and the men's children by their first marriages: Jake had, at last, the kind of welcoming, nonjudgmental extended family that he used to only imagine he had.

In time to collect social security, Helen experienced pleasures she had not planned to see again, and she didn't just mean the sex, which, contrary to her ob-gyn's dire warnings, was more along the lines of once you know how to ride a bike, you don't forget—at least after the initial pain, almost as if she'd been restored to virginity. Getting dressed up for a wedding (Mara Lowell and her lawyer—Helen hadn't been able to make Mara's publication party) and having Harry say, eyes alive, "You look great." Watching out the window as a man you didn't have to pay for the service mowed the lawn, bringing him out a cold drink. The pleasures, in short, of living in her body again. Even a simple thing: grasping Harry's head with her hands around his temples, where his last remaining hair, a close-shaven silver bristle, glistened. Seeing her own strong hands do this.

They began to talk about whether Helen should sell her house, or Harry should sell his, or whether they should sell both houses, and buy a new place together. Or simply rent. She would miss only the garden if she left. There was no hurry to decide. In fact they savored the conversations. The word *future* now conjured up things other than decline and death—a European vacation, say. Helen had not been abroad since her honeymoon. And Harry, amazingly, had never been. He'd barely left New Jersey.

Would it be unreasonable to say they had Crystal to thank for all of it?

•

The other happy tangents, too. The congratulations that the Haddonfield Police Department, the tactical team, and the negotiator got for a
job extremely well done. Haddonfield had had some bad press in recent years, including a teenage party gone sour where a group of the
town's inebriated youths did things like spray a grand piano with a
Super Soaker full of urine. And of course it would have been preferable
if the siege had happened elsewhere—people from the surrounding,
less ritzy boroughs of South Jersey were always so delighted when bad
things befell Haddonfield. Nevertheless, praise was a welcome change.

Alan's success with the wedding photos—money, a show, even a
big glossy art book. Not only was the hostage taker pretty, but she
seemed to have staged the event to assure its photogenic posterity.
With the famous actor who starred in shows about just this kind of
siege as a wedding guest, and the lovely actress who was his girlfriend
as supporting cast, Alan's photos generated a lot of discussion about
mockumentaries, reality TV, and the ever more fungible line between
truth and fiction. Still photographs hadn't gotten this much attention since—well, since Mapplethorpe. And these didn't even have any
sex in them. One image of Crystal in the gas mask and sunglasses,
hoisting the rifle, became iconographic. Not exactly Che Guevara,
but girls at the Jersey Shore wore Crystal T-shirts that said things like
"You *better* call me, mothafucka" over their bikinis.

The bartender, who never had the chance to execute his chin jab
on the hostage taker: after the siege, he signed up for a tae kwon do
class and started to work out at the gym. He looked better and felt
more confident. He gave up fried food. His complexion improved.
He got new glasses. His transformation from dork to dreamboat took
less than a year.

It turned out he'd long been nursing a quiet crush on Amy. The
two dated for a while. He promised Amy that if Kevin tried anything, he'd be ready for him.

Although Amy and the bartender didn't stay together, the
wonderful thing was that it didn't destroy either of them. They were

able to wave to each other on campus without feeling threatened. Back at school, Amy's professors allowed her to finish the classes she'd had to drop at the height of her troubles with her stalker. In fact, her abnormal-psych professor was doing a project on this very subject, and when he agreed to give her independent study credits to help him with the research, she learned that she was connected to him in a surprising, small-world way.

The private investigator who had broken the news to Crystal about Amanda had felt bad when she read the news coverage about the Haddonfield siege. It forced her to question the "tough love" approach she took with lovelorn female clients. She might have been the last human contact of any substance the woman had had, before going off the deep end. Clearly she should have said something different, but what? She didn't know. For this reason, the PI would enroll in a night course in abnormal psychology. And although the client never paid her bill, she gave the PI something much more valuable. The PI and Amy's psych professor fell in love, and married.

As for Amy's stalker, Kevin never tried anything again—and, though they were unaware of this, they had Crystal to thank for that as well.

The last life radically changed by the hostage event was Idris Deby's.

It was an extremely busy night at the Haddonfield police station, and they never got around to releasing him. They would have had he asked, but he'd fallen asleep. They'd given him a blanket. The holding cell was not uncomfortable. In the morning, when they realized he was still there, they were very apologetic. Idris was good-natured about the mistake.

In truth, he had been very tired. Not just jet lag, and the ordeal, but an unexpected emotional upheaval: he had found himself deeply drawn to Mark, the SWAT commander.

Idris's attitude about his own sexuality could best be described as don't ask yourself, don't tell yourself. He had had some girlfriends, but his work with Médecins Sans Frontières did not really allow for long-term relationships, and besides, he had not felt toward these women the kind of jolt to his being that he experienced when the big policeman with the ghost-white skin offered him a cold bottle of water.

Nothing happened. There was no evidence that the man was even a homosexual. But Idris knew what he felt. It was as if his whole life—Paris, London, Chad, the cacophony of needs in MSF, illness and poverty enough to stifle desire altogether—had been burned to the ground, and sifting through the smoldering ash, he found a tiny piece of gold that was his real self.

After he was freed, Idris went back to his hotel and took a long shower. Then he found a gay bar. At thirty-three years old, in Philadelphia, the day after same-sex marriage was legalized in New York, Idris Deby had his first sexual encounter with a man.

It was not easy for him to come out. The first people he told were Tess and Gabe. They were accepting about the revelation, in an appropriately low-key way, and did not let on how shocked they were. How, Tess asked her husband, could her gaydar be that seriously off? Tess noted that Idris had never seemed the least bit gay to her, and Gabe retorted, Well, what does he seem, exactly? He's not really African. He's not really French. He's always been running. Maybe that's what he was running from. Tess shook her head and said, A cliché, but true—no one knows anyone else, ever. Well, no one knows except my mother. The woman who had the totally bizarre idea of disarming a lunatic with a rifle by offering to take her picture.

*T*hough Helen's life was improbably full and happy, Crystal was often on her mind.

Helen thought about the countless hours Crystal must have spent in her house, hiding candy, bedpans, microphones, and guns. Did Crystal leaf through her photo albums? Did she notice the lack of a master's things in the master closet, notice that the children's rooms were frozen in time like museum dioramas of adolescence, Helen without even enough of a life to convert them into dens or guest rooms? Did she lie down for a nap in Helen's bed like Goldilocks? As she slept, did Maynard snore beside her, his twitching paws in her face smelling of fresh dirt, a surprisingly pleasant smell?

Crystal had ruined Tess's wedding. Delbert Billips Jr. would have shoulder pain for the rest of his life. Still, Helen found she felt intensely sorry for Crystal, and so eager to see her that even Helen, no lover of psychoanalytic theory, had to admit it probably was about something other than Crystal herself.

But what did it mean? Well, it meant something about mothers. Mothering and being mothered. What didn't? Alone, abandoned, and lost, Crystal had wandered into the empty house where a family had once lived. She was looking for something, but it wasn't Van. Tess had married, become a mother herself, and didn't need Helen anymore for much other than occasional babysitting. But Helen got Crystal. Such a girl thing, to need to feel needed.

In no handbook of approved therapeutic practices would it be acceptable for Helen to visit Crystal in jail. But Helen wasn't a conventional therapist and did many things that other practitioners would find improper or ill-advised. Besides, she wasn't Crystal's therapist.

As a bona fide mental health professional, Helen could have called the prison, spoken with Crystal's doctor. She could have discovered whether, and how, it would be productive to pay a call. Still, she procrastinated, partly because the man she lived with—she lived with a man!—came down so firmly on the side of no. Once she visited, Harry asked, would she keep going? What was the game plan exactly?

A dream: Helen in a little glass-walled booth, waiting. As in the movies, Crystal didn't seem to have been told who was there but was just led out—"You have a visitor." When Crystal saw Helen, she grinned. But as she sat down and looked hard at her visitor, her expression changed. She said, in a tone half-pleased, half-reproachful:

"You're in love!"

And Helen found herself looking down at the hands folded in her lap, bashful.

"If it can happen to me . . ." Helen murmured, and Crystal slowly nodded agreement.

When she told the dream to Harry, told him how real it had felt, so real that the glass on the booth was smeared and scratched, he said, "So you see, you've already seen her." Not sarcastically: he knew she believed in dreams, in ways that Jake would find naïve or laughable.

In the dream, seeing Crystal was like being reunited with a lover you have fervently missed. Or a long-lost birth mother.

Strangely, and frustratingly, most of her memories of Crystal were from the rear. Brushing her hair. Touching the sharp scapula on her naked back as she stood by the door in her underwear. "Never say never," Harry said, consolingly, but surely the makeup session in the living room was not the last time that Helen would ever see the poor woman's shiny, freckled face.

*T*hey'd lied. Again.

They never let the hostage taker confront Van. They never had any intention of letting her talk to Van.

Crystal had followed the bullhorn's instructions. She was shaking hard as she left the house, but she tried to strut with an underwear model's panache. She opened the door and put her hands in the air. As they commanded through the bullhorn, she took five steps and stopped, raised her hands higher. She took five more steps. Turned. Five more steps. Faced the other way.

"Now take off your underpants," the bullhorn boomed.

They hadn't forewarned her about this. "Pull them down quickly. Put your hands right back up."

Then they tackled her.

They hadn't mentioned the tackling, either.

A swarm of SWAT men in gas masks and full bomb swaddling appeared from behind the bushes and shoved her down. Another swarm thundered from the front, some with shields, and behind them, some with rifles cocked. One man wrestled her into the handcuffs. Another man shoved fingers into her ears to check for earpieces.

And then they all just ran off and watched from a distance, instructed her by bullhorn not to move a muscle, leaving her naked and facedown in the grass for a long three minutes.

When she did not blow up, they thundered back. Several felt her breasts and private parts—necessary, once she mentioned body cavity detonation. The Kevlar-Nomex suits weighed eighty-five pounds but their hands were just in rubber gloves for this task. If a bomb went off they would live, handless. As one man squashed down her nipples to feel for wires and spread her ass cheeks, another one, lubeless, now probed her vagina and anus. They were not minutes she would soon forget. It was like a gang rape by Michelin Men.

She did not explode, and neither did they.

The bomb guys continued to the back of the house. True to the HT's word, the bomb was a dummy, which means that at any point in their ordeal, any one of the hostages could have taken that dictionary, broken the glass, turned the handle, and left the room. Of course, as Colonel Billips had explained, they had no way to know that. And they could have been shot from an upstairs window.

They wrestled Crystal around the corner. There was no robe involved. They'd lied about that, too, as they lied about the cameras. With her arms twisted behind her back, people grabbing her elbows and still more people pushing her forward, her breasts abob, it was hard for Crystal to look self-possessed. She was visible to the snipers, all the personnel in the safe zone, and the command team watching recorded footage from the trailer.

It is untrue that SWAT would have been delighted to bring her down. The hours the men spent planning a rescue that never happened were not wasted. Their goal was for everyone to live, the hostages and the HT, too. But that isn't to say they couldn't enjoy the spasm of justifiable brutality that was her surrender. Or the knowledge that, after all that, she still wouldn't get what she wanted.

But that doesn't mean that Crystal's efforts were in vain. On the contrary, by many measures, the hostage event was a success.

The first and immediate result of the siege was that it split up Van and Amanda. The officer and the negotiator had been dating for half a year, the longest exclusive relationship Van had ever had. While he had confessed to Amanda that before meeting her he had been a bit of a rake, he hadn't told her to what extent. Only because she worked in a different county fifty miles away, too busy with single motherhood and her job to properly gossip or fraternize, had Amanda been insulated from a fuller report on her boyfriend's reputation. She had been in the van with the other negotiators when Crystal surrendered, and, having herself been married to a philanderer, had felt bad for the woman. She certainly wasn't going to trust a man who could be so callous to a woman's suffering. Granted, as Van pleaded, the bitch was crazy, but Van, Amanda said, should have known that. This seemed totally unreasonable to him, blaming the victim. But Amanda was adamant.

Van found himself devastated by the loss, as mournful and moon-eyed as a girl. He did not get over it. When he tried to return to the field, he found, to his mortification, that for the first time in his life, he could not maintain an erection. While his cock was squishy, the rest of his being was hard as a needle magnetized to the true north of Amanda.

The badge bunnies could not be trusted to keep a confidence, no matter how much gusto he brought to otherwise satisfying them. He assumed he was now known far and wide as a limpdick. Humiliated and depressed, he began to drink, which did not ameliorate his erection issues.

It also didn't help his job performance. For the first time in his life, he failed a monthly weapons qualification. He would be allowed to retest, but as the guys teased him, he was mortified.

The one thing they told Crystal that was true: Van was forced to undergo a Psychological Fitness for Duty exam. This was partly because a complaint had been filed against him. After reading about Van in the newspaper, a woman had come forward to report that a year ago, before the hostage siege, she and her then husband had gotten into an argument that turned violent and she'd called the police. Van was one of the officers who had come to the house, and he actually tried to hit on her *while handling the domestic violence report*. The woman recognized she had waited too long to call, but she was in therapy now after her divorce, and was thinking about what drew a certain kind of man to her. Van was that kind of man, and she thought they should know.

Van wasn't suspended, but he was reprimanded and forced into counseling. The therapist was competent, because despite Van's resistance, he was soon discussing post-traumatic stress from all the horrible things he'd witnessed in SWAT—for he had blown away drug dealers, had been splattered with people's brains and guts—and attending AA meetings.

As step eight of his twelve steps, he and the therapist considered how he should make amends to Crystal. He sent Crystal a letter of apology, and said he would be happy to apologize in person. At first it seemed that the letter must have gotten waylaid, for she did not answer. He sent a follow-up, and Crystal wrote back, stiffly, a short note that thanked him for getting in touch but added that right now she didn't think it would be productive for them to meet in person.

Crystal refused to see him!

There was little more satisfying than getting to blow off Van McCormick. But there were other letters that Crystal received with pleasure in prison.

Despite scouring the computer of Amy's stalker, Kevin, they could never pin anything on him about the catering company break-in, or tie him to Crystal, because he had no ties to Crystal, except feeling that this was a woman after his own heart. When he saw Crystal's photo in the newspaper and read the coverage about how she'd planned her event, the kinship with his own mind amazed and thrilled him. He and Crystal had been staking out the schedule of the catering company *at the same time.* On the same night, both he and Crystal were subjected to body-cavity searches. He wrote to express his fervent admiration.

Kevin was hardly alone in so doing. Scores of websites serve as matchmaking hubs for people who seek prison pen pals. Some of these people are psychos, like the hybristophiliacs, women attracted to violent serial killers on death row, women for whom someone like Ira Einhorn, "the Unicorn Killer," a man with the chopped-up, decaying body of his ex-girlfriend in a trunk in his apartment, seems like an alluring mate. But some supplicants claim to be opposed to the death penalty, or want to offer succor to a lonely soul. Since the siege had been national news, the "batty bride" immediately got plenty of epistolary attention. Add to the visibility of her case the fact that Alan had sold photos of their shoot to places like *People*, and that Crystal looked sensational in the photos, and she was almost a movie star.

Kevin's letter stood out for her because of its sincerity. He said he understood her pain, and she believed him.

Crystal also heard from her father. He felt guilty. He wished he'd kept in closer touch when she was growing up. ("'Closer'?" Crystal exclaimed to her therapist, for she had a therapist now. "How about 'at all'?") He wanted Crystal to know that he would never have left if her mother wasn't such a total cuntrag. To whatever extent he was responsible for Crystal being mistrustful of men, her father apologized. He said he would visit, when he was next in the States. But Crystal's mother never visited her—a fact that would figure prominently at the trial.

Crystal declined an offer from Mara Lowell, a guest at the wedding, to write an "as told to" book. After all, Crystal had her own book. Of course, the book could not really be finished until they knew the outcome of the trial. Crystal's therapist, and her lawyer, exhorted her not to shop for a literary agent, which would not be a good public relations message about her remorse, and she complied. No one could accuse her of not being able to wait. She occupied herself with making an extremely complete record of how she'd planned the event. Kevin, for one, never tired of hearing the details of how she chose this wedding. Casing out Helen's house, and making friends with Helen's dog so he didn't bark. The anxiety that Van would be out of town or otherwise indisposed and would not show up with the tac team, that all of this effort would be in vain. But he had showed up, as she knew he would.

Excellent luck of the draw: like her negotiator, like her state-appointed therapist, her public defender was highly competent. He

got her branded as a serious suicide risk and moved from the county
jail, a horrible place where she really *was* suicidal, to a psychiatric
prison to await trial. He was working up a temporary-insanity plea.

She responded well to antidepressants. They didn't even have to
go through a series of brands and dosages until they found the right
SSRI-inhibiting cocktail. She was equally responsive to therapy. The
psychiatrist struck a balance between earning her trust and establish-
ing boundaries when she declared him the best psychiatrist in the
history of civilization—the kind of borderline overbonding that had
gotten her into this mess to begin with. Although branded a suicide
risk, in truth, she no longer seemed very suicidal. In fact, she barely
seemed depressed, especially for a person in prison—given New Jersey's minimum sentencing requirements, a person likely to be in prison
for a very long time.

The state threw a whole slew of charges at Crystal to see what would
stick. Kidnapping. Criminal Restraint. Criminal Intent: Homicide.
Aggravated Assault with a Weapon. Possession of a Weapon with Intent to Commit a Crime. Possession of Prohibited Weapons (sawed-
off shotguns are illegal). Reckless Endangerment. Two counts of
Burglary. Then the whole list of charges for the bomb: Possession
of a Destructive Device. Soliciting or Providing Material Support or
Resources for Terrorism. Terroristic Threats. You'd think the fact
that the bomb wasn't real would get her out of those charges, but in
fact New Jersey had just upgraded the penalties for False Alarm.

At the arraignment, the judge asked Crystal if she understood
the charges. In her orange jumpsuit, Crystal held her head high to
declare that whatever she did, she did for love. The prosecution rec-
ommended no bail due to danger to the public, which was hardly a
stretch. The public defender explained to her that it would take a
year, maybe as many as two years, for her case to come to trial.

She would not tire of telling her story, over and over, to so many
people brought in to evaluate her and interested in even the most
minute details of her mood and method. The prospect of the trial

itself—and, probably, the appeal—were all fascinating to her, a different kind of performance, during which, no doubt, Van would be put on the stand. There were set pieces not only about Van's cruelty (his kiss-off message on her answering machine preserved, of course, to be played for the jury) but about her abandoning father, and the sound-studio guy who had sexually harassed her. Not that she was *blaming* these people. But they didn't help, if you were clinically depressed.

If you'd asked Crystal how she imagined she'd fare at an all-girl institution, she would not have been very optimistic. But she was actually quite well liked at the psychiatric prison. In that population, she hardly qualified as seriously off the deep end. There was a general feminist agreement about the evil men do, what they can push you to. She came to serve as a sort of unofficial union negotiator, to fight on such issues as changes to the hospital's four-page written haircut policy. There were still men around—doctors, guards. If it got to the point when she needed to have sex, there would be candidates, though for now she was heeding her therapist's call for a temporary moratorium. She had her own room, small but reasonably clean. The environs were hardly luxurious, but, to look on the bright side, they were not so very much worse than Dispatch, where she'd spent so many of her hours as a free woman.

More than the bad food and the constant noise, the thing Crystal found hardest was not having a computer. They had no e-mail in prison and no Internet access. Whole chunks of Crystal's life had been spent Web browsing. The withdrawal was intense, and the books in the prison library were a joke. But when Kevin came for his weekly visit, she'd relate any topic in which she'd developed a strong interest, from area churches that might be approached about sending a manicurist to the prison now and again, as a charity mission, to legal precedents for her criminal case. He would print pages out at home and mail them to her, or bring them on the next visit.

Although Kevin was sweet, she still thought about Van. She did not know about his recent troubles. If she had, she would not have gloated. She would have been moved and concerned. She had the most vivid dreams about their reunion. Satisfying as it had been to finally get to blow him off, she would still dream about him. In one repeated dream, she collected her sad bundle of belongings as they opened the door to the prison, and Van stood beyond the gates to greet her. Just his face—its stillness, its intensity—was enough to make her wake up in happy tears.

Crystal didn't get to see her shrink often enough. Sometimes it seemed like the same old disappointing dating days, waiting and waiting. The shrink had taken a real interest in her, though. He was a younger guy, and reasonably good-looking. He encouraged her to be suspicious about the notion of love as destiny. The only love that was unquestioned, unconditional, and permanent, the shrink said—or should be—was the love of a parent for a child. So sometimes she told him about her dreams. And sometimes she didn't. She was trying hard to believe him.

GUEST LIST

MOM: I put some notes in brackets here to help you out with who's who. Not many of the Needleman tribe are making the trip. And the ancient Billipses are mostly staying home, too.

I don't see any way to assign tables. Have tried. Failed. If you can, feel free.

V = Vegetarian/Vegan

US
Tess Nathanson
Gabriel Billips

(We don't want to sit alone at a separate table, staring soulfully at each other.)

Helen Burns
Agnes Burns
Simon Nathanson
Daniel Nathanson
Cole Nathanson
Rosalind Nathanson
Lauren Burns (not coming last minute)
Jake Nathanson
Mary Nathanson (plus the infant Jesus)

(Can we put Dad and Mary at a separate table? Maybe in a separate room?)

Dr. Sarah Barrett
Matthew Barrett
Theodore Nathanson
Rachel Nathanson (also bailed—is it something I said??)

THE IN-LAWS
Delbert Billips Jr.
Salome Billips
Miranda Mobley a.k.a Billips V
Trevor Hunter

Delbert Billips Sr.
Winona Billips

Dr. Ira Needleman
Sylvia Needleman
Phillip Needleman
Janice Needleman
Joe Needleman
Eric Needleman
Jennifer Needleman

THE SHRINKS PLUS ONE GI DUDE
Sam Gold, M.D.
Lucy Gold
Marty Feldstein, M.D.
Myra Feldstein, M.D.
Richard Silver, M.D.
Donna Silver

DAD WAS ALLOWED TO INVITE TOO MANY PEOPLE!!
SILVER, GOLD, WHERE'S THE STAINLESS STEEL?

AT LAST, OUR FRIENDS
Kenneth Schmidt (best man)

Ben Kramer
Britte Jorgenson Kramer
Mara Lowell
Zach Whitehead

NOTE: DO NOT SEAT THESE FOUR PEOPLE TOGETHER.

Alan Smith (photographer)
Alyssa Waters V
Allison Piccollo (bringing baby)
Joseph Piccollo
Madison Matthews V
Mike Matthews
Jason Matthews (their 5-year-old)

Ngarta Adoulaye
Acta Adoulaye
Idris Deby
Souleymane Samake

NOTE: DO NOT SEAT ONLY BLACK PEOPLE TOGETHER
(obviously). And do not seat the Doctors Without Borders people
with the Billips side. They will NOT get along.

Lindsay Rosenblatt V
Rick Martin
Eric Landesmann

NOTE: HOPEFULLY ONE OF THESE GUYS WILL TAKE
LINDSAY HOME.

Martine Lafont
Madison Whittier
Peter Thomas V
Arden Thomas V

ACKNOWLEDGMENTS

My gratitude to the following people who served as "eyes on" to guide me through facts and situations that are radically outside of my normal workday:

Sean Clancy, Commander, Atlantic County Emergency Response Team; Officers Joe Guerrier, Kristi Kinsi, and Sergeant Tim Graczyk, Hamilton Township Police Department; Officer Glenn Hausmann, Atlantic County Emergency Response Team and Township of Hamilton Search and Recovery Dive Team; Richard Norcross, Law Enforcement Liaison, CSI Technology Group and Commander (ret.), Intelligence Services Team, Camden County Prosecutor's Office; Christopher Mote, Training Officer, Camden County Department of Public Safety; Lieutenant Gary Pierce, Haddonfield Police Department; and Signe Lundberg, Ph.D.

Most special gratitude to ace diagnostician Dr. Gary Glass, and to Jay McKeen, Police Chief (ret.), Hamilton Township Police Department. Jay vouched for my sanity to many of the people above, had the guts to put a weapon in my hands, and combed a draft for humiliating inaccuracies.

Thanks to the Corporation of Yaddo, the Virginia Center for the Creative Arts, and to the artists' colonies formerly known as Kind Friends with Vacation Homes: Sidney Wade, Milli Weiss, Julianne Baird, and Ed Mauger. Thanks to Rutgers University. Thanks to James Marcus, Rafael Yglesias, Jane Bernstein, Lauren Grodstein, Gary Krist, Ellis Avery, and Beth Kephart for the literary advice, and to Tyler Hoffman for the conversations about suburban parenthood. Thanks to Sarah Crichton and Dan Piepenbring at FSG. Gratitude to the amazing Ellen Levine at Trident Media. Lastly, thanks to John Lafont, for being a great reader and for providing essential tactical support on the SWAT team called married with children (and dogs).

A NOTE ABOUT THE AUTHOR

Lisa Zeidner has published four novels, including the critically acclaimed *Layover*, and two books of poems. Her stories, reviews, and essays have appeared in *The New York Times*, *Slate*, *GQ*, *Tin House*, and elsewhere. She directs the M.F.A. program in creative writing at Rutgers University in Camden, New Jersey.